Seventy-Six Trombones

ISBN-13: 9781548829155
ISBN-10: 1548829153
Library of Congress Control Number: **2017911399**
CreateSpace Independent Publishing Platform
North Charleston, South Carolina

Seventy-Six Trombones

LIFE AFTER THIRTY-NINE MADE EASY

* * *

A Treasury of Three
The Answer—Finally!

James A. Fragale

"This one's for you, wherever you are"—*any and all of you who are still abusing substances (yes, including video games) and want to quit.*
Just stop, damn it! Stop. "If you keep doing what you've always done, you'll always get what you've always gotten," said John Maxwell.
(If you don't like this dedication, try this one: "This is dedicated to the one I love..."*)

*As the Shirelles sang in 1960. *Rolling Stone* named these female singers, at the time sixteen and seventeen years old and friends from Passaic High School in New Jersey, as one of the best pop acts of all time.

In case you're one of those heartily welcomed young readers unfamiliar with the intended meaning of "thirty-nine" in the subtitle, it refers to the age that comic and actor Jack Benny celebrated every year on his birthday. What a gift never to be older than that. PS—if you don't know Jack Benny, he's worth a Google and a giggle.

Mission Statement

* * *

For any and all,

This book was compiled for only one audience: you. So I don't think it's going to make me a lot of money. I'm OK with that. Some folks set out to become millionaires or movie stars. I'm not about to become either. My *raison d'être* is to be of help, to be of assistance in any way I can, to any and all who need a hand with addiction, whether it is alcohol, video games (yes, even online video games), cell/smartphones, over-the-counter cigarettes, compulsive shopping, pot, porn, prostitution, private-parts websites, web-surfing, another human being, love, romance, tweeting, texting, social media-ing, Facebooking, Instagramming, Snapshoting, television; a feeling (yes, hooked on a feeling), gambling, internet gaming, submission/dominance roll play, (the two latest additions) sex and food, (and I'm not even going to go there:) kleptomania—*any*, most any, area. And, presently I'm going to tell you how to handle what I call Addiction Reflex when you get an urge.

Your life can change with a wave of your hand, a twinkling of an eye, a shadow of a smile, a tip of a hat, a kind word, a gesture of support, a seductive nod, a dollop of tough love. Scoop them all up, accept them, *paesano*, take them into your heart, and thrive. (If you think this is all totally uncool—psst, no one's looking.)

Footquote
And as they invariably suggest (insist?) in 12 step meetings, "Take what you want and leave the rest."

> *The Master gave his teaching in parables and stories, which*
> *his disciples listened to with pleasure—and occasionally*
> *frustration, for they longed for something deeper.*
>
> *The Master was unmoved. To all their objections he would*
> *say, "You have yet to understand, my dears, that the shortest*
> *distance between a human being and Truth is a story."*
>
> —ANTHONY DE MELLO, ONE MINUTE WISDOM
> (PENGUIN/RANDOM HOUSE)

I'll tell you mine if you tell me yours.

Setting Up the Set-Up before Settling In

$*$ $*$ $*$

BOOK ONE, *THE ANSWER TO Life*, was my autobiographical novel. As Nino Pino, I portrayed what it was like being me: an appealing, hunky, unexposed-to-life, in-my-early-twenties Italian hillbilly West Virginian and ambitious singer-songwriter. It followed Pino's adventures in New York City as he sought fame and fortune—only to bump into a reality for which he was wildly unprepared.

I dedicated the book to my mother with an apology, but fortunately, the memoir fiction (or fictionalized memoir) was well received and garnered multiple five-star reviews. But was I forgiven?

Book Two was *F.U.! (Follow Up)! The Answer to Life Revisited.* In this f.u., my Nino Pino had made his way to awe-inspiring, unforgiving New York City to make it big in the competitive music industry. And he did, sort of. This smart and snarky sequel catches up with him later in life. We can be honest here—Pino's gotten older, frozen out by ageist agents. Dismissively, "they" even shot down his idea for an automated gourmet hamburger-meatball joint back home in West Virginny. As Pino tackles the aging challenges, he reminisces about life as an Italian American West Virginian hillbilly. Pino details his serious struggles as well as triumphs amid the uncertainty about his newfound demon (when under pressure, he drank too much). Pino was older, but would he grow up? More than fifty original coveted recipes handed down from the author's mother are included. Before going forward, I'd like to hazard a theory that I don't explore but deeply feel. In my case, when I got overserved, it was somehow a generational curse, and when I stopped drinking, I was for not only doing it for myself but for my entire family, a generation back.

In Book Three, *Seventy-Six Trombones*, our imperfect hero reaches age seventy-six. He works out in the gym every day—or tries to. He has sex a couple of times a week (honest)—at least once—with or without the help of erectile dysfunction meds, but he has prescriptions if he needs them. And…well, you have to see for yourself what you think of the crusty, crotchety yet youthful septuagenarian, Nino Pino.

Previews of presents and gifts to come: More on Studio 54. Roy Cohn's chauffeur. Insights on forgiving yourself. Scientific studies that prove that "aging liberals have more sex than most." Pathways to getting your ducks in a row, your shit together. Some laughs. Savor "the middle years." Get familiar with Martin Buber. And the answer to life (oh, that again). "I will give you hidden riches, stored in secret places" (Isaiah 45:3). You can count on it in *Seventy-Six Trombones*. (Hint: seventy-six is the new seventy-five.)

Footnote. End quote. Antidote.

"Loathing and self-hatred are always very good for writers…A degree of anger at oneself makes you better at something you're doing" (Author Aravind Adiga opined on National Public Radio, January 8, 2017, promoting his coming-of-age novel about fathers, sons, brothers, and the butch game of cricket. *Selection Day*, Simon & Schuster, 2017).

Book Two on Amazon.com: *F.U.! (Follow Up)! The Answer to Life Revisited*
Book One on Amazon.com: *The Answer to Life*

Preface Now. Afterface Later.

$$\ast \quad \ast \quad \ast$$

Old age is not for sissies.

—BETTE DAVIS

ON FEBRUARY 13, 2016, I woke up to the realization that I had just turned seventy-six. Nino Senior, my father, had passed on at seventy-six on August 5, 1989. Then and there I decided that everything from that moment on would be gravy. Ha!

These days I still get up at seven. ("Morning's at seven…" suggested Robert Browning in "Pippa's Song").* After breakfast and three cups of coffee, I write. Sometimes, I admit, as Truman Capote accused prolific Jack Kerouac of doing, I type, not write.

At forty-three minutes on the hour, 7:43 a.m., New York Channel One has a chap recap what's in the New York dailies as well as the *Washington Post*, the *Wall Street Journal*, and some regional rags. While sipping my first cup of java, I can get an overview of what the newspapers think is big news since yesterday.

Breakfast. And I keep filling the six cups of lovingly brewed coffee (a different brand every morning: variety is the spice of good coffee).

I have lunch at about twelve-thirty (precooked food, delivered at ten) while watching Channel 7, ABC TV News. The number-one news station in the city brings one up to date, midday, with smart, snappy, savvy commentators and the weather (maybe too often, but OK), and at 12:30 p.m., they announce midday lottery numbers.

After lunch, on alternate days, I shave. For some reason, shaving is more of an ordeal these days. You need to know I use several kinds of shaving cream (gels, foams, creams) as well as an oil lubricant (on my face, thank you) and several razors. Excessive? No, I have craggy skin, and when I do give in to shaving, I go to the max.

Then I tidy up the place—essentially a lick and a promise, as Mother used to say—dress, and head out to exercise at the health-club gym.

The ideal would be to exercise every day. (A hundred percent of anything is rare, and it's best to always aim for it.) As for the workouts, as Lewis Carroll once said in *Alice*, "It takes all the running you can do to stay in place" (see the appendix). Recently as I did my warm-up, hanging from a high bar, lifting my legs, a younger gent walked by and without stopping said, "Not very many seventy-seven-year-olds can do that." Seventy-seven? Wait a friggin' minute. I'm seventy-six.

Gym whim: great compliment at the gym. But leg lifts are one of the few exercises I did with ease and, to be honest, not that many repetitions—most of the time about a half a dozen these days, down from a dozen or so. I tread lightly. My workouts* are performed gingerly. I start at the lowest weight and work up as far as I can go. When the law of diminishing returns sets in, I go on to the next exercise.

Yes, I work out daily and have sex an average of once a week, sometimes twice, but at least once a week. (A bit of self-aggrandizement here: my therapist—Thursdays at 2:00 p.m. for him—said, "Nino, you get three times the invitations to get laid as my patients one-third your age. Say yes more often."). I resolve. (But let's not tempt fate here with hubris.)

While on the subject of my life: I'm now more enamored of my Upper West Side neighborhood. I reveal that since I used to be out and about in Manhattan at all hours, in every neighborhood, sans an ounce of fear. Apprehension started creeping in after 9/11. These days, though, I find it more comfortable to stay within walking distance of the apartment. Why? Recent uptick in attacks on the gray-haired set; slick, professional pickpockets; subway stabbings; increase of shoving(s) on the tracks; toppling of folks on walkers...again, why tempt fate? When I get the urge to go on vacation, I see a Broadway show. Afterward, I feel as if I've been on vacation for two hours.

Up here on Manhattan's Upper West Side, restaurants are decent. Folks are friendly. Acquaintances tip their hats. And, no small thing, the 12 step meetings in these parts are filled with engaging, *gemutlich* people, folks who fill the gap. It is imperative that I come clean: in the old days, you could find me God-knows-where at all hours, doing who-knows-what or whom. For now, for me, I stick close to Seventy-Second and Broadway (one block away) most of the time. One could do worse.

As of this typing, my second novel, released several months ago, has received ten five-star reviews on Amazon.com. (Five is Amazon's highest rating.) On that subject, I've published five pieces on the *Huffington Post*, boast a popular-music CD that listeners find decent (*Oil and Coal*), and, in the hamper/hopper, I'm holding on to twelve sets of song lyrics, not yet musicfied, waiting for some young, unsung Puccini to write the unforgettable melodies. What's the adage about old hope springing from human pectorals?

My income is derived from two checks every month, directly deposited into a credit union—one from Social Security, the other a small pension from Walt Disney Company in honor of my twenty-plus years at Disney's television subsidiary, ABC. I'd like to boast that I'm well fixed, but hey-ho, I am not. (It's relative anyway, isn't it?). I subsist/survive/make do. But am I prudent? Not really, but I do buy overpriced necessities during frequent preannounced "sales" in West Seventies stores, where most everything is overpriced. In olden days, who bothered with discount coupons? I didn't even hazard a white sale.

Some people are curious about royalties. Most who know me unfailingly broach that subject. Song royalties stopped long ago. The two novels haven't even broken even yet. And for those well-done, well-received five hard-fought efforts on the *Huffington Post*, the blogs didn't bring in a dime. Oh, I'm proud of that work, but when Miss Arianna Huffington drove the train, I was not paid a farthing. Before I submit anything else to the new, tough *Huffington Post* powers, I am going to ask for compensation; the new mahoffs, a government term for bosses, might be more generous. One can't pay the rent with an impressive writing credit.

I state again and probably should not tempt the gods any further: I did not become a writer to get rich. (You know what they say about self-fulfilling prophecies.) I do confess, however, that if I had to do it over again, I'd tweak my intentions. Banking seems like an awfully appealing alternative. And so to round out to the nearest cent.

Income outlined: I earned my Social Security. I began working in high school at a local shoe store and then in college at the sloppy produce department of a supermarket. Later, I endured a one-year internship in Washington, DC, in a government agency where they took out money. Remarkably, I worked for decades for the not-very-fat check that comes once a month.

To further digress:

Dear Uncle Sam: I wish you'd increase SS more every year, but maybe there is not enough money to do that; however, the powers-that-be can always find the money to make war, to subsidize missiles. Subsequently, why not reward your old folks a little bit more merely because they're still around? Other countries revere their old people.

A therapist once told me, "Nino Pino, you care a lot about details, the little things in life." Case in point: one of my favorite efforts was an article in *Newsweek*, included in the appendix section, on the humblest of coins, the penny.

My Wage, by Jessie Rittenhouse

I bargained with Life for a penny,
And Life would pay no more,
However I begged at evening
When I counted my scanty store;
For Life is just an employer,
He gives you what you ask,
But once you have set the wages,

Why, you must bear the task.
I worked for a menial's hire,
Only to learn, dismayed,
That any wage I had asked of Life,
Life would have paid.

Now you tell me?

Pippa's Song, by Robert Browning

The year's at the spring,
And day's at the morn;
Morning's at seven;
The hill-side's dew pearl'd;
The lark's on the wing;
The snail's on the thorn;
God's in His heaven—
All's right with the world!

One of my better friends, the late Lloyd Lee, much-loved lifestyle guru, used to say to me, "Nino, you are successful. You just don't have any money."

"Then what's the point?" I would reply.

*Prayer, daily at 4:00 p.m., before entering the gym: Dear God, yes! "They shall run, and not be weary..." (Is. 40:31, King James Version). "But they that wait upon the Lord shall renew their strength; they shall mount up with wings as eagles; they shall run, and not be weary; and they shall walk, and not faint."

Gracia tutti: Before moving on, I'd like to thank you for getting this book, especially after I learned that 42 percent of high-school graduates never read another book entirely.

INTERJECTION: INQUISITIVE EDITOR'S QUESTIONABLE QUERY: Yet another question I was asked by the editor: "What does the main character look like today? We know what he looked like in the past," she added, "but what does he look like now?" He has a full head of salt and pepper hair–a generational gift/blessing. Around the eyes, there are three-lined crows feet. He has a fairly tight jaw and the body of a 76+ year old who does some type of exercise every day of his life, even Christmas Day--if they'll let him in the gym. Nino does eat too much pasta and therefore, sports a soft belly. Fortunately, he retained all of his teeth, a firm handshake, and a superb memory that gets him into hot water with family and friends. Nino's been told many times, he has beautiful hands--a mixed blessing for a grown man. *Better to hold you, my dear.*

CHAPTER 1

A Sliver of Ice in the Heart

* * *

"The pigeons are flying again..."

I LIVE ON A HIGH floor in a 1940s-built apartment building that looks down on a brownstone-like dwelling below and faces a five-story brick brownstone that is now a Moslem mosque. (These small dwellings were typical uptown in 1910, when the subway came further uptown and apartment buildings were then a necessity.) Many beautiful buildings were torn down to make room for the *messes*, as Greta Garbo pronounced "the masses." During the mosque's recent repairs, the Moslem management installed a mysterious apparatus that attracts hundreds of pigeons to its rooftop. In a swirling motion, the scavenger birds light on the building's top, suddenly fly *upward* in a wide circle, and land back on the building's roof. After a few moments, abruptly again, they rapidly rise up and fly in that wide circle around and around and then land back on the rooftop. The birdies duplicate the exercise all day long. It's downright mesmerizingly—a joy to behold.

More important: Why is this happening? What is their secret?

I would like the inside poop on this flying-pigeon phenomenon, although poop is primarily more accustomed to being outside with these avian. But I don't have the chutzpah to knock on the mosque's door to ask, "How do they do that? And why?" I'm simply satisfied in enjoying the circling bird phenomenon as I sit at my kitchen table, sipping my third cup of coffee and gazing out on the Hudson and Riverside Park. The decision today: Should/could/would/ought/must I hazard a third novel? American psychologist, originator of cognitive-behavior therapy, Dr. Albert Ellis calls this mental machination "*musterbation.*"

Missed blessing: Marathons/triathlons begin and end on the corner across from that house of worship, below my window, and sometimes their queuing-up noise begins at dawn. During the competition, participant friends and loved ones egg the runners on with loud shouts of encouragement that last throughout the races and can drive one to narcosis. But then again, sometimes the competitions are mesmerizing to watch.

Fourth cup of coffee and back to the subject at hand.

In his 1971 autobiography, *A Sort of Life*, Graham Greene detailed a moment he experienced as a young man when he was recovering in Westminster Hospital from appendicitis. Suddenly the child in an adjacent bed, who had been diagnosed merely with a broken leg from playing rugby, passed away. As the boy's parents arrived, a screen was drawn to let them grieve in private, and most people on the ward looked away or put on earphones to offer the couple space. Not Mr. Greene. He wanted to be close to the emotions, to capture them.

"There is a splinter of ice in the heart of a writer," he wrote. "[That day] I watched and listened. There was something there which one day I might need: the woman speaking, uttering the banalities she must have remembered from some woman's magazine, a genuine grief that could communicate only in clichés."

Powerful. *A splinter of ice in the heart of a writer. Do I have what it takes?* I ask myself.

After reading my first novel, *The Answer to Life*, my youngest and closest brother stopped speaking to me (three years now), nary a word, not one e-mail, not a birthday greeting, bottle of wine. Hey-ho…or is that hi-ho? I begin with that revelation at this juncture, and unhappy to further add, a first cousin on my father's side is also incommunicado, and a cousin on my mother's side who used to regularly contact me has distanced himself.

I belabor here my standing joke to anyone who will listen: "Don't let your daughters be writers."

I heard secondhand my sibling's objection: "Nino made our mother and father look bad. Nino told family secrets." Gulp. It's a novel. The younger but no longer a youngster and I are ten years apart. Our experience of our parents and Lewistown, West Virginia, are a decade different. You'd think youngest sibling would find my take intriguing. I certainly would welcome his if he were inclined to report it.

I love this analogy, and admit I often cite it: I, like the nondescript, clueless, unattractive silkworm who weaves on, methodically, mesmerizingly, ceaselessly—I, Nino Pino, write every day with the prayer and with love in my heart that someday, something—hoping against hope—there might be a delicate piece of silk at the end of the web's tunnel. If not, an appealing, accurate analogy, at least, a lovely one.

Endquote:

"And I want people to understand something I learned only recently: that for those of us lucky enough to live the American Dream, the demons of the life we left behind continue to chase us." Oh God, yes, Mr. Vance, right on.

Granted, I wrote more about demons in my first novel. And I responded to the above quote enough to jot it down—from the articulate, evenly appealing, to-be-admired J. D. Vance in *Hillbilly Elegy—A Memoir of a Family and Culture in Crisis*, a bestseller included on several ten best books lists of 2016, HarperCollins. For more, see chapter 8. I can't seem to say enough about this memoir. I bought several copies.

Well worth noting: Mid-2017, cognitive-behavior therapy is still being recommended for anxiety, depression, and like ailments. I can't tout founder Dr. Albert Ellis enough for any of us with addictive personalities. More on him later.

The sound of jackhammers is unfailingly present in the background most everywhere in New York City, like right now below my window. The continual cacophonies of clamorous New York City noises nudge me and positively *contribute* to my productivity every day: those jackhammers below my window. Ear-splitting sirens blaring down Seventy-Second Street bound for the Highway. At Seventy-Second and Broadway: the hubbub of automobile and foot traffic not to mention nonstop tearing-up-above, then-mutilating-down-below, street work. Yes, sometimes I actually grit my teeth, but I totally feel I am a part of, *a component to*, that constant, deafeningly chaotic, contagious-to-me energy. Consequently, candidly, I don't think (and I may be wrong) I could write anyplace else in the world.

CHAPTER 2

Mama, Trauma, and Italian Opera Drama

✳   ✳   ✳

"...ISOLATED TRAUMATIC EVENTS RARELY MOLD individual lives," wrote George E. Vaillant in *Adaptation to Life* (Harvard University Press, 1977). Really, Mr. Vaillant? *Really?*

Deep-breath time.

Friends chide me for writing over and over again about the eviction. I don't always know I'm doing it, and I can't seem *not* to. I find myself interjecting that traumatic, horrifying event into every kind of writing: novel/blog/humorous effort/punchlines. And so, once and for all, may I please put this to rest?

1. Cousin Antonio came by our basement apartment on West Main Street with a cinder in his eye. Mother may have been overwhelmed with her burdens or not in the mood, experiencing postpartum depression. Maybe Cousin Tony should have gone directly up the block to the pizzeria where both his parents were.

2. Mother, knee deep in her own children with housework, cooking, diapers, and that speculated post–whatever depression in that basement apartment.

   Her response to Antonio's hangnail *du jour*: "Go to the restaurant"—a pizzeria Uncle Bruno and Aunt Maria owned three blocks up.

3. The overreaction of Uncle Bruno. It didn't take long—moments, it seemed—for my mother's sister's husband, Uncle Bruno, to charge the length of his long front yard, leap down the steep gray

steps, and pound on the door of our basement-level apartment. He was on a mission. He stormed into our square forty-by-forty kitchen with the one window that looked up the stairs to Uncle Bruno's giant front yard. Then in his high-pitched, overheated, overwrought voice, he screamed at my mother. "Why do you think I have you here? To look after my children also when they need it. Why?"

Mother casually, in an incongruous, slow, rhythmic, circling motion (out of sync with the atmosphere), continued to wipe the porcelain on the Magic Chef with a thick white cloth. For the first time in life that I actually saw someone in someone's face, Mom then picked up one of the round, black, cast-iron burners that hold the pasta pots on the stove and waved it in his face. "Hit me," she chided, cajoled. "Go ahead, hit me." Without a beat, red-faced, he spit out, "Get out, get out, get out. I want you and your kids out of here as soon as you can...out!"

He turned and retraced his journey: out the door, up the painted gray wooden stairs, with long strides up the brick pathway to the sidewalk and a military sharp left, up the block.

Finally, I found my voice. And it was whiny. "What are we gonna do?" I sing-songed.

Mother looked down at me. Stunned, shocked, scared, and I suspect resisting the temptation to whack me across my face, she said, "Shudddd uppp." I did.

The following Sunday, in several trips, our belongings were transported to my maternal grandparents' basement in St. Paul's Graveyard's pockmarked pickup truck. I didn't have to enhance the atmosphere here; it began to rain.

I ask now, what must they have felt? Although they seemed old to me, they weren't even middle aged, but Mother and Dad must have felt shame, hurt, humiliation, disappointment, anger. If so, they didn't show any of it. What they did was tackle the situation directly in front of them. No looking backward or forward. Dad went to work at dawn every morning to the neighboring town's A&P as meathead, manager of the meat department, with white shirt and tie tucked inside the middle of the shirt, dress pants, and work shoes covered by spats. (Spats were a material shoe coat that covered the top part of a shoe as well as the shoestrings to protect them from dirt, dust, and in his case, sawdust.)

At our new place with Grandmaw, Mother struggled tirelessly to hold house and home together—cleaning, washing clothes, dusting, vacuuming, and cooking those gourmet-like meals on a peasant's budget, wonderful, scrumptious meals. I can still smell the kitchen when she made spaghetti sauce on the Magic Chef, keeping all the plates in the air.

So you can understand why I'd like this to be the last time I write about the eviction, ever.

Except...

...some decades later, I was visiting Lewistown on some holiday. Cousin Antonio was also back in town during school break and was helping his dad, Uncle Bruno, at the pizzeria. We started talking, chatting, munching on a pepperoni roll when Uncle Bruno said something totally out of left field. He said, "Nino, I hope you're not mean to me when I'm old." In his own memory, he could not forget that I was there the night he threw us out. Was he asking forgiveness? And would I grant it?

May I now put the eviction to rest, let it go. As popular 1970s guru Louise Hay might say, "I forgive you, and I set you free." More on Ms. Hay later.

And I'm going to say once more/state emphatically that Mother and Dad got up every morning and did what was in front of them—sure, occasionally with a small complaint or two but usually not—daily doing what was there to do, what *had* to be done, and in the process chipped away at our lot in life, whittled away our poverty until one day it was no longer there. Contrary to popular belief of unfriendly family critics and cranky cousins, after my first novel, with boundless, exorbitant respect, I commended them.

Questionable Quotes

"...isolated traumatic events rarely mold individual lives," wrote George E. Vaillant in *Adaptation to Life*, Harvard University Press, 1977. Really, Mr. Vaillant? *Really?*

In another of the *New York Times* ten best books of the year, Harvard sociologist Matthew Desmond's spellbinding landmark, *Evicted, Poverty and Profit in the American City*, evocatively exposes the harrowing world of the ten million low-income households that pay half of their incomes in rent and utilities, a long-overlooked population whose numbers have recently soared. Desmond directly *contradicts* the above George Eman Vaillant quote with this insight, "eviction can brand a person for life." Evictions "leave lasting emotional scars...Yet (the evicted) have been an afterthought."

From *Evicted, Poverty and Profit in the American City*, by Matthew Desmond, Crown Publishers, a Best Book 2016, *The Week*, and 2017 Pulitzer Prize winner for general nonfiction.

Author Matthew Desmond takes it one step further. "Then there is the toll eviction takes on a person's spirit...One in two recently evicted mothers reports multiple symptoms of clinical depression, double the rates of similar mothers who were not forced from their homes. Even after years pass, evicted mothers are less happy, energetic, and optimistic than their peers." OMG.

And finally I'm compelled to report that the *New York Times* printed these words on Sunday, December 11, 2016, page 11: The book *Evicted* "reintroduces the concept of 'exploitation' into the poverty debate, showing how eviction, like incarceration, can brand a person for life." Amen.

Now I put the eviction to bed for all time and rest my case. Honest, Bruno.

Before moving on, I'd like to mention an aside that haunts me. Mother worked tirelessly. While at her chores, she often evoked the deity, loudly, en passant. One of her frequent petitions was, without a pause, "God, give me strength." Not "Heaven, remove this problem." Or "Lord, take this away." No. It was, "God, give me strength."

So I share with you:

Colossians, chapter 3, Apostle Paul: *Paul prayed that the people would have the strength to endure whatever came their way. Apostle Paul didn't* pray that God would remove every difficulty. He didn't pray that God would deliver them instantly. He prayed that they'd have the strength to go through the trials that they were facing and going to face.

Sometimes we pray, "God, you've got to get me out of this situation today. I can't stand it any longer. If it goes on another week, I'm not going to make it." But a better way to pray is, "Father, please give me the strength to go through this with a good attitude. Help me to keep my joy. Help me to keep my peace." Our circumstances are not going to change until we change. Remember, you are more than a conqueror, a victor and not a victim.

From *Thoughts for the Week*, www.danburycoc.org/s

CHAPTER 3

Life at Grandmaw's

*   *   *

Hashtag: Crash pad.

DOING A-WHAT COMES NATURALLY IN the early 1950s.

I'd like to gloss over this painful, formidable preteen period. Here's what it was like:

1. I slept nightly on auto mechanic Uncle Al's authentic army cot.
2. Every evening, in Grandmaw's master bedroom, as a family we would gather 'round, even Paw, get on our knees and, in unison, say the rosary as the glow from lit candles flickered around the darkened room. The church passed out 3 x 5 cards that read, *"The Family that Prays Together, Stays Together."* That was us.
3. For work, I bundled newspapers and picked up scrap metal, for which I was paid pennies per pound at a bona fide junkyard (complete with *two* junkyard dogs).
4. And then when Uncle Albert bought me a wagon with removable sides so I could get more newspapers, coat hangers, scrap metal in the vehicle and I thought it was a great gesture, it turned out I had to pay him back fifty cents a week.
5. I later got a job cleaning pans at a bakery up the block. (While I was scrubbing pots, I could hear the sounds of the neighborhood boys playing sandlot baseball next door. This pathetic story even made my German therapist sad. Not easy to do.)

6. I was smack in the center of a traumatizing tug of war between my mother and my sixth-grade teacher, which resulted in the principal of the school recommending that I attend school where Grandmaw lived.
7. Grandmaw said no way.
8. Ridicule was a way of life. While at Grandma's, Paw once made fun of a book I was reading about dogs instead of encouraging me.
9. Did I mention no girlfriends allowed? Maw used to make fun of the girlfriend I was fond of, beginning a pattern that followed for years. I think Sweetheart #2 got put down in a nursery rhyme whine. Girlfriend Three, Mother wouldn't even acknowledge, giving her the classic cold shoulder on a visit. (*Is this productive parental behavior?* I asked.)
10. Well, one bright spot: My folks eventually found a three-story house at the end of the block, at the bottom of a steep hill, beside a river that actually made a turn at our house. It was in a family-connected neighborhood and was half a dozen blocks from school. Whew.

The side faced the hilly street on the left. Cars made a left turn at our house onto Dennison.

In every room there were working fireplaces, which Maw immediately had removed and plastered over. The place smelled of cats, but slowly, over the years, the scent finally went away with Mother and my sister Toni's constant cleaning, spraying, scrubbing. From my bedroom window, I could look out at where the river turned left. The trickle of a waterfall could always be heard, which was really a wide pipe emitting runoff water coming down the hill in the near distance. Cutting through the middle of the hill was a train track. Every night at the same hour, about midnight, the Baltimore and Ohio chugged through without forgetting to blow its whistle. All these sounds receded into the background after I'd lived there a time.

Grandmaw and Grandpaw Pino always seemed old to me, and my memory has held up thus far. I do think Grandpaw got a bit crankier, but more important: he was *always there*, under foot. Grandmaw was not used to having him around during the day. He was forced into retirement in his midsixties, and somehow Grandmaw resented this new arrangement.

He did work his garden, which reaped homegrown herbs, the most golden corn, beefsteak tomatoes as big as grapefruits. And I recall he worked with bricks, concrete retrieved from a dump in the distance, but then after that he was there, and Grandmaw was required to wait on him hand and other hand. She occasionally threw her own hands up in exasperation when he wasn't looking. I reported elsewhere a memory of the shuffling sound his feet made in his size-twelve Lorne and White leather slippers, at all hours, down to his wine cellar for a nip or two.

Grandpaw Pino had one friend, short, round, heavyset Mr. Butcheo who owned a little bodega/fruit stand near the Fourth Street Bridge's end. Grandpaw and Mr. Butcheo spoke regularly on the phone and frequently went to the movies, at least once a week or so. One day, without explanation, without note, Mr. Butcheo strung a rope near the bridge's end, yards from his business, and within viewing of Grandpaw and Grandmaw's house, and hung himself. No explanation, no note. Though the incident speaks volumes, I have little to say about it--I have no more information and there is no one around to ask. I did find it stunning. Grandpaw never again went to the movies and the incident was never again mentioned in their home. Life was strange even in the early 1950s.

Eventually, television got to Lewistown via coaxial cable and Grandpaw spend a lot time on a lounger in front of the tube. Back then, during the day, dozens of old black and white Western were recycled. Invariably, you could hear him say, "I think I saw this... I think I saw this...".

When we played in the yard with a beach ball, he would make fun of us; mock our squeals, squeal for squeal. I've already reported Aunt Conchetta's rushing out of the house one afternoon to butcher-knife the beach ball, a gift *from* her, when we were making a racket unnerving her (amateur diagnosis: rage-aholics, hungover, the both of them.) We were kids, for God's sake.

As the years went on and he aged, Grandpaw was keen to dredge up, over and over again, old incidents referring to his failing memory, "I freget, I freget." He was keen on dredging up fregets, regrets, upsets, old debts.

And later, another of his unabashed emotional blackmail warnings, "I don't know how long I'll be around," which he trotted out on holidays. Blessing? It was customary, a tradition at Easter time when everyone lined up—and I hated and avoided this and never did it—to kneel and kiss the back of his hand. As he'd say and accept your kiss on his hand, "I don't know how much longer I'll be around." So much for not being around very long; he lived to be ninety-two. I should be more endeared to him. As a child and into young manhood, he continued to call me "handsome," never Nino. It was always handsome. If I responded to anything, it was the fact that he had a favorite song, a Spanish quasi-folk tune, "La Paloma (The Dove)," written a hundred forty years ago by Sebastian Iradier, which has the distinction of being one of the most recorded songs of all time.

Speaking of, the early 1950s, I was ten, eleven, twelve, and what I remember most of all, "the cheap, potent," popular music that wafted in over the radio, and I might add all of the time, in every household I was part of.

Before television, before computers, before iPads, iPhones, iTunes, lubricant eyewash, there was radio, and our Philco was on all the time. And I listened and learned the words to songs. Many of them still run around in my brain as contemporary as ever.

The Weavers—"Goodnight Irene." Red Foley—"Chattanooga Shoe Shine Boy." Eileen Barton—"If I Knew You Were Coming Id've (sic) Baked a Cake." Phil Harris—"The Thing." Patti Page—"Tennessee Waltz." Ames Brothers—"Rag Mop." Bing Crosby—"Dear Hearts and Gentle People." Les Paul and Mary Ford—"The World Is Waiting for the Sunrise." Ella Mae Mores—"Blacksmith Blues." Johnny Ray—"Cry." Mills Brothers—"Glow Worm." Eddie Fisher—"Anytime" *and* "Wish You Were Here." (Note: "Wish You Were Here" was from a Broadway musical of that same name and a number-one record for Eddie Fisher).

Billy Eckstine—"My Foolish Heart" *and* "I Apologize." Nat King Cole— "Mona Lisa." Tony Bennett—"Because of You." Rosemary Clooney— "Come on-a My House." Perry Como with the Fontaine Sisters—"You're Just in Love." (Also: "You're Just In Love" was from Broadway musical, *Call Me Madame,* and Como's record reached number five on the charts). Jo Stafford—"You Belong to Me." Mario Lanza—"Be My Love." Frankie Lane—"High Noon." Don Cornell—"I'm Yours" *and* "I'll Walk Alone." Margaret Whiting with Jimmy Wakely—"Silver Bells." Teresa Brewer— "Music, Music, Music"…on and on…Kay Starr, Georgia Gibbs, Doris Day, the Andrew Sisters, Dinah Shore…

Why Sinatra's name is *not* on the above list: In the early 1950s, Frank Sinatra's career had stalled and then (was) reborn again in 1953, when he was cast in the lead in the feature film *From Here to Eternity.* (Revered LP recording "In the Wee Small Hours" didn't come along in 1955.) Did he not host the Oscars in 1953?

*Although Teresa Brewer's "Music, Music, Music" was a number-one million-record seller, some radio stations banned the smash hit in light of this lyric—remember it was 1950: "I'd do anything for you /Anything you'd want me to." *Shocked!* I'm knocked, rocked, socked, and shocked.

CHAPTER 4

Blue Dog. Blue Balls. Code Blue.

✳   ✳   ✳

THE BIG FUNK OF 2016. "Has anybody seen my mojo?" Mock writer's block investigated.

The funk began when daylight saving(s) time ended, November 6, 2016, at 2:00 a.m. The change(s) didn't sit well with me. Suddenly the light was different and downright disorienting; *time* was not where it was supposed to be. I was all mixed up, messed down, thrown off for several days, and then two days later...

Election 2016: November 8. The candidate expected to win didn't, a monstrous shock to me. A jolt! The winning candidate then-president-elect didn't seem quite right for the country; he appeared undignified, brash. Sometimes terrible words came out of his mouth; his tone was nasal; he was unattractive (to me anyway), at times unappetizing. What was curious—it's been reported, ironically, that he selected his vice president and cabinet mainly by their physical appearances. Forget politics for a moment. I find Donald Trump unappetizing, unaesthetically (is that a word?) pleasing—both in look and voice/tone. And I find Kellyanne Conway unaesthetic in look and her voice/tone. Could it be that Kellyanne Conway is Ann Coulter's grandmother?

Ladies and gentlemen of the jury, Donald Trump does not need for me to find him appealing; apparently plenty of folks do. And I pray he doesn't have an enemies list a la Richard Nixon. Hmm. A world leader in a red baseball cap? (Think dignified presidents: John F. Kennedy. Ronald Reagan. Bill Clinton. Bush One. *Donald Trump?*)

As someone pushing seventy-seven, I am concerned that we have a president who might have been helped into power by Russia, a leader who says things like the United States is not so innocent. Word is the White House is in chaos—*defined* by chaos. Not to mention, North Korea wants to bomb us.

Note: I consider myself an independent. I emphatically say I am and want to stay an independent! But I'm accused of other leanings. For one, my friend Clark Adams frequently says, "You're a Blue Dog." Another pal, D K W, says, "Your haircut makes you look like a Republican; are you?" It's herculean to remain an independent. Just ask the Swiss.

May I remain uncertain for now?

I wondered: if I were watching the six o'clock news with my teenage nephew Jack, and the commentator, a reliable fact checker, offered that the candidate who won the electoral vote lied more than 75 percent of the time and distorted the truth in his favor at other times, what would I say to Young Buck: "Don't pay any attention to that. *You* tell the truth all the time"? (In the back of my mind, I wondered what's going to happen to Social Security.) Let me add out of fear, guilt, ambivalence, I am open to loving and supporting this new president. I am pulling for the country and for everything to be all right. For now, at this typing. [At press time, President Trump's (un-)approval ratings, according to Gallup, is 34%, while 61% of those polled disapprove of his performance.]

As a Catholic priest might say somewhere sometime during a Mass, "Let us pray."

Oh, this kind of untimely bewilderment had happened to me before. When John F. Kennedy was assassinated in Dallas on November 22, 1963, forget Democrat or Republican; we all saw the charismatic president of the United States killed before our eyes on television. And, yes, I had bought into the Camelot thing, I admit, that innocent era of good feeling. Fact: At the time, I was about to graduate from college and was busy with finals, as well as juggling the necessary arrangements to move to New York, and a goddamn bloody assassination puts a pall on my hopeful young life (not to mention his). Did the assassination affect my finals exams, I now wonder?

Gratefully, fortunately, when I did get to New York City, I got caught up in the whirlwind of transformation. I had little time to think about the assassination then here in the frenetic Big Apple.

Whirlwind: First stop: Vanderbilt YMCA. Fast: new job, 1964 New York World's Fair. (I could type 114 words a minute on an electric, and that impressed the interviewee.) Got an apartment share with some gents in Queens. Charge Account Number One: Brooks Brothers. Met one of "the swells" and started getting invited everywhere: cocktail parties, art openings, apartment closings—and said yes. Booze at every event: slowly embraced drinking. Joined a gym. Noodled in my free time (huh!) with my writing. Branched out: began writing songs with a World's Fair gent from Hawaii. It appeared as if I was lucky at most everything. Years later, writer Dotson Rader said I prevailed because—en route I said yes; I invariably said yes. Where was I? Oh, yes...

Not long after, during dinner, actress Elaine Stritch, who I'd just met, told a story about overhearing a cleaning woman who had been asked what she thought about the Kennedy assassination. The maid's punch line, and I envision her methodically, continuing the circular cleaning chore at hand, was, "Better him than me." A table of New Yorker dinner companions laughed. That helped. I later learned that nothing is off base for guffaws in New York City.

Next, I threw myself into New York life: Parties. Job search(es). The workouts. Sex. Booze. Pop music, my first love, in the background, American popular music of all kinds (off the record, even country/ Western).

Then my favorite, Bobby Kennedy, was shot. By that time I was deeply ensconced in a lifestyle that took time, money, work, energy, drinks, and lots of Bayer aspirins. I started seeing a therapist and expressed multiple concerns, especially after, without explanation, a strapping, healthy, over-sized weightlifter, gym-rat-friend committed suicide. Dr. German Accent said during one of my weekly whines, "I never worry about you in that way, Mr. Pino. You have the gym, booze, and sex." My friend Lloyd Lee joked, "Yes—all of those things, dancing as fast as they can to keep you afloat." What? I was being held up by shallow fortification?

Back home, Father O'Reilly would be appalled. And now I interject a bad-taste, politically incorrect expression, frequently used in Lewistown, West Virginia, and I never heard once in Gotham City, "I was so busy I didn't know whether to shit or go blind."

Fast forward: Then Al Gore won the popular vote, and for days there was this back and forth, up and down, in and out, and before you could say "Jackie Robinson Parkway," George W. Bush was in the White House. That, too, I had a hard time processing. Again for a minute, forget Democrat/Republican; somehow it didn't quite compute, didn't seem quite honest, or fair, or right. I wish my sensibilities leaned more toward politics; I wish I knew more in that arena. (Should I have taken more political science classes in college? Or law? Most successful television shows involve lawyers, courtrooms, crimes, and criminals. Had I chosen the wrong career?)

Fuck Republican. *Fuck* Democrat. With Global Warming, melting icebergs, "monster" storms, tornedos, hurricanes, record heat, dry spells, forest fires, (what have I left out?) and maybe, just maybe, we should have paid more attention to Al Gore a couple of decades ago...

The truth is I'd rather be listening to Frank Sinatra caress "The Very Thought of You" any day than talking politics.

More...New York life, repetitious but never the same: Parties. Job searches. Sex. Booze. Pop music. Dinner. Out every night. Writing now, I fancied myself a writer. The German therapist with that annoying guttural accent said to me, "Don't say you don't know what you do, who you are, Mr. Pino; you're a *writer.*" Thank you, sir! How does one find the time? Take two aspirins and start all over again.

And back to: Did we pay a price for George Bush's presidency? Just asking. The following eight years, more war and economic uncertainty. As you can tell, I don't pretend to go below the surface in/on politics. Didn't Bush go into the White House when the economy was solid, after Bill Clinton? Wasn't the country in solid shape? Just asking. And I don't mind being contradicted. Yes, I should have taken more history classes. Yes, that's it. History classes. Issues! I need to know more about issues!

And now in 2016, here we go again.

Subsequently, after the election on November 8, 2016, I dragged my ass for days. It smacked of 9/11. Other New Yorkers expressed similar sentiments.

Then the Thanksgiving holiday began, and I didn't feel a bit thankful. I was still spiraling down, and now the holiday blues swirl into the heady, messy mix setting in. Yes, still in a funk from the election, in a downward spiral.

Then on December 3, 2016, I hurt my neck at the gym, doing some exercise I had been advised *not* to do. I'd been warned multiple times even by a known TV sports commentator that that exercise was no longer acceptable, obsolete: pull-downs behind the neck. (My defense, "I did it when I was young.") For days I couldn't move my head very far to the right or left without out an "ouch" out loud. Forget sleeping. (For the first time, I got to experience acupuncture.) For the record, it took more than two months for the pain to completely go away.

Attention, ladies and gents, it is now incumbent on me to get back on track. Do I want to write a third novel? Am I able to write another novel? Do I pursue the big hunt, that private search that began in secret when I was a teenager back in Lewistown, West Virginia—looking for the answer(s) to life? My mother might say, "Get on a stick, Nino!"

Get back in the saddle, guy. Get a move on. And as Liz Taylor told a reporter when he asked her if she was sleeping with Michael Jackson: get a grip!

What the fuck do I do now? If you haven't guessed, all this is really about a selfish, self-centered attempt to get my mojo back on the third novel.

Wrap Map

From nonpartisan Washington, DC, "fact-tank"-respected Pew Research Center's list of Americans' most historical (hysterical?) events, at least in summer 2016:

1. September 11
2. Obama's election
3. Tech revolution
4. JFK's assassination

5. Vietnam War
6. Iraq/Afghan Wars
7. Moon landing
8. Fall of Berlin Wall/end of Cold War
9. Gay marriage
10. Orlando shooting

Clarification and an Inspiration

When I read Joan Didion's *The Year of Magical Thinking*,** I was struck by the inordinate amount of quoted material in the work. Didion's account of the year following her husband's death was immediately acclaimed a classic and went on to win the nonfiction National Book Award. Not a bad role model, Ms. Joan Didion. As the chorine sang, "I can do that. I can do that." I love quotes and will keep that/her in mind. Thank you, Joan Didion; more on you in the appendix.

** *The Year of Magical Thinking*, by Joan Didion, Vintage (2005), and I restate National Book Award winner.

See a tidbit or two on Trump in the appendix.

Editor's note: "Not everyone feels the way you do about Donald Trump." Wait a goddamn minute, hon. I said I was perplexed. I said I was pulling for him *and* the country. Communication is impossible. I will reread what I wrote to see if she's right. Jeez.

Quick query: Have you ever had the experience of reading a concept in the newspaper that was one you were thinking? On Sunday, April 16, 2017, journalist-author Lesley Stahl did a Q&A about her soon-to-become bestseller, *Becoming Grandma*, Penguin/Random House, this way: If you could require the president to read one book, what would it be? Her answer: The United States Constitution. (And, I ask, do you suppose that document is out of date these days?) And what a timely idea for a television program, documentary, or series on the US Constitution.

From the Bible: Ephesians 5:16, "Take advantage of every opportunity, redeem the time, because the days are evil."

Divertimento: My mother always knew when I was stalling. "You're stalling, Nino," she would chide. And right now I'm stalling. (But, Mom, the White House seems to be chaotic.) I'm guilty of using what the German shrink calls my "avoidance mechanism." I'm not sure what to think and/or how to feel about the country right now, so I'm going to take a brief detour. You can move on, skim, or hang with me.

After the April 3, 2017 issue of *Time* magazine, cover story "Is Truth Dead?" (reminiscent of iconic April 8, 1966, *Time* cover "Is God Dead?"), I found myself in heated and sometimes disturbing debates, again and again at the health club, over truth and President Donald Trump's smartphone tweets. We have a president, I argued, who most evenings on the nightly news invariably not only gets many facts wrong but also treats truth as a toy. (Donald Trump shamelessly exaggerated the size of his inaugural crowds...voter fraud...wiretapped NATO funding). Is this gentleman a serial liar with his fake-news rants and fibs about Obama *or* a smart spinner with a highly effective "alternative facts" syndrome? OK, historically presidents have gotten the country in or out of hot water with their beliefs, half-truths, strong points of view: war, delayed peace, allies alienation, appeased enemies, freed slaves, a spaceship on the moon. This time it's different, and frankly, I'm perplexed.

The bottom line for me here, I belabor, is I'm not sure what to think and how to feel—and sometimes find myself apprehensive. When I was young, I was in awe of dignified presidents, and now I'm confused, embarrassed by, and downright offended by the leader of the free world's unappetizing countenance. *I want Camelot* even though Camelot may not ever really have existed. I thought it did, and now, pushing seventy-seven, I long for yesterday, when most of my troubles were so far away.

A positive takeaway on the above from this lover of details: I was so taken by *Time* magazine's April 3, 2017, cover that I did some research. Obviously, *Time* was paying homage to its April 8, 1966, issue, "Is God Dead?" which was the first one since its 1923 inception to appear without an image. This simple, effective, under designed red type appearing through a full rectangle of black impressed me and many others while shocking some with the sentiment and the look. However, an even more

fascinating fact to me was that the type on the cover was hand drawn—
each letter in "Is Truth Dead?" was drawn by hand. The art director found
no comparable of the typeface used on the original 1966 outing. I find
these solid facts reassuring—the terra firma under it all. The therapist
will have a field day.

CHAPTER 5

Always Something There to Remind Me

∗   ∗   ∗

Twice-told tale: I'm not above duplicating a footnote or two and/or quoting myself. Mary Ann Dolby Madden, New York Magazine puzzle maven, and a friend, once joked at dinner, "Old! Old! We hate old!"

I WAKE UP EVERY MORNING and shuffle to the front door and pick up the three newspapers that were delivered during the early-morning hours, while all the world is fast asleep. Three newspapers, four inches high, several pounds of information. Yes, the world has changed some while I was sleeping. There may not be very much new under the sun, but if there is, it's said somewhere in those three dailies. And I'm reminded once more, again and again, day after day, every single morning despite what's going on in my life—the world and the universe move on, with or without me, and I'd better make goddamn sure I keep up or else.

Lest I forget for a moment, there is always someone, some*thing* there to remind me.

In the mid-1980s, at all times, I carried my gym bag and toted a brown leather weight belt with my initials on it. Back then I worked out hard every day. The neighborhood diner I favored was Utopia at West Seventy-Second and Amsterdam Avenue (it's still there). My favorite booth was in the back, and I even had a regular Greek waiter, who liked to joke about my oversized weight belt, which I hung on a hook next to my windbreaker. Greek waiter Frank fancied trying on the weight belt and taunting me with my nickname, Caballo. In fact, even the cashier, George the Greek, greeted me daily with a hello and a Caballo, Spanish for "horse"; this

Greek waiter had picked up the word from the busboys. In their minds, they associated this wide weight belt with a (work) horse, hence Caballo.

Years passed, and, sadly, Waiter Frank had a heart attack and went to his reward.

Recently, in 2016, I went to the Utopia with a group of local pals, and that original register man, short, graying, part owner, Greek George, now retired, was filling in for the vacationing counterman. Go, George!

"Now," he said to me proudly, "I'm seventy-one" and greeted me warmly. "Nino, Nino, Nino, I remember you from 1986. You came in every day with your gym bag and your weight belt, and Frank—you remember Frank—he died. He called you Caballo. He liked to try on your weight belt and dance a little, remember?" Yes, George, I remember. That was thirty years ago.

"Yes," George plowed on, "you were young with dark hair and hand-some. Now you have gray hair, and you're old." Why, thank you, George, nice to see you too. Glad we're both here some thirty years later. What is it that Confucius says about how a man in business should always have a smile on his face?

More recently, this *dees*, *dems*, and *dos*, sixty-fiveish-year-old asshole, sporting an obvious gray toupee parted on the left, (or was it hair trans-plants? Don't blame Rogaine.) I might add, he came up to me with this queer question, "I see you almost every day working out. How old are you?"

"What?"

"How old are you?"

"Seventy-six," I said, trying to get away from him; he was following close behind.

"I wanted to ask you, when did you start feeling it?"

"Feeling what?"

"Feeling old?"

"Fuck off, *gavone*."

Now when he is coming my way, I turn and walk the other way. As Barbra Streisand asided in *Funny Girl*, "In this pickle, what would Sadie do?" To be honest, I'm not always sure how to treat other people—what's appropriate in interactions—even bores. I like being fair, and I'm not always sure how to be. Keep in mind this is New York City, where you bump into thousands every day, and sometimes you want to say "fuck off."

Grace:

"…adults sixty-five to sixty-nine are more likely to be working than teenagers, except during summer…older workers are increasingly less likely to be part timers. Nearly two thirds of workers older than sixty-five hold full-time jobs…working at least thirty-five hours a week…We're also working longer because we can. True, health crisis can strike at any point, but lengthening life spans and improved health, at least among higher-income seniors, have contributed to extended careers."*

Thank you, Paula Span. Thank you, *New York Times*. Thank you, Jesus.

*From Paula Span's article "65 Is Just a Number," *New York Times*, August 2, 2016.

"We are always the same age inside." Gertrude Stein.

CHAPTER 6

Grandfathering My Grandfathers

* * *

MY PATERNAL GRANDFATHER WORKED IN the coalmines until he was forced into retirement at age sixty-three. My maternal grandfather also worked in the mines, but as a carpenter, until age sixty-five. My mother often referred to Cooks Mines in her dialogue. I never had the wherewithal to ask her if she'd lived near the mines before moving to Lewistown proper.

Although Grandpaw Pino could not write his name (he would make an X, and I filled in his signature), he was a master bricklayer and a celebrated (why not?—he gave it away) winemaker. What's more, he had a garden that would make Pepperidge and Boone Farm envious: beefsteak tomatoes larger than baseballs, silver-dollar-sized strawberries, and sweet corn sweeter than sugar cakes. He made his own wine and drank some of it every day of his life. He was not a whoop-de-doo guy, downright cranky and angry a lot (hung over?). I hesitate, but include anyway, and I rehash: he used the word *kotz* at the end of every sentence whether he was swatting flies or referring to a local politician or the president of the United States. *Kotz.* Alternated with fist-in-the-air *managia!* Or *Man-a-gia, Ah-mer-re-ca!* Cursing the country that opened its arms to him.

Early memories of him are preferable. When we were young children, he'd drop by occasionally to help us on a holiday to get everyone (on foot) to his house. On one of my early birthdays when Dad brought me the unorthodox record player that hooked up and played through the radio, Grandpaw Pino was there celebrating with us, helping to change the ten-inch vinyl discs on the turntable.

As we grew older, he never came back, not once, to that basement apartment on Main Street nor to the two-story on Dennison Lane, where we ultimately moved after the eviction after that painful stay at Grandpaw Bia's. Closing argument on Grandpaw Pino: I did not identify with him. He was too inarticulate, too belittling, too disgruntled (hung over?). There are multiple degrees of separation here. Why, he disliked cinnamon to the extent that my Grandmaw Pino had to invent a new way to make pumpkin pies. She then substituted chocolate for cinnamon, and, yes, folks loved her Thanksgiving invention, but the point here: cinnamon is my favorite spice. I add cinnamon to any dish and dessert that will take it.

Though not vocal, my reserved maternal (he had green eyes) Grandpaw Bea, on the other hand, read newspapers constantly, smoked a pungent maple-smelling pipe, and could drive a nail directly into a two-by-four faster than I could lift a hammer in the air. With a handsaw, he could cut through a straight line on a piece of lumber equal to the precision of the electric option. Grandpaw Bea used to add chocolate (there's that additive again, chocolate) to his coffee (decades before chocolate was considered a healthy boost) until the doctors made him stop. Grandpaw Bea smoked that sweet, smelly, maple-pungent pipe until his daughters made him stop. Oh, by the way, he lived to be a hundred, and I'm told could still get an erection. He terrified nurses in the hospital with "Look! I'm a hundred."

I introduce these gents now to disclose I am fascinated by the coal business from afar. I never tire of reading stories about coal, oil, gas in the detailed New York dailies. You get the real story about coalmines, etc., here in the New York dailies, and, I suspect, the media back home hold back on some questionable details. Why bite the hand that feeds ya? (Only speculating.) More pertinent, I distanced myself from those local professions mentally, physically, and emotionally. Personally? I was never hugged by either of this gents. Why, I don't even remember shaking their hands or kissing their rings (as some did as Eastertime).

What I'm really doing now is lifting the cover on the subtext. I didn't even consider working in the mines, or the fish market, or a pizzeria, or a graveyard, or any of the local businesses akin to my male kin. My interest in coal and carpentry, brick-oven pizza, meatball hoagies, and pepperoni rolls as well as digging graves is more intellectual curiosity than professional interest.

As early as junior high school, I wanted to be a writer. And I suspect that yearning sprang from the inability as a kid to be heard, listened to by my family, as well as a lack of the vocabulary to genuinely communicate with them.

As you might have heard, I was quietly reading books that might shed some light on—that clued me in on the answer(s) to life. (Those wrapped-in-brown-paper volumes were not something one flaunted around in Lewistown, West Virginia, in polite company.)

My legacy? A vocabulary of Calabrian dialect spoken phonetically and listed here, at the end (see Calabrian dialect glossary). A shitload of my mother's precious original recipes. And Grandpaw Bea promised me a gold railroad pocket watch. When I was grown, I held him to it, and he gave it to me. I passed it on to my youngest sibling, trusting it would be better taken care of in his possession, more lasting in his hands.

Yes, that brother.

CHAPTER 7

As Bette Midler Reminded Us, "But You've Got to Have Friends"*

∗   ∗   ∗

*"Friends," 1973 Bette Midler hit written by Buzzy Linhart and "Moogy" Klingman, published by Sony/ATV Music/Universal Music Group.

I USED TO HAVE A savvy friend in Washington, DC, the late Oklahoman Burton C. Wood, who was an Ivy League lawyer and a lobbyist for MBA (Mortgage Bankers Association). It was his wont to jokingly poke me in the shoulder with this: "Nino. Make young friends." (He'd grown older, mideighties, and most of his pals had dispersed.)

On the other hand, Mr. Cole Porter found friendship a perfect *blendship*. Sounds nice, a perfect blendship, but these days I'm not sure *what* to think.

Take the *Boston Globe* editor who recently opined that "middle-aged men have no friends." I don't know if that's true, but reading that sure does get one to thinking. Yes, in the past I have written ad infinitum about friends, "the swells" who changed my life with a wave of a hand, the young people I met when new to New York who died early from ill-chosen lifestyles, etc., etc., etc. I even wrote in Novel Two, *The Answer to Life*, "It is uncool to admit you're lonely." But I'm no closer to any meaning, and as you've suspected, I'm always looking for answers.

Now at seventy-six (do you hear those trombones a-blasting?), I have learned to socialize in new ways, although I admit it doesn't really solve the loneliness problem 100 percent: the health club, any kind of 12 step meeting, a gentlemanly nod to the workers near the windows in every business I pass walking the long block east to Broadway. As my mother would say to me, "Nino, you're stalling."

Maybe I am. I'm not sure how to address this sensitive subject, and, in life, it's the crux of getting one's ducks in a row. I have admitted before that after a certain age, it *is* harder to make new friends, and one must factor in the *mishagoss*,** the resistance to exerting the effort to making new pals. (When I pray, I oftentimes begin with a petition around relationships; after all, what else is there?)

For openers to friendship, we find our time now is more valuable, more precious, at a time we have finally learned to like our own company (sometimes).

We like looking at the news and/or at least reading the daily papers. Darn shame. We got this far, and now we have to worry about these damn new findings. "They," the experts, are saying the older you get, the unhealthier it is not to have close friends. Someone even wrote a cheeky book about it: *Loneliness: Human Nature and the Need for Social Connection*, by John T. Cacioppo.***

J. C. claims that social isolation has an impact on health comparable to the biggies like high blood pressure, lack of exercise, obesity, or that killer, smoking. Other recent scientific studies imply that social separation is bad for sleep patterns, immune systems, stress-hormone levels. What's an alter-cocker to do? A bookend *closer* here to friendship—as Cy Coleman and Dorothy Fields asked as a tag to their song "Where Am I Going?": *You* tell me.****

**Mishagoss: Yiddish term for craziness.

****Loneliness: Human Nature and the Need for Social Connection*, by John T. Capioppo and William Patrick, W. W. Norton & Company.

****"Where Am I Going?" is a showstopper from big hit Broadway musical *Sweet Charity*, by Cy Coleman and Dorothy Fields. Note on that: The story circulated that Barbra Streisand left off that kick-ass last line, "You tell me!" on her rousing recording. When questioned why by composer Cy Coleman, Streisand supposedly said, "Nobody tells me, Cy."

Jane Brody, the *New York Times*, June 13, 2017, quoting Emma Seppala of the Stanford Center for Compassion and Altruism Research and Education and author of *The Happiness Track:** "social connectedness generates a positive feedback loop of social, emotional and physical well-being. A societal decline in social connectedness may help to explain recent increases in reports of loneliness, isolation, and alienation; and may be why people seek psychological counseling. Sociological research revealed that more than 25 percent of Americans had no one to confide in...They lacked a close friend with whom they felt comfortable sharing a personal problem." For those seeking a health-promoting lifestyle, Jane Brody added that it's not enough to focus on eating your veggies and getting regular exercise. Dr. Seppala advises, "Don't forget to connect." Emma Seppala, **The Happiness Track*, 2016, HarperOne Publishing.

More on friends in chapter 16. These days, I find myself saddled with an ongoing rumination on friendship and all the avenues between generation gaps filled up with minutiae. I pray daily, "Dear God, help me know what's appropriate in relationships and to do that."

CHAPTER 8

Bold Editor's Note to Me. She asks, "What about wrinkles, aches and pains, bunions, loss of strength, etc., etc., etc., Nino? Aging! While you're at it, include stuff we all go through. Plus *your* reaction to it. Then include some suggestions on how to *deal* with it." Bunions? Phooey. (I tried my best here and even threw in a couple of beauty tips). *Bunions?!!*

*　　*　　*

AA axiom, rubber stamped: Take what you want and leave the rest.

Moi?

At my most recent annual physical, the doctor said, "You need to take more vitamin D, two thousand units a day. Cholesterol, excellent. B12, adequate. Blood count and blood sugar, stable. Blood cell platelets slightly low; we will take this blood test again in three months."

Immediately after, less than a week, right hip and right leg started hurting. Amateur diagnosis: arthritis and sciatica. It aches periodically but not always. I don't let it stop me. I work out every day anyway and occasionally pop an aspirin or two. Fuck it.

In the past, I had a series of gym injuries, including:

1. Lower back.
2. Tennis elbow, twice, which was drained.
   (My wont: I let the injuries heal and then go right back to the health club, come hell, high water, low tide, and nagging pain: ignored.)

3. Tried something, a fancy exercise I saw some young buck doing with a pumped professional trainer (cables, pulling from below and up). My hand swelled to the size of a grapefruit. Went to emergency room. Took meds and soaked in hot water. There is still a bump from that incident on my left hand, which I ignore.

4. Some bloke at the gym said to me one day near the treadmill, "You don't perspire enough. You need to do more when running." I increased my speed and hurt my foot: foot, too, swelled. The foot soon healed, but I went back to my original speed, 3.5, and from then on ignored most suggestions from gym rats half my age.

5. Cool it! A TV personality came up to me and said, "I wouldn't do that exercise; it is no longer viable." (While seated, pull-downs behind by neck. I did it every day as a young guy.) When he wasn't looking, I went back to it. Phooey, I seriously hurt my neck and was out of commission in that area for about six weeks. Unwisely (?), I worked out anyway; I did leg work and other nonpainful, acceptable exercises.

6. There was a left painful knee thing that in the early days would have required an operation and was cured with medication. I don't know if it was caused by gym exercises or a physical therapist strong pull during a session. Nutshell: I lived.

In 2003, I was hit from behind by a young man driving an SUV while texting on a cell. Extended bout with physical therapy.

In 2001, I suffered a mini stroke that began a regimen of Aggrenox and Lipitor, twice a day. Another brief stint with physical therapy. Decades later, I still take Aggrenox and Lipitor once a day. (No one believes I didn't miss a day at the gym. I can't always do what I call "full workouts," but I showed up, nurturing my working-out obsession.)

Brief bout with shingles on chest. The reddish rash came on quick, hot, and painful and then went away.

Later, another persistent rash on chest, cured with an inexpensive medication. Dr. Dermatologist called this new red menace Grover's Disease (did the doctor make that up?) and recommended a new salve costing hundreds of dollars I did not have. I saw a second (opinion) skin doctor, who recommended an inexpensive medication called Clindamycin Phosphate topical solution. Red Menace Number Two cleared up rash in a week.

In the late 2010s, an operation (?) on my left little toe to remove a bunion, which hurt when I wore cowboy boots. The scalpel scarred my left pinky toe.

I had a cyst on my lower back, basic fatty tissue, removed twice, producing little pain but mild inconvenience. Curbed my workouts for a short time—can you believe such a thing?

Skin: Ongoing skin problems, acne, adult acne. Started cleansing treatments with New York's then-most-prominent dermatologist (Howard T. Berman, MD) once, twice, sometimes three times a week for a thorough cleaning. To show you how high-tone it was, Fifth Avenue and Sixty-Ninth Street. I saw Jackie Kennedy there on my first visit; Joan Kennedy on a subsequent appointment; *Vogue* editor Diana Vreeland dictating to her secretary in the waiting room. Elaine Stritch went there for treatments also and other actresses and Upper East Side matrons. I got in under the wire and the red velvet rope via my (for a short time, agent) longtime friend, famous Gloria Safier. May she rest in peace and God bless her nurturing, motherly soul.

Berman's treatment: steam on face, nurse opened pustule (?) and squeezed out blackheads, and then the face and any other treated parts got a once-over with stinging, hissing dry ice. (One glowed for a day.) But Mother Nature always has the last word. Within ten days, I needed the treatment again. (When I worked, insurance paid a large percentage.) Endlessly irritating to me, the things that money can buy (and I can't).

Dentist: My first root canal, a wonderful thirty-nine-year-old dentist walked me through it. I hated the damn rubber dam on my face. The following week he had a heart attack and died. I felt it was my fault. I admit I do *not* visit the dentist with ease. But my teeth are my teeth, and I take credit for them. When I was a teen, that lower back tooth broke, and I looked up a dentist in the phone book (my aunt had dated him). He pulled the tooth, and after that I went to the dentist regularly, paying for it with my paper route money. When I got to NYC, I had my teeth cleaned at least every three months. That's why I like to say: my teeth are my teeth.

Therapy: Early on, after arriving in New York City, my friend LLB suggested therapy. His advice, "A therapist will help you with your work, if nothing else." Not long after, Dr. Thick German Accent straightened me out when I was whining about not knowing what career to choose. He firmly stated with assurance, "You're a writer, Mr. Pino. You're a writer." I was and am.

While on one of my (extended?) stays in Los Angeles, taking those darn screenwriting classes, I contracted a persistent sinus infection. Finally I saw a friend's doctor out there who prescribed Seldane and an antibiotic. The symptoms soon went away. (California, I like to say: all dirty air and derriere.) Seldane was presently taken off the market. The story went that Seldane caused heart attacks. Then I heard, and can't confirm, one ingredient was removed, and then it was back on the market as Claritin. I have no idea if that's true or not.

Once I contracted a good, old, garden-variety body itch: crabs. I went to a doctor near the office, who gingerly lifted my pubes with a pair of twisters and then pronounced a little too loudly for my money, "You have crabs, Nino." Ewwww. He prescribed baths and washing with tincture of green soap, followed by several days of A200 in that area. They were gone in a jiffy, never to return or see the light of day again. Eminently embarrassing and difficult to be a human being, isn't it?

While in college, living in a rented room in a one-story house with two other men, I got a bad case of athlete's foot—so bad my foot swelled and I limped a little. University infirmary gave me a soaking cure that turned my toenails black but dispelled/cured the affliction lickety-split.

Breather: Do you get a sense of how pedestrian my aches and pains are, editor dear? (I pray I'm not tempting fate here by inventorying them.) That first broken tooth when I was a teen turned out to be a blessing. I was able from then on to make sure I brushed and saw the dentist regularly, pulling my own money together not only to buy the toothbrushes but also visit the dentist. A classic wake-up call.

Before that, not much else. Oh, yes, I recall one dog bite by a big black dog sicced on me by a local boy who walked with a limp. Sent me to a doctor for a shot (tetanus), 1945–1946. I was humiliated in my white panty-like shorts. I had not yet started wearing grown man's underwear. (What were they thinking?) Maybe it was less expensive and easier to launder the same kind of underwear for all six of us.

Luckily, I didn't visit another professional of any type until that broken tooth, circa 1951.

Miller time, light-up time, wind-up time…

And I'll close with some beauty tips: I read somewhere that men had an advantage over women—they shave their faces, which allows them to remove outer layers of dead skin, and they are less likely to develop wrinkles. Thus, when I shave, I go as close to the crow's feet as I can, assuming I'm shaving years off from my age. Fat chance.

I'm often asked about the full head of hair at seventy-six-plus. After a shower, when I dry my hair, I use several, as many as four, sometimes five, bath towels to vigorously dry. Never a hair dryer. Subsequently I have a full head of healthy Italian hair, which people like to reach up and touch. (Probably better locks prevail with good genetics and have nothing to do with Nino's towel-drying regiment.) And the final touch, still, after fifty-five years, I work in a little dab of Brylcreem.

I have the usual size grown-man's prostate and get up a couple of times during the night to take a leak. However, I drink an inordinate amount of water, always have. Not for health reasons, simply I'm saddled with a big thirst. I love the taste of cold water in a cowpoke's tin cup. (I'm just glad it is no longer alcoholic liquid.) Of an evening, while reading the papers, with one eye on the boob tube, I chugalug gallons of ice-cold water out of that tin cup like a cowboy at a campfire. (I wonder if I was a cattle chaser in another life. No, I think I was reincarnated from Michelangelo's David. Maybe both. Can you be both? Those gents were alive in different centuries. That's it! I was reincarnated from both). I'll tell you about a doctor's trip up the nu-nu.

Here goes: Since Dad died at seventy-six from prostate cancer, I had a series of tests in my seventy-sixth year. (A) Cystoscopy. One involved going up my nu-nu—that's the front if you're asking—with lights and monitors all around as a gentle urologist did his good work. (Though he offered, I did not want to watch. Reminder, this is going up the male genitalia with a prod.) Prognosis, if you will: Dr. S. D. found a tiny thing, had it biopsied, and it was all OK. (B) Next, the same hospital did a CAT scan of my midsection—innocent enough. I brought a book and read while waiting and prepping. And then the nurses injected a dye and started the CAT scan procedure, also innocent enough, instructing me if I had to go, to hold it. They needed to take some pictures. I've always been photogenic, and this sounded fine. I was able to hold it—for as long as I could and finally gave in. It turned out the nurses got the pictures they needed, and I got to go home. Innocent enough.

Note: It was St. Patrick's Day, buses and cabs were stalled, and I had to take a leak every ten minutes or less. I was able to let go in several cubbyholes and driveways on the Upper East Side (illegal, by the way, in New York City) until I had to take a subway—took the long way home. I got off subway and rushed into diner near the Seventy-Second and Broadway subway stop. Phew! To all male readers: Avoid a midsection CAT scan where they are checking your urinary track. At least don't schedule the procedure on St. Patrick's Day. Footnote to all that: in the name of good health, I have been prodded up the backside and way up in the front,* neither pleasant, but this is 2017, and there are multiple ways to stay healthy at any cost.

I will spare male and female readers alike further discussion of the procedure called cystoscopy. The man is propped up on a procedure table. Women don't have the franchise on this.

Then again, I'm once more reminded, it's not easy being a human being.

BEAUTY CUTIE

At the gym I go to, there's a small refrigerator at our disposal filled with dozens of rolled-up, ice-cold, white wet washcloths. I appropriate one and hold the end of it under my chin and then move it around on my neck as I go from one workout machine to the next. (I read somewhere that ice does something to fat that makes it disappear—fact, fiction?—but that's my feeble attempt to get rid of a sagging jaw line.

At aforementioned health club/gym, I witness metrosexuals moisturizing from head to toe, back and front, even their private parts and bubble butts. I never moisturize. I don't have anything against it; I'm just too lazy to stand in front of a mirror and grease up. What's more, the thought of having goop all over makes me cringe.

That's it for my beauty tips, folks, and I trust I've helped you to stay youthful.

DIET

I eat most everything and anything and too much of it. I use olive oil on everything I heat up, along with some black pepper. I put cinnamon on anything that will take it, mostly at breakfast and then on some desserts. I never put salt on anything, ever. As a child, at home, most meals were perfectly spiced and didn't need salt or anything else (oh, occasionally a little parmesan). I never eat fried food—oh, wait: sometimes Chinese restaurants will slip something in but, by choice, never French fries or anything else deep oiled. Yes, I do love hamburgers, and I may be cribbing on that score. I can't resist a great big ole cheeseburger with lettuce, tomato, and mayonnaise once in a while but infrequently. I love pizza and have it de temps en temps. New York has some of the best pizza anywhere—it's anti-Gotham not to (fuck you, Chicago). I'm aware we should not eat excessive amounts of sugar, and I know many foods have white sugar in them, but I generally dive in anyway. I do not add sugar to coffee or breakfast cereal, but sugar is always lurking there in the background. I suspect I'd look and feel better without sugar, but I indulge anyway. But never sugary or diet soft drinks, ever. Then there are days when I have six cups of coffee (with half and half)—not saintly here. My maternal grandfather lived to be a hundred. My paternal grandfather, ninety-two. When we were speaking, my youngest sibling warned, "You'd better start taking better care of yourself." Hey, I'm seventy-six; can you hear the trombones blasting? Or am I starting to hear things? Wait. *Where's my cell phone?*

And since you brought up the subject of food, check out fifty of my mother's original recipes in Book Two: *F.U.! (Follow Up)! The Answer to Life Revisited,* Amazon.com.

No MSG, please: I *never* knowingly consume MSG or tenderizers of any kind. My system knows when it's been slipped into some food, Chinese, and/or a hamburger.

Vitamins

I take one vitamin D every day at breakfast time. After I swallow the capsule, I shake the bottle in my ear, adding one more faction to help me remember I took the vitamin D. Don't get old.

Spices

Quickly, spices I favored: Ground cinnamon on everything breakfast. Oregano and rosemary on any dish with red sauce, both of which I'm told are healthy. I add cayenne red pepper to salsa with chips, *hot*, but I hear it's good for you and tasty. Then there's turmeric added to mustard dishes, an acquired taste. (I'll mix three kinds of mustard on a dish, sprinkle on a healthy helping of turmeric into the mustards, then slap mixture on a ham and Swiss cheese on whole-wheat sandwich.) Finally, pepper on everything and anything that will take it (mashed potatoes, rice). But salt? Never on anything. Ever. Healthy whole-wheat-bread sandwich suggestion: ham, warmed, with a small amount of rosemary and thyme, topped with a slice of Swiss cheese. (On October 26, 2016, the *New York Post* devoted an entire page by Molly Shea to the spice rosemary. Here's what Ms. Shea said, "New studies suggest rosemary may be the key to a long and healthy life." Failing that, it sure tastes good.)

Constipation and Portnoy's dad. In Philip Roth's classic *Portnoy's Complaint,* the narrator referenced his father's constipation multiple times. Let me tell you a little secret, and keep in mind, I'm not a doctor. On everything I warm over, on the stove or in the microwave, I put a thin layer of top-of-the-line olive oil and some black paper. Every dish. I suspect one who does this never has Portnoy's father's complaint.

Olive oil is the cornerstone of a Mediterranean diet and boasts a multitude of benefits. *Possible* health benefits: olive oil reduces inflammation, kills cancer cells, reduces risk of type-2 diabetes, "might" help prevent strokes, assists in keeping the heart young, claims to fight osteoporosis, maybe protects from depression, found to (possibly) help prevent skin cancer, "might" help in preventing strokes, and on and on.

Cup o' Joe

I read somewhere that caffeine seems to undo some of the disruption caused by aging. Hallelujah! I'm certainly glad to hear that since I sip the brew all day long. I'm a democratic type; I alternate: Maxwell House. Dunkin' Donuts. French Roast. 100% Colombian. Hot java is a healthy habit. A regular regimen is a cancer-fighting antioxidant while it's keeping heart vessels clear and at the same time lowering the risk of type-2 diabetes. Thank God the drug companies didn't find out about this way back. Under no circumstance am I giving up coffee for Lent. I suspect coffee is in my bloodstream. When I was a child, my parents always had a pot of A&P Eight O'clock coffee brewing on the back burner. When they grocery shopped, one of the stops was the red, outsized grinding machine that would grind their whole beans to taste. (I suspect Mother often had coffee and cake when she was pregnant with me, and it's percolating in my bloodstream.)

New findings: "Men who drink Italian-style coffee can significantly reduce their likelihood for prostate cancer, according to a new study." Brewed this way: high-pressure, 190-degree-water temperature, with no filter (might lower risk of common cancer that affects one in seven American men by 53 percent). Researchers tested coffee extracts with caffeine and without caffeine and found the benefits were mostly likely due to the caffeine rather than other substances in the coffee. The specific way Italian coffee is brewed lowers loss of bioactive compounds, and it's now being further studied in the prevention of not only cancer but also other dreaded diseases.

The above, from a fine writer with a curious name, definitely not Italian, Joe Dziemianowicz, in the *New York Daily News.*

CHAPTER 9

Moving It Around on the Desk and in Other Places. I'm reminded of the television commercial set in a health club where a rep is showing a hulk around as he keeps repeating, "I pick things up, and I put them down." The gym rep gets the message and ushers oaf out through a side door. I do the same. I pick things up and put them down.

✳   ✳   ✳

WHEN DOING THE INFREQUENT (FOR me, anyway), loathsome chore of going through old income tax files (circa 2008), dreading, vetting, and shredding, I ran across a smudged 8½ x 11 sheet with three columns: (a) a name on the left, (b) home numbers next, and (c) in column three, office/work numbers. This document guaranteed I could have drinks and dinner with someone every night. Someone on the list would be willing.

As I skimmed the sheet, I realized all of the friends on it were gone. Gone: a few, I didn't know to *where*, but the rest, the majority of them were dead.

Wonderful, fun, intelligent, savvy, snappy, hip New Yorkers I could tap any night of the week to have drinks and dinner—drinks for sure. And they are all among the missing—gone.

I witnessed Lloyd Lee go from trim super sport—out on the town most evenings around the city, invited everywhere, the ultimate sport, superb company, successful lifestyle guru, man included every time—overnight, with a snap of a finger, to stroke-ridden old man, withering away. Virtually overnight, literally shut in, with 'round-the-clock nurses and other caretakers. It was hard to watch and personally threatening. Is that what happens to everyone, even the most blessed?

No pity party here: I admit from the get-go, I had a good run. Fun from the minute I arrived in New York City, a big city that embraced this small-town, penniless, newly graduated, unexposed West Virginian Italian. Yes, New York put its arms around me. I was invited everywhere and went come hell, high water, hailstorm, or Hail Mary. I showed up. Way back, I was already admitting, "I had a good run," a high time,* even at the expense of reality. I was always behind financially (who cared?), and, for decades, I went out every night. The heavenly upside to all this? Now I can look back, and I can say with impunity: I had a good run.

*It's High Time

It's high time that we all got stinkin'
High time we were gay
It's high time that we did some drinkin'
But in a strictly American way.

*From Broadway musical *Gentleman Prefer Blondes*, music by Jule Styne and lyrics by Leo Robin, book by Joseph Field and Anita Loos, Music Sales Corp. Publishers, 1949.

Dead poets and other friends...where have all the flowers gone?

...In a perpetual state of mourning...nothing chases the blues away or alleviates/erases the feelings beyond *deeper* than sad...T. McB., that actor in the wheelchair in *Halloween*, pushed down the stairs...the aforementioned lifestyle editor, bestselling author Lloyd L....Peter P., Central Park park ranger...Peter C., artist and photo re-printer...Lucy C., royalties head at CBS/Columbia Records/Sony...Jim P., brother of name baseball player and better looking than Cary Grant...David T., Roy Cohn's chauffeur, where did you go? (A scene in *Angels in America*: Roy Cohn and his chauffeur in a hospital room, forcing a dying man to sign a document. In reality, the chauffeur was a warm, gentle, appealing drinking buddy of mine. At one juncture, he telephoned me from Florida, where he "had to stay for a while." I never heard from him again. Where did you go, David T.?)…Grace V., fun, funny, "fabulous," fierce friend of mine and Lorraine S.'s housemate…L. J., florist, on and on and on. B. James, E. Stritch, T. Kelleher, P. Pappas, P. Catzanero, T. Findley, D. Haraway, J. Africano, T. Arnold, S. McIntosh, B. Courtney, B. Wood, J. Pfile, Phil A., Werner C., H. Cook, C. Lunnin, P. Botts, D. Haraway, R. Green, S. Cruthers, L. Lee, M.A. Madden, G. Vann, A. Bolesta, A. Calcagni, D. Eaton, J. Kirkwood, J. Desmond, C. Brosnan, J. Molthen, etc., etc., etc.—*all have gone to their rewards. A mixed message—today, no one to drink with, thank the Lord and pass the sarsaparilla.* Just a little glass of white wine?

A sad, somber, shocking reflection:

I got a telephone call at 8:46 on 9/11, after the first plane hit the World Trade Center, from best friend R. C. He worked at the bank next door to the center. Debris was falling outside his office window; he said a plane had hit a tower and his building was being evacuated. A few minutes later, I received a second call from R. C., now on the street below. He had just thrown up. Bodies were falling out of the WTC onto the pavement. Go uptown, I said, alarmed; go home! Nothing's running, he answered. Walk. Walk! He hung up and went uptown on foot with soot falling all over him. At that moment, he did not know that both towers had fallen behind him. He learned that news when he got home on the Upper East Side.

For weeks after, R. C. had vertigo. Therapy and medical help were offered. He accepted neither entitlement. R. C.'s bank transferred him to a Park Avenue branch temporarily until new arrangements could be made.

It is with remorse that I report R. C. was never the same after the September 11 attacks. The vertigo hung around for about six months and then finally, fully went away. Little by little, he began to distance himself from me. He was a close friend; I felt hurt. Not long after, he left town. The last I heard he had taken early retirement and was living somewhere upstate. A decade has passed. I still can't shake the sadness, the soreness, the anger. On holidays, I send a card to his old address and leave a message on his cell phone as well, but essentially he, too, I'm sad to say, is gone from my life. And he took his wok pot with him.

Grim 1980s interjection-recollection-misconception:

When visiting Greenwich Village in the 1980s, they were everywhere: You could see young men withering away, some wearing white gloves to ward off any infection from something they might touch, from another person, from anything. They were afraid of you, and you, you were afraid of them.

Note: In 1982, the first case of what would become known as AIDS was reported. At that time, there were no established prevention methods and no effective treatment options. Thank God that is no longer true.

But then there were wonderful memories and the free and easy 1960s and 1970s, and now I'm left with recollections that sometimes sustain me at seventy-six.

So I can use my energy to sit down every morning at a computer and write/type. As some are quick to point out: "You often knock off yourself." Yes, and will now conjure up one of my favorites. In the smart, eminently, *geminately* quotable film *My Dinner with Andre*, the hero looks into the camera and says he doesn't know if he has any talent, but every morning he gets up and moves *it* around on the desk. I now get up every morning and move it around on the computer table. And thank the Lord, and pass me the coffee mug, I have a backlog of memories to sustain me—and most of the time, I don't feel one damn bit deprived or the like. Editor suggested a summary.

1964–1965 New York World's Fair. Writing songs; making contacts (networking, they call it now). 1968, New Orleans, Mardi Gras. 1969–1970 Producing records and advertising commercials. Blackout on November 9, 1965: sexy. Cover stories for GQ, *four in a row, Reeve, Gere, O'Neal, Hart Bochner. People magazine credit. Fire Island. Cocktail parties. Writing more songs now. Openings. Closings. Theater. Movie screenings. Articles I authored in various periodicals and newspapers. The Hamptons. The Hamptons. The Hamptons. Jury duty. Early draft of a novel. An agent. A second agent. The novel disappears—lost. (Where did I put that last draft?) Flown to Los Angeles to write a story and interview Joan Darling, Susan Dey; to visit a movie set; to work in a tiny office on the Paramount Pictures lot. To do that cover on Christopher*

Reeve. Competed for the title tune to feature film The Swimmer. *(Came in second. Damn.) Next month, trip to Palm Springs to write an article,* After Dark Magazine. *Blackout: July 13–14, 1977, scary and tedious. I take more screenwriting classes. (Screenplays look as if they'll be made into feature films.) They are not. Two-year stint with Liz Smith/*Daily News *as New York "legman." Late 1970s, maître d' job at the hottest restaurant in town, Joanna...*I woke up one morning and it was 1980.

Back to the present. Friends and new people I happen to meet these days ask, "Are you retired?" (It's the gray hair.) I'm typically taken aback. I work every day, attempt to write pages every morning of my life, and when I'm not at the computer, I'm reading something that might be of value, of use, in my pages. New pages, every day, or else. Yes, I've always chased rainbows. "Busy," that absurd word that encompasses all "busy," is my quiet search for the answers to life. What about all the songs I wrote and wrote and wrote, once in a while recorded, incidentally, without too much reward except an occasional pat on the back? And, oh yes, one or two advertising jingles. The long-playing records (LPs) I produced; ad copy I wrote for record companies; music publishing stints. All the while drawing a paycheck, which, without fail, withheld money for the future. I was making an income to support my creative endeavors and accruing some Social Security but never, in my eyes, I confess, fully catching the brass ring. But I did it; I plied my trade, which chiefly included using words, words, words. Who cares if I never made it big (in my eyes, I didn't)? No number-one record. No Grammy award. And, yes, there was occasionally a pat on the poo-poo for a couple of magazine-cover stories. It was never big time for me. Trust I'm not tempting fate here. I have to remind myself I came from a small glass-factory/coal-mining town with two hundred dollars in one pocket and a thousand dreams in the other.

(AA suggests: Be grateful, my man, be grateful. And while you're at it, make a list of "things" for which you are thankful. And words from my favorite writer, Arthur C. Brooks, president of the American Enterprise Institute: "Make gratitude a routine, independent of how you feel—and not just once each November [on Thanksgiving Day], but all year long." Then a tidbit from poet Sir Thomas Gray's poem "Ode for Music": "the still small voice of gratitude." Can you hear it? Before moving on, **conversely**, it might be wise to make a list of the things you find bothersome, challenging, difficult. Just a thought. You don't have to be Christian to appreciate the fact that Jesus Christ said thank you before performing every miracle.)

And now I'm seventy-six with a readable résumé, but I'm not dancing in the streets, yet to answer your original question, no, I am not retired. As my friend Liz Smith liked to remind me, "Better than a kick in the ass, Nino, better than a kick in the ass." And, then again, another voice, my West Coast editor buddy S. A. W. used to say, amid putdowns, "...but, Nino, you have such spirit." Spirit. Can I take that to the bank? How about a song to take us out of all of the above? Wait.

[Deep breath. S. A. W. (not S. W. W.) couldn't have guessed that I might years later be more drawn to spirits (alcohol) of a cocktail-hour kind. Then, even further down the yellow brick and cobblestone roads of New York City, that might take me to petitioning help from the 100 percent spirits above. Then—abandoning that—to solicit assistance from the Ultimate Spirit Up There for a more practical solution down here, where twelve steppers took multiple opportunities to quote the Latin word for spirit: *spiritus*. How it all fits, I do not know. But I am sober now twenty-eight years, and I am still here through Herbert and J. Edgar Hoover. Before the song, I'd like to add for S. X. W.'s benefit, in the Hebrew, the word "spirit" means "breath." You couldn't have guessed back then you were right. Exhale. Ours is not to question why, or is it?]

A song:

This Is My Life*

Funny how a lonely day can make a person say:
What good is my life?
Funny how a breaking heart can make me start to say:
What good is my life?

47

Funny how I often seem to think I'll never find a dream
In my life
Till I look around and see this great big world is part of me
And my life

This is my life
Today, tomorrow, love will come and find me
But that's the way that I was born to be
This is me
This is me

This is my life
And I don't give a damn for lost emotions
I've such a lot of love I've got to give
Let me live
Let me live

Sometime when I feel afraid, I think of what a mess I've made
Of my life
Crying over my mistakes, forgetting all the breaks I've had
In my life
I was put on earth to be, a part of this great world is me
And my life
Guess I'll just add up the score and count the things I'm grateful
for
In my life

This is my life
Today, tomorrow, love will come and find me
But that's the way that I was born to be
This is me
This is me

This is my life
And I don't give a damn for lost emotions
I've such a lot of love I've got to give
Let me live
Let me live

This is my life
This is my life
This is my life

Giving credits where it's due, and it's due:

*"This Is My Life," a favorite record of mine with a complicated history worth knowing. The most popular version was recorded and released by Brit Shirley Bassey (1968) and was much played here and as sung in Italy as "La Vita." [Years back we might call this a "turntable hit," a popular song that doesn't show up at the top of music charts but is much heard and often played elsewhere (radio).]

"This is My Life" was written by Bruno Canforo with Italian lyrics translation: Antonio Amuri, and then partially *re*written in English by Norman Newell. If all that's too weighty, consult Mr. Wikipedia. I *love* hearing this song every time out, never ever tire of it. Music publisher: Curci USA.

Play it again, Shirley.

CHAPTER 10

"Somebody Stole My Weight Belt"

*   *   *

"Somebody Stole My Weight Belt" originally appeared in the West
Side YMCA's newsletter, which I wrote and edited all through the
1990s—and for which I was paid nothing. Somewhere in the mid-
2000s, I put in for the fifty-year free membership they promised
back in 1963 when I joined. They reneged. Salvaged from all that?
This story—and maybe, in retrospect, not such a bad inheritance.

"SOMEBODY STOLE MY WEIGHT BELT." That's not as bad as somebody stole my
gal but almost. It's not the first time either, and that's another story.

I left the belt hanging on a hat tree in my office, and my suspicion is
the "night people" took it. You know the night people—those phantoms
who come into your office in the wee small hours of the morning, empty
your waste basket, run a feather duster across your desk, and take anything
not nailed down. You think I'm being harsh? The following items have
disappeared from my area. I know of: a large coral seashell, a magnifying
glass, one digital radio, a book promising WordPerfect would be made
easy, a banana, half a corn muffin, a gift certificate to Barnes & Noble,
a homemade CD (carefully copied from an old long-play album) called
"Ringo, Will You Marry Me?" by McFarland, and my credit card number,
after which twenty-seven dollars in burgers was charged at a Wendy's in
New Jersey. They have no mercy.

The belt is essential for back support while exercising at the YMCA.
It's tan, several inches wide, made of genuine leather, with a double-
pronged buckle. My name, address, and phone number were burned inside

by Ming. I'd had the belt for three years, and it was a perfect fit. It had a homey, worn look. Even as a child, I never did like things that looked new, a defense probably since I was heir to hand-me-downs from an older, generous, more prosperous cousin. Aha, that's it. It's a throwback. I had five younger siblings who continually went through my stuff. I had no privacy, no off-limits possession. Loss, despite the size, is devastating to me.

The saddest point about this whole affair: it's happened before. Once, I left a different belt in the gym long enough to shower and change. By the time I remembered the belt and went back for it, some gym rat had made off with it. He knew a good thing when he saw it. Fifty bucks is what it's worth, maybe more with inflation being what it is. Oh, yes, the story.

My next move was more creative. I typed a sign and tacked it on the Y's bulletin board:

"Lost,
One workout belt,
Mr. All American brand,
Sentimental value,
If found please turn it in to
Sports fitness office,
Be a mensch,
Turn in the belt."

A savvy YMCA member found the message amusing enough to jot down. The next thing I knew my words turned up in Ron Alexander's Wednesday "Metropolitan Diary" column in the *New York Times*—verbatim. The item mention netted me a lot of congratulations from friends who knew it was my sign. It didn't turn up the belt.

The scenario doesn't end there. Oh, no, it went into double overtime. What happened next, somebody else sent the New York "Metropolitan Diary" item to All American brand belt company in Chattanooga, Tennessee. Aren't New Yorkers resourceful?

I mean they had to know that All American brand was in Tennessee. It does read Chattanooga below the belt's logo, but how did he get the company address? And they took the trouble to put it in an envelope, address it, and stamp it. Awesome.

Next, All American brand telephones me at home. Honestly, a nice guy with a public relations voice and easy with words calls and says, "We'd like to know your size, sir. We want to send you a new belt."

Oh, yes, they did. Mr. Nice Guy from All American brand belts, Chattanooga, Tennessee: it's size thirty-two or thirty-three. Within days, a new belt arrives in the mail. Brand new and smelling of genuine leather with no sweat stains on it.

I loved my new belt. And I wasn't taking any chance with this one. That's when I took it to my genius friend Ming, who burned on my name, address, and phone number with area code inside the belt.

Now the guys at the Y come up and ask me about my new belt. I must have told the *New York Times*-All American-brand-new-belt story a hundred times. That was three years ago.

Then disaster struck. I rushed out of the office to do a full workout. I had this start-up routine I don't recommend: it might not be healthy. Half an hour before quitting time, I washed down two aspirins with a cup of coffee. By five o'clock I'm like a jittery race horse at the starting gate. Sometimes I'd even put on my gym clothes at the office not to waste a second of time when I get to the gym. All I wanted to do was get to the Y and pump iron. That Thursday in question was one of those days.

That's when I charged out of the office and left the belt hanging on my hat tree. When I got to the gym, I was too eager to begin the workout to worry about that belt. I just assumed it would be hanging there on Friday morning when I got to work. A knave had another thought. You can imagine how panic set in when it wasn't there. For the next week, every night before leaving the office, I taped an 8 x 11½ piece of paper on the waste basket with these words right in the middle: "Return the belt."

This gesture pissed off those "night people." Now they empty my wastebasket and fail to put a plastic bag liner like they do for everyone else. I don't care. I want my belt back. A concerned workout buddy gave me a gray Velcro one. I hate it. Velcro. Ugh. Maybe that night, the person who stole my belt would get a pang of conscience and return it. Lesser miracles have happened. By then it was a month, as unluck would have it, on the thirteenth.

Yesterday, a Catholic secretary at the office told me there was a patron saint of lost articles, St. Anthony or St. Jude. She's going to ask her mother. But I can't wait. Tonight I'm going to the library to find out how you pray for lost articles to St. Anthony, St. Jude, Mother Theresa, anyone up there. It's worth a shot. Velcro, ugh.

Old! Old! We like old:

After being stiffed by the Y for my fifty-year largess, angrily, I investigated every gym and health club within walking distance of my flat and now workout at a more upscale venue I can barely afford. Moral? (1) Get it in writing and safely file it away? (2) Change sometimes turns out to be better than you thought? (3) Occasionally, you luck out when you least expect it? (The other day, Arnold Schwarzenegger pumped iron at the new gym with three bodyguards.) (4) Sometimes I feel I'm now becoming one of the "swells" I wrote about in my second novel. Conclusion: Ultimately, the Y did me a big favor?

Now that I'm older, I get to enjoy an upscale health club I would never have otherwise joined. (I inherited a "Depression mentality" and would not have opted for the higher fees.) Occasionally, I miss the dusty West Side YMCA, but I'm older, wiser, and now deserving of this healthier environment—right-on appropriate for a seventy-six-year-old man, gray at the temples, short in the tooth.

CHAPTER 11

Editor's Pencil-Note Question to Me: "Nino, *your* take on *Hillbilly* Elegy?" (*In lieu of being one?* I wondered. I didn't ask.)

$$* \quad * \quad *$$

BEFORE I BEGIN, I WOULD like to admit I may be out my league. Here goes anyway.

Hillbilly Elegy is a moving memoir by Protestant-heterosexual-white-male writer J. D. Vance, who grew up Rust-Belt poor in a formerly flourishing Ohio steel town—now a burg with few jobs and little hope—and he got out. (The full title, *Hillbilly Elegy: A Memoir of a Family and Culture in Crisis*.)* Author Vance, thirty-one, was actually born in Kentucky and moved to Middletown, Ohio, a dying, once-thriving Armco Steel town where he was raised by his grandparents. J. D.'s immediate dysfunctional family struggled with poverty and domestic violence. His own mother (an aunt became a surrogate mom) was addicted to drugs and never got off. Many of his neighbors were jobless and welfare recipients.

The boy got away by joining the marines and soon after served in Iraq. After he was discharged, Vance graduated from Ohio State and then soon after was accepted at Yale. *You see where this is going?* The takeaway from this poignant personal story: J. D. Vance pulled himself up and out by roots, suits, and bootstraps, suggesting in his memoir that you could do it too.** Now Vance is married and lives in San Francisco, where he works at Silicon Valley investment firm Mithril Capital.

Vance's memoir-sociological analysis of the white underclass, white working-class and its discontent has been appropriated by conservatives, who responded to this mostly empathetic portrait of Poor White Working

Class's disaffection, shamelessly trotting out poverty-stricken-white-Rust-Belt Americans and tapping into the Poor White Working Class's disaffection. (Note: Donald Trump's name is never mentioned in the work.) During those randy days leading up to the election, bestselling former-hillbilly Vance became liberal media's darling-white-trash spokesperson. Yep, TV pundits and talking heads fixated on the anguish of white impoverished Appalachia and trotted out handsome Vance as the(ir) man who got away. Was it Vance's intention to become a guide to Middle America's landscape during and after the election, I wondered, or was this merely a fortuitous by-product?

Dissenting quote from savvy Sarah Jones, in highly regarded New Republic: *"Remember that bootstraps are for people with boots. And elegies are no use to the living."*

Much of Vance's sometimes puzzling, other times controversial, and (for sure) sympathetic narrative in *Hillbilly Elegy* revolves about the plodding, painful, excruciating hillbilly culture from which he escaped.

A digression from one hillbilly to hill-Williams everywhere: Hillbillies are a proud lot—loyal, honorable, tough, unpretentiously patriotic, hard-working, family oriented, and swift to act when justice is required. Where did Vance stand on all that? Was he paying tribute to his family?

I was riveted to his exceptionally well-written memoir. I envied the thorough background information and his use of data. Had the author done it all himself? What's more, all through my reading, I underlined passages, identifying often, agreeing frequently with the multiple insights and varied sentiments, continual observations and a-ha realizations, even down to the minutiae. My identification was ongoing, even though author Vance and I are different kinds of hick.

Questions. Questions. Questions. As I read, I wondered: How much should we hold the hillbillies responsible for their own bad luck? Sorry, politically incorrect. Strike that.

I admit I'm a country boy, and there's little getting away from it; no matter how hard I try, I can't escape it. And I'm often caught off guard. Say, in New York, when I'm too relaxed, people consistently ask, "You have an accent; where are you from?" Oops, so much for losing my twang. (For sure, when I used to have a couple of drinks, the West Virginia accent came forefront.) And a p.s. to that thought, everything I write has a little Southern in it.

To remind myself, when I was in line opening day of my freshman year in college to buy my books in a supermarket line set up, I chatted up an appealing Doris Day blond, who asked, "You have the nicest accent. Where are you from?" Encouraged, I answered, "West Virginia." Without missing a ballet swirl, she said, "Oh" as she turned away. At that moment, I began getting rid of my twang.

Am I any different from J. D. Vance? Purely coincidental? My hometown was the county seat. Occasionally, motley types sat on the marble seat-high ledge that surrounded the Court House Square, but I don't ever recall seeing a drunk or a beggar there. Looking back, downtown was always neat and clean, with diverse shopping, Lane Bryant clothing stores, furniture, books, jewelry, bakeries, a couple of truly good restaurants. Yes, exceptional food. Newly Italian baked bread, scrumptious pepperoni rolls, hot dogs with chili the likes of which you can't get anywhere else in the world, red sauce and meatballs from a coveted, old-world, secret Calabrian recipe. And yet, amid all this, I was a hillbilly. But then my family was noble and poor, hardworking though also enterprising. And I, too, pulled myself up and out, paying for my own dental work and then working my way through college, ultimately coming to New York on a dime and making a little something of myself.

OK, six points of light that jumped out at me.

1. Mr. Vance preaches personal responsibility and has little patience for some of his people: one acquaintance who told him he had quit his job. The slacker hated waking up early and then reverts to Facebook to blame the "Obama economy." Another capricious coworker at a tile warehouse missed work once a week even though his live-in girlfriend was pregnant.
2. Vance resents local welfare recipients, many on the dole, accepting food stamps—working the system. These bums resold their soda

pop for cash and then availed themselves of luxury items—that is, cell phones and HBO. Vance says, "I could never understand why our lives felt like a struggle while those living off government largesse enjoyed trinkets that I only dreamed about."

3. A direct quote: "Every two weeks I'd get a small pay-check and notice the line where the federal and state income taxes were deducted from my wages. At least as often, our drug-addicted neighbor would buy T-bone steaks, which I was too poor to buy for myself, but was forced by Uncle Sam to buy for someone else."

4. Summer 2016, *American Conservative* columnist Rod Dreher wrote of Vance's memoir, "*Hillbilly Elegy* does for poor white people what Ta-Nehisi Coates's book does for poor black people: give them voice and presence in the public square." I'm not well versed enough to know if that's true or not.

5. And then there's savvy Joshua Rothman in *New Yorker Magazine*, September 12, 2016: "When we pursue education, we improve ourselves both 'economically' and 'culturally' (and in other ways); conversely, there's nothing distinctly and intrinsically 'economic' or 'cultural' about the problems that affect poor communities such as widespread drug addiction or divorce. (If you lose your job, get divorced, and become an addict, is your addiction 'economic' or 'cultural' in nature?) When we debate whether such problems have a fundamentally 'economic' or 'cultural' cause, we aren't saying anything meaningful about the problems. We're just arguing— incoherently—about whether or not people who suffer from them deserve to be blamed for them."

The initial copy of *Hillbilly Elegy* was mailed to me early on by childhood friend S. W. W. Then I bought copies as gifts for friends and family and highly recommended the memoir to others folks. I found it articulate and fascinating, though sometimes perplexing; Vance is, as I pointed out, to be admired and, on television, (is) both appealing and credible. I can't pay enough tribute to J. D. Vance. Dinner on me, bud.

J. D. Vance's *Hillbilly Elegy—A Memoir of a Family and Culture in Crisis*, was a bestseller and included on several ten best books lists of 2016, Harper/Collins, including picky, prestigious *The Week*. I'm glad Vance wrote it, and I suspect he is too. I hope some-day to shake his hand. Meanwhile I pray the above take helps to sell even more copies. The book was number one in the *New York Times* last time I looked. Not least, the memoir is even on some recommended high-school reading lists.

As a septuagenarian, I point out once more, I loved this book; I found it riveting. But I wonder how I would have felt about Vance's take if I had read it when I was in my early twenties, new to New York City: soaking up as much as I could as fast as I could, trying to fit it in, striving to make it, attempting to be as articulate and amusing as "the swells," to be as interesting, to be one of the crowd. Would I have liked this book? Maybe not so much.

CHAPTER 12

Hay House Is Not Always a Home

∗   ∗   ∗

*Research reminds us: A midlife crisis is a transition of identity and
self-confidence that may occur in middle-aged (and sometimes in
younger individuals.) It is a psychological and behavioral observation
that commonly happens with folks between the ages of forty-five
and sixty-four. Alas, it differs from person to person. While some
may experience feelings of anxiety, depression, and remorse, others
may take on a longing for youth which sometime lead to drastic
(sometimes disastrous) changes to their current lifestyles.*

*Should I buy that vintage, red, like-new, refurbished
Corvette convertible and get a crew cut?*

I'M HERE TO TELL YOU the syndrome really exists, and I had a big one in
1984.

Succinctly: Somewhere in the mid-1980s, it started to catch up with me.
Long about forty-four, something clicked. Sure. At that time, there was
little trace of that West Virginia kid. I'd learned a few tricks; I had a few
friends; I enjoyed a solid social life—and we have to be honest here (or it
doesn't work): (A) I looked good. I worked out every day. A man's body
doesn't look its best until his forties, I read somewhere, and I had a classic
six-pack abdomen. (Sad to say, none of that is now true.) (B) I had friends
in Los Angeles, San Francisco, Chicago, and even a few in Miami, Florida.
(C) I chalked up a few credits and a decent résumé. But, my reader friends,

something started to buzz in the back of my head. Yes, I admit I wrote sometimes, I took classes, I submitted ideas here and there, but off the record: my career had stalled. Aha! New York was my problem; I had to go to Los Angeles to study and get connected to movies. Reasoning: I'd had some luck with songs; hadn't I even produced records? After that, when I decided one day to be a journalist: I placed articles and even had cover stories in international magazines. Shucks, getting a movie made would be a cinch.

I now chased a new rainbow. And after all, Los Angeles had just come off a big high: the 1984 Summer Olympics. July 28 through August 12, 1984, were "the most successful Olympics ever: LA, 1984." The city shined. Yeah! What to do? What to do? I got it. I needed more classes, and I had to take them in Los Angeles. (Let's ignore the facts. I'd taken New York classes at The New School, NYU, the West Side YMCA). There was no stopping me. I had to go to Los Angeles to study with screenplay writer-teachers in order to make it in my new career: screenwriter. The expert-gurus out there were Robert Mckee, Syd Field, Linda Something or Other, and even some I can't remember. I ruminated: if I got myself to LA, if I took some master's classes with the masters, I could pitch ideas to the studios in the meantime and keep turning out new work. It sounded just great.

Pith/inventory/to the tune of "Fascinating Rhythm:" I won a couple of minor contests and was even mentioned in *The Hollywood Reporter*, but to be honest here, nothing much came of what AA would later label "L.A.—a giant 'geographic.'" In defense, socially I was invited out to events and to dinner (in whatever city I was in). [A big interjection: In a session before I made the trip, the German therapist with the thick, guttural accent made this mocking gesture, an obvious putdown: next to his chair, he filled an invisible bucket with air and spoke these words: "You're going to Los Angeles to scoop up buckets of gold from the streets." (I'm not sure what his message was. "Don't go"? "You're filled with illusions"? I don't know.)

I wish, in reexamination, he would have been more specific, but I don't think it would have made any difference—being specific was not in his Freudian nature anyway. I want my money back.

Defiance (one of the more irritating characteristics of an alcoholic) abounds: I'm including a chapter here that my editor doesn't like. Why? The period was a big part of my Los Angeles experience; it was indicative of what was going on in big cities in the mid-1980s—the tumultuous mid-1980s, when AIDS was rampant—and, lastly, I was going out to dinner and for drinks every night. I partied too much without giving it first thought. Thank Yahweh for my friends Master Card, Visa, and American Express. The limit was the limit. It might be noted that I did not stop drinking for another four more years.

And So Here Goes Defiant Chapter Twelve

"I love and approve of myself. I love and approve of myself," as Louise L. Hay used to emphasize ad infinitum and suggested you do the same.

During the 1980s, I spent a lot of time in Los Angeles chasing rainbows—taking screenwriting classes with masters Messrs. Robert McKee and Syd Field. With my penchant for books with answers, I hopped aboard the controversial and much-maligned (and loved) Louise L. Hay bandwagon, absorbing her self-help books and attending her well-stocked weekly gatherings in West Hollywood with hundreds of young and mostly attractive Hollywood locals, several hundred on a given evening. I'm including all this here. It was a scene. I was there, in the middle (thick?) of it.

Miss Hay's prevalent philosophy was to love the self. She preached blatant self-love and self-approval, often the subject of her weekly Wednesday night seminars. In fact, the thrust of her program, a suggested all-day-long affirmation was: "I love and approve of myself. I love and approve of myself." In addition, the guru-self-proclaimed-healer-minister advocated that her followers look in the mirror and affirm, "I love you. I love you." *This* attendee, I confess, found it impossible to do that. However, I admit I did enjoy her evening, self-styled "Hay rides."

Back then, in print, psychologists and psychiatrists as well as the media were not always kind to Ms. Hay, either out of envy or genuine concern that her advice might be harmful to some already challenged victims. Not to mention she was pulling in a great deal of money every week. (I swear it was a sociable scene And, I liked it for that reason.) As you know I am not a professional. I do know I was having a damn good time as well as getting familiar with unconventional (to me) philosophies (reiki, for one). I'd never heard of reiki or any of the old and new-age thinking she touted, and I always liked learning new things. (Lloyd Lee always reminded me of that: "Nino, you like learning; that's why you went to AA, to scrutinize it. You like to dissect new things.") And, oh, did I mention I enjoyed the company of those young and attractive Tinsel Towners who likewise flocked to her Wednesday night scene, so-called West Hollywood "Hay rides." Oh, right, I did.

How it was. New-age music played in the background as Hay held court from the stage in a flowing gossamer gown. She began with moving, eyes-closed, relaxing exercises; then lectured a bit; and many an evening introduced a new-age personality or two, and, oh, yes, offering for sale several well-stocked tables full of paraphernalia (books, tapes, affirmation cards). It is obvious to note, during that time, one of Hay's books, *You Can Heal Your Life,** even landed with a plop on the *New York Times*'s bestsellers list. I suspect some well-trained, highly educated professionals and practitioners were beside themselves with envy. (It's human nature.)

Hay House Books, 1984 (read: self-published). In the same week, after appearances on both Phil Donahue and Oprah Winfrey, March 1988, Louise Hay's You Can Heal Your Life *landed on the* New York Times *bestsellers list. Coincidentally, 1988 is the year I decided I didn't want to drink anymore. Sheer coincidence.*

Deservedly or not, as I mentioned, she got flak from professionals and the press, but, in her defense, the story circulating went this way: In the early 1980s, before anyone knew what AIDS was, during a time when hospital orderlies threw food into the afflicted patients' hospital rooms (those supposedly safe havens, a hospital, that even some doctors and nurses refused to enter), Louse L. Hay visited the sick and dying at their bedsides *to rub their aching feet.* (During this time, there was also a New York City case reported that someone went into a dying, AIDS-afflicted patient's hospital room and mercilessly beat him up.) Unselfishly, the much-criticized Louise L. Hay not only went into the off-base hospital rooms, but she ministered to them in a way no one else did or would. Simultaneously, she was amassing a fortune in book sales and publishing. I say: *vee-cha via-cha* (Italian dialect), a God bless with a touch of flip sarcasm. I don't begrudge her her success. No one else was putting themselves out there at that time, not even the president of the United States of America.

Why am I telling you all this?

And now to make a 180-degree turn: Years later, I am still reading work that might have insight into the meaning of it all. And recently I ran across an old paperback in a used bookstore published in 1980, which we can assume was written in the late 1970s and then released with a publishing date of 1980. In that volume, I hit on some specifics that sounded suspiciously familiar. (Note: I'm not accusing anyone of anything. I am, as a curiosity, merely pointing this out. And we're all aware there is nothing new under the moon.)

Maybe a stretch here, I admit, but there's a quote in that crumbling, yellowed psychology paperback book that was awfully similar to Ms. Hay's philosophy. See what you think.

"Self esteem can be viewed as your decision to treat yourself like a beloved friend. Imagine that some VIP you respect came unexpectedly to visit you one day. How might you treat that person? You would wear your best clothes and offer your finest wine and food, and you would do everything you could to make him feel comfortable and pleased with his visit. Do it all the time if you can!...This attitude embodies the essence of self-love and self-respect."

**From *Feeling Good, The New Mood Therapy*, by David D. Burns, MD, Avon, 1980.

Friends, it is quite possible that the collective consciousness and unconsciousness was working overtime in the early 1980s, hence the similarity here and in other places (Werner Erhard?).

As for this perennial student, I wrote fifteen screenplays between 1984 and 2004, some of them while in Los Angeles. None was made into a feature film. However, I did write a detailed article that many aspiring screenwriters have reprinted and passed around in film-school classes, "Who Is Syd Field and Why Does Everyone Own His Books, or How to Write a Hit Movie," *Creative Screenwriter*, winter 1995. The point: For writers, everything is fodder—screenwriting classes, Louise L. Hay, yellowing paperbacks discarded at the local senior center, and songs my mother hummed around the house. Oh, did I mention I stopped drinking in 1988 and explained it this way: "I don't want another hangover as long as I live"? (Reason enough.) I'm uncertain the dots connected here fit (on paper), but something suspiciously smacks of similarity from Louise Hay, Werner Erhard, and every other new-age guru that slid down the firehouse pole in the 1970s. As William Shakespeare said twice in *King Lear*, "Nothing can come of nothing." Then later, "Nothing will come of nothing."

Coveted old paperbacks found in used book stalls:

"Achievements can bring you satisfaction but not happiness. Self-worth based on accomplishments is a 'pseudo-esteem,' not the genuine thing! My many successful but depressed patients would all agree. Nor can you base a valid sense of self-worth on your looks, talent, fame, or fortune. Marilyn Monroe, Mark Rothko, Freddie Prinz, and a multitude of famous suicide victims attest to this grim truth. Nor can love, approval, friendship, or a capacity for close, caring human relationship add one iota to your inherent worth. The great majority of depressed individuals are in fact very much loved, but it doesn't help one bit because *self*-love and *self*-esteem are missing. At the bottom line, only your own sense of self-worth determines how you feel."**

**From yellowing-paged, highly regarded *Feeling Good, The New Mood Therapy*, by David D. Burns, MD, Avon Books, New York, 1980, which brilliantly outlines a drug-free cure for anxiety, guilt, pessimism, procrastination, low self-esteem, and other "black holes" of depression with a knockout preface by genius therapist Aaron T. Beck, MD, Dr. David D. Burns's "personal teacher."

With a slight turn of the screw, *Feeling Good, The New Mood Therapy* changed my life some, at least made me aware. I tip my hat to you, David D. Burns, MD.

It's not a bad concept to this searcher of wisdom-truth/respect chaser to be reminded that "the paths of glory lead but to the grave," a line from Thomas Gray's "Elegy Written in a Country Churchyard," one of the world's best-loved, best-known poems and not really an elegy. (If you don't know that poem, your high school failed you.)

Note to self: Get Burns's workbook that goes with his book.

And do you suppose those 1970s new-age gurus (Louise Hay, Werner Erhard, et al., mostly in Los Angeles) studied Martin Buber? I'll think about that tomorrow. At Tara.

I Confess I Talk to Myself. Maybe You Do Too. As Well As up to My Ass in Asterisks.

✳   ✳   ✳

A back story to begin chapter 13: I was born on the thirteenth
(February), sandwiched in between Mr. Lincoln and St. Valentine,
and I'm not superstitious (well, a speck) and trust chapter 13 holds up.
(I like to say about myself, almost a sweetheart. Missed Abe Lincoln's
birthday and St. Valentine's Day by a few hours, the story of my life.)

"I talk to the trees, but they don't listen to me..."*

To BEGIN, I HAVE TO confess I've used this report somewhere before, but it bears rehashing just as I find myself doing more and more the older I get. Someone did a scientific (?) study that purported that we talk to ourselves up to thirty thousand times a day. The findings did not specify if, on some of those occasions, we speak to ourselves aloud. I think we can assume maybe a few of those times we did.

Back home, if people walked the streets mumbling, they would be thought crazy, loco, loony, *botza*, and dismissed or jeered at. Here in New York, many folks talk to themselves—and for sure, many certifiably insane, psychos, schizos, too, but in Manhattan, this is not considered abnormal. On occasion, you can catch a Gotham Joe talking aloud, reminding himself of something, or acknowledging he forgot to perform a task, or that he/she just, on the spot, made a mistake. Remember, in archery, a *sin* is merely missing the mark. None of the above is farfetched.

A lot of the time my mind races, especially after three cups of just-brewed Eight O'clock, and there are times I recall a memory I don't want to entertain at that moment; hence, I speak out loud, even if it's merely to say "stop!" To dispel the thought. And in addition—and/or when, for sure, if I'm tempted to take on someone else's drama, and let me tell you that's easy to do for a recovering codependent*******—I say "stop" or something similar to quiet the mind and move on to activities more productive.

Furthermore, fellow septuagenarians, there is substantial evidence that talking aloud to oneself is actually beneficial.

In my case, I find myself doing every action these days a tad more deliberately, even that. When I move around the apartment in an attempt not to bump into furniture and sharp corners, I move around with more care. To avoid dropping or spilling things (my wont), I maneuver cautiously as I try to stay alert or, if you will, as a wise man advised me in a book, more "conscious."**

For sure, at the gym, it is necessary for me to be more alert these days in an effort to not hurt myself (and sometimes I do anyway). I have to be more cautious while exercising, and if that includes talking to myself to avoid disaster, I do. Too many times I've rushed headlong into a movement—even those I used to do with ease—hurt myself, and/or bruised my thigh.

Hurts these days take too damn long to heal, too much downtime, too long to get going again. At intervals, if I have to stop, think, get (again) "conscious," and possibly speak aloud before the task before me (to *stay* conscious**), I do. Borderline crazy? Not so much.

A downside: if I'm in a public place, someone nearby might ask, "What? What'd ya say? How's that?"

"Oh, I'm merely talking to myself."

With multitudes speaking on cell phones, who can tell the difference anyway? Talk away.

Editor's note: "Nino, what about all those folks who talk to their dogs? Reportedly, they are more intelligent than the average bloke." You mean I've missed something out there in print? Damn. Mea culpa, mea culpa, mea culpa.

✳   ✳   ✳

Back-up evidence:

1. Three tidbits from Gigi Engle:***

"Thinking out loud helps me materialize what I'm thinking about. It helps me make sense of things."

"The smartest people on earth talk to themselves. Look at the inner monologues of the greatest thinkers. Look at poetry! Look at history!"

"Talking to yourself makes your brain work more efficiently."

***From the article "People Who Talk to Themselves Aren't Crazy, They're Actually Geniuses," by Gigi Engle, October 27, 2016, American online news platform Elite Daily.

2. Dead-right, right on fodder from Live Science:****

"…saying things out loud sparks memory…solidifies the end game; and makes it tangible."

"A child learns by talking through his actions. By doing so, he remembers for the future how he solved the problem. Talking through it helps him or her make sense of the world."

From the science news website Live Science, owned by PURCH.

3. Renowned psychologist Dr. Linda Sapadin,**** PhD, thinks talking out loud helps you validate important and difficult decisions. In her own words, "It helps you clarify your thoughts, tend to what's important and firm up any decisions you're contemplating."

Sapadin goes on to say, "Verbalizing your goals out loud focuses your attention, reinforces the message, controls your runaway emotions and screens out distractions."

****From Dr. Linda Sapadin, PhD, psychologist and success coach.

* * *

4. Life-changing quotes from towering psychiatrist David D. Burns, MD*****

"The best way to solve a problem is to talk it out. And it's your problem, you can do it with yourself."

To boost self-esteem: "Talk back to that internal critic. A sense of worthlessness is created by your internal self-critical dialogue. It is self-degrading statements, such as: 'I'm no damn good,' 'I'm a shit,' 'I'm inferior to other people,' and soon, that creates and feeds your feelings of despair and poor self-esteem. In order to overcome this bad mental habit three steps are necessary:

a. Train yourself to recognize, to write down self-critical thoughts as they go through your mind;
b. Learn why these thoughts are distorted; and
c. Practice talking back to them and develop a more realistic self-evaluation system."

*****From David D. Burns, MD, *Feeling Good* (full title: *Feeling Good, The New Mood Therapy*, New York: Avon Books, 1980)—To *re-state*: outlines a drug-free cure for anxiety, guilt, pessimism, procrastination, low self-esteem and other "black holes" of depression with a useful preface by Aaron T. Beck, MD, Dr. Burns's "personal teacher." Furthermore, we're told there is even a helpful workbook to accompany this masterpiece.

Dear Reader, I have to stop talking now—I'm out of breath and getting hoarse.

*******If you're unfamiliar with codependency, I suspect it's not what you think. Check out Melodie Beatty's *Co-Dependent No More*, Hazelden Publishing. It could alter your perceptions in relationships.

Revelation—theory of:
According to Einstein.org, Mr. Albert Einstein himself "used to repeat his sentences to himself softly." If that's not talking to yourself, I'm Ish Kabibble.*******

Post-it postscript: Under a pile of papers, I found these words scribbled in pencil on a Post-it note and don't know from whence they came: "Talk back to that internal critic!" May I add, consider talking back to the *outer* critic.

******Ish Kabibble (Merwyn Bogue), (1908–1994), American comedian and notable cornet player, who studied law at West Virginia University, until his comedy antics took over and he became a successful entertainer. I suspect he regretted it. After that, he was never taken seriously as a musician, merely a comedian.

Opening asterisk: *"I talk to the trees…" Big number from Broadway musical *Paint Your Wagon*, lyrics by Alan Jay Lerner, music by Frederick Loewe. Publisher: Chappell-Co, Inc. ASCAP. On Broadway from November 12, 1951, to July 19, 1952. The 1969 film version starred Clint Eastwood with the book rewritten by Paddy Chayefsky.

CHAPTER 14

Alzheimer's Remembered

$*$ $*$ $*$

NOT SUCH A FUNNY RUNNING joke, it's a reoccurring reality: "Where *is* my damn cell phone?"

Occasionally, I place things in the wrong place. And I sometimes struggle a tad to remember a fact, although I find eventually my memory does come across; my ability to recall rarely totally fails me. Though there are those incidences when I do ask myself, *Am I losing it?* (Where is my other shoe?)

SUPER AGERS TO THE FRONT

Off the record, there are Alzheimer's disease studies on the brains of some older dead people, autopsied (unfortunately, after death), that found that many of the alert older ones had the same lesions on their brains, plaques and tangles that technically qualify as full-blown Alzheimer's, although those people (when alive), *never* had actual symptoms of the syndrome. Nope, none. They showed few, if any, signs of Alzheimer's (when alive). How can that be? Their minds: clear. Their reasoning: excellent. Their memories: sharp. And it's been reported that many, but not all, had a positive outlook on life. These folks are called "super agers."* On the whole, they were hopeful, productive, and were blessed with a positive outlook on life.

In an effort to not waste your time and to be honest here, let me tell you the bottom line upfront; in the words of one expert, "they just don't know." Here goes anyway:

As a postscript to all that, two startling facts:

a) According to one report, about 30 percent of people over seventy have "amyloid residue" in their brains and no symptoms of the disease.
b) Why is it: Alzheimer's is curable in mice but not in men?
c) If some people are protected from the toxic effects of plaques on their brain cells—if a factoid—how? What damn factors, dammit, contribute to the protection of the neurons' environment? Is it lifelong pursuit of knowledge (education)? Or genetics? Obviously a multitude of unknown mysterious mechanisms?

I wish we knew more. I keep telling friends, without any backup, that they are going to come up with a cure for Alzheimer's in our lifetime. More wishful thinking than scientific fact, I'm afraid.

I devoured a promising article by Gretchen Reynolds in a March 2017 *New York Times* that looked hopeful to the aging: brisk walks may help bolster physical abilities and slow memory loss, citing a new study from the University of Kansas, PLoS One. PLoS One experimented with simple walking exercises along with stretching/toning classes for people with early Alzheimer's. Some "walkers" were thinking and remember better. The study concluded that others gained endurance and "generally" improved their ability to think. The conclusion: progression of Alzheimer's slowed. Fitness rose. But as I neared the end of the piece, I realized, in their words, they "just don't know." Overall, disappointing, yes, but more studies are underway.

Check out these three articles:

New York Times, March 14, 2017, "For Early Alzheimer's, Try Exercise," by Gretchen Reynolds.

Huffington Post, by writer Bahar Gholipour, "When 'Super Agers' Get Alzheimer's, They Don't Exhibit Any Symptoms."

**Science News Magazine*, the Orwellian think tank, and neuroscience writer Laura Sanders, PhD, November 16, 2016.

✳   ✳   ✳

Warning: Which brings me to the most troublesome article (essay, piece, lovely piece of work) I've ever read in a magazine. Oddly enough, ironically, the effort appeared in one of my favorite periodicals, *The Atlantic*, in October 2014, and I rue the day I read it. Editor's note: *Why does it bother you so much?*

"Why I Hope to Die at 75," by Ezekiel J. Emanuel.

Did I establish that this article haunted me? I did. Here are some excerpts.

"Seventy-five. That's how long I want to live: 75 years," begins Ezekiel Emanuel.

"...here is a simple truth that many of us seem to resist: living too long is...a loss. It renders many of us, if not disabled, then faltering and declining, a state that may not be worse than death, but is nonetheless deprived. It robs us of our creativity and ability to contribute to work, society, the world. It transforms how people experience us, relate to us, and most important, remember us. We are no longer remembered as vibrant and engaged but as feeble, ineffectual, even pathetic." *Huh!*

"Americans seem to be obsessed with exercising, doing mental puzzles, consuming various juice and protein concoctions, sticking to strict diets, and popping vitamins and supplements, all in a valiant effort to cheat death and prolong life as long as possible...manic desperation to endlessly extend life is misguided and potentially destructive.

"In 1900, the life expectancy of an average American at birth was approximately 47 years. By 1930, it was 59.7; by 1960, 69.7; by 1990, 75.4. Today, a newborn can expect to live about 79 years.

"Right now approximately 5 million Americans over 65 have Alzheimer's; one in three Americans 85 and older has Alzheimer's. And the prospect of that changing in the next few decades is not good.

"Japan has the third-highest life expectancy, at 84.4 years (behind Monaco and Macau), while the United States is a disappointing No. 42, at 79.5 years."

This is Nino, your friendly author, speaking and speculating: One wonders—well, *I* wonder—what *Atlantic Magazine*'s founders, Ralph

Waldo Emerson and Henry Wadsworth Longfellow, would think of this article/essay. Emerson lived to be nearly eighty (May 25, 1803, to April 27, 1882), while Longfellow passed on at seventy-five plus one month (February 27, 1807, to March 24, 1882).

"Why I Hope to Die at 75," by Ezekiel J. Emanuel, October 2014, *Atlantic Magazine,* Washington, DC. For the entire piece, contact their back issues department. You may be bowled over. As for me, I wonder and wondered: (A) What was the point of this piece? (B) And I wonder, now that I'm pushing seventy-seven, does the author believe all that? (C) If so, let's question him when he reaches our age.

Song lyric: *"And if you should survive to a hundred and five, look at all you derive out of being aaaah-live…"**

Lyric from "Young at Heart," music (came first) by Johnny Richards, lyrics by Carolyn Leigh, and a million-selling record for Frank Sinatra that reached number two on Billboard's record charts—then afterward, the title was appropriated as a movie title for a feature film, bumping the original title after the movie was already in production. Music publishing: Sony/ATV Music and June's Tunes, LTD, 1953.

Oh, the early 1950s—were they not the best?

HOPE AGAINST HOPE

In an attempt to go out on a more positive note on a bewildering subject: an oversimplification. A Massachusetts Institute of Technology team of neuroscientists and engineers has devised and is experimenting with a method called temporal interference that might skip surgery by reaching deep brain areas with a pulse of electricity to affect some cures. From a journal, *Cell,* (then picked up by other publications), of course, in experiments with mice, the specialists activate specific parts of the brain by electrical stimulation without interfering or harming other healthy parts of the brain. Yes, a small step, but the electrical method may be the answer and may have potential for neurological and psychiatric treatment. An oversimplification, I'm aware, but I need hope for a cure for Alzheimer's disease.

The Last Hurrah? I have to confess, from time to time, usually in the morning, I say to myself, I don't know how many hurrah's I have left in me. I get up anyway and do what's in front of me.

CHAPTER 15

And Now a Few Words from a Couple of Drunks, Some Old and Some Not So Old. (This is the editor's *favorite* chapter. Go figure.)

$*$ $*$ $*$

IN MY CASE, FREQUENTLY...NIGHTLY, I met polite company, or many of the folks I considered "swells" for dinner in some hot new restaurant. We'd never enter an eatery that failed to serve booze, ever. (See the list in the Appendix but don't forget to come back here). I would have two Scotches before dinner, a couple of glasses of wine with dinner, and a Brandy Stinger after dinner. Does that make me an alcoholic, or merely a "sport?" Yes? No? Maybe? (In AA, that's called "The Debating Society.) The answer: It all depends who you ask. I will admit this: if you do it often enough, it catches up with you. In my case, it did. On the other foot, I feel lucky to have known the dinner companions and often hum the song Peter Allen wrote about his friendship with Judy Garland, "I've Been Taught by Experts."* Of course, you know Allen later marry Garland's daughter, Liza with a "Z."

*"I've Been Taught By Experts," All Music/Universal/A&M.

$*$ $*$ $*$

People confuse blacking out with slumping over. In a blackout, a drunk is "anything but silent and immobile," tells Sarah Hepola in her amazing addiction memoir, *Blackout*. Ms. Hepola could "talk and laugh and charm people at the bar with funny stories of [her] past," she writes and includes in her personal story examples of calamitous karaoke and the like.

76

Meanwhile, her blood alcohol level could even shut down her brain's long-term memory center and then recall none of it.

From *Blackout*, by Sarah Hepola, a stunningly written must-read for substance abusers. Grand Central Publishing.

HOLD THE PHONE! STOP THE PRESSES! THIS JUST CAME IN OVER THE TRANSOM.

Columbia University medical journal *JAMA* Psychiatry, from lead author Deborah Hasin (of Columbia),* a new study reports that high-risk drinking increased among US adults about 30 percent between 2001-2002 and 2012-2013, and dependence has risen 49.9% since the 2001-2002 study. Ms. Hasin goes on to describe the findings as "a public heath crisis." (High risk drinking in women, four drinks a day; five in men.) Nearly 13% of American adults meet the criteria for alcoholism, defined by the "Diagnostic and Statistical Manual of Mental Disorders." These upticks in drinking were highest among women, older adults, racial and ethic minorities as well as folks people with low income levels and little education. Why, oh why? A) A change in social norms and B) people are using alcohol as a coping device. (Didn't we always?) Look out for more heart problems, strokes, and infections, reports Ms. Hasin. NOTE: *The Washington Post* cites Bridget Grant as "lead author" of the study. We suspect it took more than two people to compile the report. We thank them all. August 2017

OVERHEARD OUTSIDE AA MEETINGS

In my previous novel, I beat my drinking to death, in detail. It would be redundant to bring up booze and boozing war stories. I have been asked since I evoke the nineteen seventies again and again, what about drugs? I occasionally I tried a drug here and there, but not much. I was more attracted to Johnny Barleycorn.

Sixty-nine nifty tidbits overheard outside AA meetings while sucking on a Camel. *A Lucky?* And/or over hot coffee or iced tea at a nearby New

York diner—did you know there's a coffee shop on every corner in Old New York? It helps a lot.

1. What I have in store for me is smaller than what God has in store for me.
2. My disease and the desire to drink are stronger than my maternal instincts.
3. Writing out my resentments makes me hate the person I resent less.
4. AA meetings are a refuge for me.
5. Eighty-two years ago, we didn't know what to do with a drunk.
6. When I go to AA meetings, somehow I feel good; I feel *better* afterward—every time.
7. AA is not a spectator sport; you have to participate. And, I admit, I have a hard time speaking out and drawing attention to myself in AA meetings, in most of the classes I took in college, and after. It's a specular kind of shyness I can't shake.
8. When you pray, God has three answers: 1) yes, 2) not yet, and 3) "No, I have something better in store for you."
9. "AA gives me a structure, an overview, I can't and don't get anywhere else or, for sure, on my own."
10. (Diner dish): In Alcoholics Anonymous, I hear the truth, I hear the truth in the meeting rooms of AA and not anywhere else, not even in my own home.
11. Drinking is like living with a roommate who wants to kill you.
12. Once a pickle, never a cucumber again. (Once you get sober, drinking's never the same.) Yes, the program ruins drinking for you after a few meetings and hearing the stories.
13. (A handshake): Thank you for your horrible story. It keeps me alive.
14. Most of us in AA are trying to be our best selves. Nowhere else in the world are folks trying this bloody hard. (The newcomer looked glazed as he buttered his scone.)
15. During my first meeting, I thought they were passing the basket to pay the speaker. It never occurred to me they had to pay rent for the basement room.

16. One woman to another, in a whisper: I woke up with the pizza delivery boy in my bed.

17. I'm a terrible person with an audience for that all the time in AA.

18. Overheard more than once in diners or out front of a meeting place: "The pull, the desire, the temptation of alcohol was greater than my love of/for my children. I tried to quit for the love of my children. It did not work. I needed more. I had to have the help of the program of Alcoholics Anonymous to finally quit drinking (for good, I hope and pray). Addiction is stronger than love."

19. The medium of the message is *identification*.

20. What do people who don't drink do in the evenings?

21. To have self-esteem, buddy, you have to perform estimable acts. I pray every day for God to help me "be of service"—it's holding the door for the person behind me on the bus and small actions like that.

22. Overdosed, in a hospital, and I was looking for a cigarette while attached to oxygen apparatus.

23. Don't love me; I'm rotten inside. (That got a hug for the person out front of the diner.)

24. Be good to others and kind to yourself.

25. Another member remembered my name the next time she saw me—and it changed my life. It's amazing how someone will remember that and a lot more after months—years, even.

26. I have to stay present. I can't get sober on yesterday's meeting and/ or get stressed out on tomorrow's problems, to be *clean* on yesterday's showers. If not, as sure as shit, I'll drink.

27. Focus on the solution. 'Get off your position, guy.' Metaphysicians said that in the 1970s, and AAers are still saying it now. They also said in the 1970s: 'uncertainty is a high space.' It's OK to be uncertain. *Huh?*

28. I came to AA because I had no place else to go. At least I didn't want to go to the places I used to hang out.

29. You have to practice these principles of AA in *all* your affairs, not just some. In order to stay sober, you need to practice these AA principles in every area of your life. *All?*

30. Someone said to me, "I want to be like you." (Oh God, what do I answer to that?)

31. I drank in the bum bars and loved it.

32. William Faulkner once said when asked why he drank so much, "For the pain." One wonders: to get rid of it or to keep it going to fuel his work?

33. A big man who looked like a former boxer pumped fists with me after a meeting and said, "Eye of the tiger." I looked it up online. Eye of the tiger—a feeling of confidence, an internal power and strength. I'll take it. *Is that male bonding?* I wondered.

34. A tall trim handsome man explaining to a newcomer in front of an Upper West Side meeting, advising him to be vigilant, "It's alcohol*ism*, not alcohol*was*im, dude. And, you need for all of the five sense to report one hundred percent of the data, one hundred percent of the time." The novice looked glazed.

35. When you, alcoholic, are disturbed by another person, maybe there was something wrong with you, and you need to examine yourself to see where that is. (Sounded to me as if it came from the literature, but credit is not something always given in AA.) "Check out the tenth step," someone nearby whispered to me, blowing smoke in my face.

36. At dinner in a diner: An alcoholic is one of the few people in the room who can look down at others from the gutter.

37. At dinner in a diner, coffee, dessert, and more coffee: Recovery takes place in relationships; it is not an abstraction. It's all about defective relationships. (Isn't *everything?*)

38. A friend and a longtime member of the program often said to me, especially when I complained, "The 12 steps of Alcoholics Anonymous are there for your comfort." The implication is you/I have to work at it.

39. AA is more than a philosophy. It is not group therapy; it is a discipline like praying or meditation. (Note: therapy *is* also considered a discipline, my shrink tells me.)

40. Outside a Greenwich Village meeting, spoken on a cigarette exhale, "I talk to myself sometimes. Talking to someone, arguing with a person, while in the shower, an individual who is not there—do you think that is a problem?" No, madam, we all do it. Keep coming back. (See the chapter in these pages on talking to yourself.)

41. Again and again: In a diner: "It's about relationships! This drinking thing *and* the problems. It's all about relationships with other people." Again, I say, isn't everything? Same conversation: "... *defective* relationships...and what's more: AA is a design for living; a launching pad for a real life." Someone else chimed in, lighting up a Lucky: "And AA is the greatest social architect of the twentieth century."

42. And over Jell-O with mounds of whipped cream at the Utopia Coffee Shop, to several groans, someone said: "I get up every morning and thank my alarm clock for waking me." (Well, not every share is a gem.) Thank you, alarm clock.

43. About to close here, something that is repeated repeatedly during coffee, dinner, sidewalk cigarettes, over and over again: "Alcoholics Anonymous is the greatest democracy on the planet; everyone is welcome." (That wasn't always true, the literature supports; it seems to be what's so now.)

44. Overheard outside an Upper West Side of Manhattan 12 step meeting, two gents off to the side, the older one says firmly to the younger newcomer, "You are where your feet are, not where your head is. May I bum a fag?" He said as he sipped cold coffee.

45. Spoken at that damn diner in Greenwich Village after a 12 step meeting, "When you're a regular in AA, you get used to the hum of people's personalities." Sure loved that comment. May be a wrap-up on life. *The hum of people's personalities.*

46. The context I can't remember, but one bloke said to another—and not exclusive to AA: "I realize 'If you don't like my peaches, don't shake my tree.' In addition: you, bud, should resign from the debating society. 'You are. You aren't.' You've stayed sober awhile now. (Pass me the pepper). If the cure is working, you probably have the disease."

47. "The unacceptable became acceptable." And then, later, "The inexplicable became understandable." Someone else at the table interrupted: "Like people on cell phones in public places, on the bus, on the train, in stores, on the street. I used to want to strangle them. Now I let it go and move on to my next thought. The unacceptable became acceptable."

48. Overheard in a greasy spoon, often referred to as the so-called Serenity Café: "Alcoholics Anonymous is a program of ego deflation." Now I wonder: what goddamn purpose is served in/by telling a newcomer that over the soup du jour? Is this not gratuitous information, and how does that help a new- or old comer? (But then I'm wrong a lot.)

49. Five stars: "I really have a problem talking to people in social situations," she shared with me. And went on, "Someone once said, 'You start dying the moment you're born, and it's *accelerated* at dinner parties." Applause here from yours truly.

50. "Nobody told me when I got sober I'd have to deal with getting older. Not sure what to do about that?" (But then that's what this book is all about—my work here on every page).

51. Someone at the table chimed in, "In AA, you get to be the best version of yourself."

52. "Getting into a relationship when you're drinking is like pouring gasoline on your character defects. I don't suggest it, at least for the first year." The newcomer looked away. I suspect it was too late for him for this advice. "OK then, wear life like a loose garment."

53. Let me interrupt you here: you have to abandon the hope of a brighter past. *What?*

54. "May I borrow a cigarette?...My first meeting was upstate and filled with little, old, white-haired ladies. One said to me, 'I knew I had a problem with alcohol when I burnt the toast.' That became the theme of the evenings, 'I knew I had a problem when I burnt the toast.'" The guy went on. "I soon moved away from that small town and found there were meetings with guys like me and you." He changed his mind about the cigarette and then changed his mind again. I was happy he was invited to dinner with us. I picked up his check. (Note: diners we frequent know to give the group separate checks, without asking.)

55. Again: Not merely honesty—"*rigorous* honesty in all of our affairs," they quote to newcomers, old timers, and to anyone who will listen. (Impossible request, I say, but nevertheless I heard it over and over and over again from day one.) "... especially when you're 'restless, irritable, and discontent'..."

56. Older member buying diner dinner for younger newcomer: The kid says, "I counted my money in pints."

57. "Forgive and forget. Don't drink—no matter if your ass falls off." Also, "Mind your own goddamn business." Tough advice from a mild-mannered, longtime-sober old timer to a wide-eyed, multiple-time slipper. Best not to say anything. Just listen.

58. An old timer but newcomer at the after-meeting diner dinner table tried to pass off some AA literature tidbit as his own words: "I took inventory of my life and then hung on to the worst items in stock." Wise, until later, in a meeting, someone reads those words from the AA literature. Everyone appropriates.

59. At the diner, sipping the second refilled Diet Coke, "I hear the truth in AA. I hear the truth in the rooms like I hear it nowhere else—" (lowered voice) "—not even in my own home." Noted this before—it's often said and invariably surprising to me, every time.

60. "I woke up one morning in pain and hung over. I felt as if I didn't have a soul...I was severely soulless." (Someone at the table picked up *his* check.)

61. I now have a God in my life who is just crazy about me. I think the late Elaine Stritch said that to us at dinner, but I can't be sure.

62. If you stop drinking and some time passes and then you decided to drink again, you don't start fresh/over; you (your drinking quotient) pick up where you left off. It's a progressive disease even when you're not drinking. Just when you think it's safe to go back into the water: *Sharks!*

63. Life doesn't get better when you stop drinking; you get better at life.

64. To a bewildered newcomer at dinner: Alcoholics Anonymous is not about self-improvement. Alcoholics Anonymous is about self-acceptance. And as I said to you yesterday, alcoholism is a self-diagnosed disease. (I wondered if that was too much too soon for the novice.)

65. It's an inside job: "Stop! Stop comparing your insides with other people's outsides. It doesn't work. Comparisons are odious anyway."

66. How do you do it? How do I do it? "I don't drink, no matter what. I go to meetings, often. And *I now have a vocabulary for my fears.*" God, how great. A vocabulary for my fears.

67. What-the-fuck-does-that-mean department: "Interpretation of the AA literature, at any given moment, is not the function of truth but more the purpose of power." Huh?

68. Most alcoholics think they are a piece of shit around which the world revolves. After they come into the AA program, many soon realize *the center of the universe is a very crowded place*, and maybe, just maybe, they should get off their position(s). Thank you, C.B.

69. "In AA they suggest you 'act as if' until you're where you want or need to be. Act like a winner, they say, until you become one." I found this concept difficult to grasp until I ran across these Scripture quotes. God speaks of nonexistent things as if they exist (King James 2000 Bible): "God, who gives life to the dead, and calls those things which are not, as though they were." "God who…calls into existence things that don't even exist." (GW version of the Bible). Recommendation: simply act as if.

70. Buddy, I'm saying it again: it's not alcohol*was*ism. It's alcoho*lism*. It's ongoing. And don't worry about other addictions right now, like maybe you eat too much. No one's ever been arrested for fat driving. Yes, I said some of that above in number 34, but then part of staying sober is hearing the concepts over and over again. At least for this one-time drinker. Fat driving? Boo. I've been without a drink at this typing for twenty-eight and one half years and counting. More on that later.

Positive addendum to all of the above:

In Los Angeles, there was a ninety-year-old, multiple-yeared sober member of AA; the other people in the rooms would pick him up where he stayed and bring him to meetings and fuss after him there and then made sure he got home safely, right to his front door. The old guy was always included in West Coast AA-style anniversary parties frequently held around a swimming pool. How wonderful is that? When I visited Los Angeles, after I stopped drinking at an ambivalent forty-eight, I was embraced by young members, many of them half my age; I was invited to their pool parties and local restaurant group dinners. Several times I was picked up and driven to a 12 step meeting. To be sure, I felt quite welcomed by West Coast Alcoholics Anonymous.

Here in New York, the elder statesmen and women are cared for—treated with reverence and oft quoted by other members in their own share/qualifications. No small thing with a generation of baby boomers nipping at our nose and heels.

MINDFULNESS: In the spirit of fairness, the following should be a headline, not an asterisk. In Buddhist philosophy, craving is viewed as the root of most suffering. There's evidence now that an offshoot—*mindfulness*--counters the dopamine flood of today's stressful living. University of Washington researchers created a program based on mindfulness more effective in preventing drug-addiction (at least, relapse) than 12-step programs.

Culled from September 2017's cover story in superb (I mean it) issue of *National Geographic*, "The Science of Addition." If you have the slightest interest, don't miss the entire issue. It knocked me out.

Before moving on, let me go out on a high note with couple of other secrets from the *National Geographic* article: 1) Nearly one of every twenty adults worldwide is addicted to alcohol. 2) The U. S. surgeon general's November 2016 report concluded that "… 21 million Americans have a drug or alcohol addiction making the disorder more common than cancer."

SCREAM!

CHAPTER 16

My Huckleberry Friends and Me

✳   ✳   ✳

THE GREEKS HAVE SIX WORDS for the ultimate feeling: love.

> *(1) Eros, or sexual passion. The first kind of love was eros, named after the Greek god of fertility, and it represented the idea of sexual passion and desire. (2) Philia, or deep friendship. (3) Ludus, or playful love. (4) Agape, or love for everyone. (5) Pragma, or longstanding love. (6) Philautia, or love of the self.*

We, in English, have one. Aha! Competitive me boasts that in Italian we have a lexicon-load of terms for the other loveliest of words: friend / friends/friendship.

In the world's most romantic language, the term heard most, of course, is the classic *paisan(o)*. *Paisano!* Then there's the appealing school-buddy term, *compagnoa*—an inviting endearment akin to companionship. I say you can't have too much of that.

Next, there are two diminutive Italian derivatives that might be uttered simultaneously with a three-touching-fingers-and-loud-air-kiss: *amico.* (Note: the feminine is *amica*, the plural *amici*.) A variation on those two, *amicizia*, to me sounds like my maiden aunt, Zia, but these days my Italian is a tad rusty.

Which brings me to the poignant phrase "Let's be friends," *Facciamo pace.* Can't you just hear yourself now: *Facciamo pace, paesano? Facciamo pace.*

My favorite Italian-friend offshoot that sounds more like a punch line than a real word: *collega. Coll-ega* opens up the party to a limitless name game.

If an at-work friend-colleague is a *collega*, I ask, is an intimate friend a "ball-ega"? Or if a colleague at the office is a *collega*, is a boring dude a "dull-ega?" An interim date a "lull-ega?" How about someone you used to go out with, a "saw-llega?" Hmmm…wonder how you'd dub a friend with benefits?

I came to New York City for good on February 5, 1964. I had no friends here and a whole bunch back home in Lewistown, West Virginia—or so I thought. On closer inspection: I had two.

Over the years, in my newfound hometown, the Big Apple, I've had variations-on-a-theme cohorts, a sizable stable that served a multitude of functions: girlfriend, drinking buddy, workout gym rat, collaborator, associate, sidekick, neighbor down the hall, corner counter guy to wave at en passant en route to work, etc., etc., etc., ad infinitum. After that giant geographic shift in 1964, moving to Gotham from ghetto, I soon chalked up an impressive roster of drinking-dining buddies, folks with whom I could bend the elbow at the drop of…the hint of an invite. (Let's not right now address the newfangled gossip magazine lingo I don't quite get: "bromance.")

Profoundly, now pushing seventy-seven, and some fifty-three-plus years after getting off the plane at LaGuardia, I'm examining the relationship: friends and/or friendship. The older ones died of natural causes; the younger ones, in one way or another, drank themselves to death and/or succumbed to their lifestyles—sex, drugs, rock 'n' roll, and not-so-comforting Southern Comfort. Either way, they left the planet. Prime time, big time, that narrowed the playing field. Period. Reader-friend-*paesano*, before going any further, it is imperative to confess once more here, now and forever, I do not drink anymore. In your wildest imagination, can you grasp how much that changes everything? Verboten these days: sociable acquaintances as well as social functions—off limits.

What's left? I confess I used to spend every early evening at the local YMCA. That gym picked up the *facciamo pace* slack. At precisely five-thirty, I could chew the fat, in between sets, with other gym rats. *Amici*, I aimed for 100 percent, seven days a week, and rarely made it—but showed up most every day. Then, after too many decades to mention (ahem, fifty years), I traded the neighborhood YMCA for a more expensive health club closer to home, leaving my workout *amicizios* behind. And I rationalized the higher fee this way: I'm buying time. (A) The new gym is closer to the apartment. (B) I save approximately ten minutes each way. En toto, (C) That's twenty minutes purchased daily. How dare I put a price on time? Downside to upscale gym: now working out at a high-tone health club, I'm obliged to make different, new workout cronies or pump iron—(huh!)— exercise alone.

Hold the friggin' iPad!

One of my first gigs, soon out of college, was writing advertising copy for Bloomingdale's. Recently, one of my old bosses from there did get in touch, decades after we'd palled around. After all these decades, Bloomingdale-boss-vita Lisa got wind of my first novel, *The Answer to Life*, read it, liked it, and looked me up. We have rekindled our *collega* friendship and frequently have lunch. (Remind me to invent a novel concept/word for old-new rekindled chums—for now, on the back burner.)

Pushing seventy-seven (at this typing), with 2017 around the corner, what do I have to report? What do I have to communicate about real friends and friendship? For openers, and not so surprising, those two childhood friends mentioned early on? The ones back in my hometown? They are still my huckleberry friends—thank you, Johnny Mercer**— into whose hands I'd put my life. I want you to meet them.

Aspettami! Is it an embarrassing footnote, late in life, to boast only two real friends? Boo-hoo? Bummer? Failure?

1. Hootie is a tall, trim, distinguished college professor-writer who, over the years, without fail, was there for me any time I needed him. I can't emphasize that enough. He's the only person I've ever known who is always on the scene to hear me out—without prejudice, envy, or eye roll, on the spot, when I hit the wall, and/or to red pencil a paragraph. More than that an insecure writer couldn't ask for. Meet Hootie: honor-roll recipient, straight-A student, boasting an established local family—the Coles—with old-world WASP credentials. An advantageous position to be in, diametrically opposed to my own Italian immigrant roots: Peno, Martino, Adamo with a touch of Perfetti. And, yes, his great-grandfather

Cole had been mayor. Somewhere across town, a bridge was named after Granddad Cole.

Not surprisingly, Hootie had all the trappings of confidence and brainpower to succeed in the world of twentieth-century United States of America. And he did—right on cue: he became a respected college professor/dean at one of the more ivy-covered (he jokes: "poison-ivy-covered") institutions of higher learning. All impressive. But for me he tops a more lowbrow list. His finest asset is that he is a down-to-earth gent. When I detail folks I knew who made me laugh out loud, he heads the list. Hootie could elicit a belly laugh from me in a snap—long before LOL was an acronym. In my book, Hootie was and is an all-around top-drawer friend.

2. Not in second place, I assure you, is Cocco. Cocco was a few years older than I. She lived down the block from my grandparents and took me under her wing during a difficult time. After my folks got tossed out onto the street (still bitter, though I'm trying), we were bunking down in the Italian neighborhood with my maternal grandparents. This tall, trim, clear-skinned, unfussy, high-minded, smart, snappy liberal with long, straight, clean-smelling hair befriended this clueless, preteen, ethnic dude—more than anyone else in that not-so-forgiving Italian neighborhood. Further evidence of her above-and-beyond-average spirituality: a few steps behind, a sweet-tempered, champagne-colored husky named Pal tailed us everywhere, loving and guarding us. To this day, when we reference Pal all these years later, she still gets teary-eyed. That's heart.

At that time, I had to walk across town to grade school, shivering with every step in my Thom McAn's. I'd become a courier for the grade-school principal, who forced me to be interceder between Her Principalness and Mother Lou, the boss of our family. Old Maid Bruta Face-a, in her stark, industry-green and mahogany office with resting-on-her-breast bifocals, would call me in. She was on my case right after the eviction to have us move from that school, one I'd been attending for six years, to the Italian-section school. On the carpet, in her office, my pits dripping, she'd dress me down, indulging herself in long tirades—all of which ended with words I grit my teeth to detail, to be delivered to my mother. (Why Miss Bruta Face-a was exercising extraordinary energy on this, I'll never know. I ask myself: because we were Italian?) The message to Mom: "You and your siblings must transfer to the grade school nearer the North Side." My mother's succinct reply, the same every time, uttered/ spoken passionlessly, with firm resignation: "It's just temporary." Please don't tell Catholic Grandmaw that Mother Lou referred to the principal as Assy-Whaley.

Cocco sure was extraordinary. Cocco and I, on my evenings off, tooled around the North Side. I'd "secured" a job cleaning cake pans in a restaurant up the block. Note: with sad violins dripping in the background, the cleaning room window, where I scraped clean—and then thoroughly greased—was positioned directly above the sandlot where the neighborhood guys roughhoused and played baseball. Their homerun cheers wafted up and into the window as I removed yesterday's crumbs from the bottom of a nagging pile of grubby rectangular bake pans. (In the future, therapist Dr. Bosco was to have a psychologist's field day with that coincidence—sandlot below my preteen job above other boys' field of play.) To say the least, at eleven or twelve, this was a rough time for me. And Cocco was my refuge, my strength, my confidant—a most admirable *amica*.

Cocco would buy us RC Colas dripping with steaming-cold frost. First we'd take a couple of sips. Then we'd drop handfuls of salted peanuts into the fizzing cola bottle. Boy, was that a great treat. And at the first whisper of darkness, twilight, we'd sneak into the bakery up on Sixth Street. From the dented, steel-gray cooling racks, we'd swipe a couple of still-warm, right-from-the-oven, vigorously glazed donuts. I suspect the bakers knew what we were doing and good-naturedly looked the other way.

After high school, Cocco went on to chalk up impressive credentials in Washington, DC, positioned in a wide-windowed office that looked down the block at the White House. She became a higher-up for the National Education Association. We can assume she was good at what she did. Even after she retired, the NEA mahoffs would telephone her at home with questions on policy and solicit solutions on current snafus.

We're still close friends. Cocco and I exchange e-mails twice a week. And her life now? Retired, in a roomy house in a DC suburb, with a sweet puppy or two. Even the new, charming, yelping, trouser-brushing pedigrees don't replace mongrel Pal, though.

Before halting here, I'd like to interject some hubris.

In midlife, as I mentioned before, I saw a therapist with whom I shared, among other *hazerai*, my confusion and confoundedness on difficult New Yorkers: friends, lovers, and other strangers—in other words, big-headed, big-city neurotic human beings (read: relationships!). Along the way, this German-accented therapist said something I never forgot and took to heart. "Sir," he said in his best official power voice, "you have stated what great people your friends are. But you fail to recognize what a good friend you are to them. You really know how to be a friend." That comment was worth every penny my employer paid Dr. German Accent on my behalf. I pray this was true then and trust it's truer now.

Closing caveat: today, realistically, I suspect that making new (close) friends at seventy-six-plus is not in the bridge game. But philosophically, I concede: ending up, late in life, with two close friends is not a bad batting average. But I ain't dead yet. Old and new hope springs. I'm still open to making future (uncomplicated, please) *paisanos*. And having said aaalllll that, I ask you: What in Sam Hill is a "bromance"?

** "My huckleberry friend," lyric from Johnny Mercer's "Moon River," music by Italian composer Henry Mancini.

Foot and shoe note: In Matthew 10:14, Jesus Christ suggested that when you leave a place, to "shake the dust off your feet." When I saw Lewistown, West Virginia, in the rearview mirror and New York, New York, up ahead, I shook the dust off my feet and went out and bought a new pair of sandals.

Thank you and to give back:

In another form, this chapter appeared in the *Huffington Post*. I was glad for the exposure. When one comes from a West Virginia coal-mining/glass-factory/Maidenform brassier-sewing town and ends up in New York City a bona fide writer, he's grateful for every bylined credit. As I've established: I did not become a writer to get rich, and I ditto: they tell me over and over in 12 step meetings, "You have to give it away to get it." I want to help someone else out there to shake, to let go of an addiction of any kind with every sentence I string together. There may be fifty ways to leave your mother.

I'd like to begin chapter 17 with a rock-'n'-roll song:

"Seventeen, hot-rod queen, the prettiest girl I've ever seen." Can you believe I plunked down ninety-nine cents to buy singer Boyd Bennett's 45-rpm record "Seventeen" in 1955? Wonder what that disc is worth today. What did I do with all those 45-rpms? If I'd kept them, I could go on Ebay and … Hold on, I don't know how to go on Ebay.

Writers: Boyd Bennett, John Young, and Carl Gorman, published by Fort Knox and Trio Music.

CHAPTER 17

Actually Not Actualized Yet, but I Can Dream, Can't I?

✳   ✳   ✳

"THE MOST BEAUTIFUL THING WE can experience is the mysterious" (Abraham Maslow quoting Mr. Albert Einstein). See there. Even the imposing Abraham Maslow, to make a point, appropriated.

SELF-ACTUALIZATION REVEALED, VISITED, REVISITED, REVILED, RETWEAKED, AND POSSIBLY BEATEN TO DEATH

As we've established, during the 1970s, I was attracted to a human-potential movement and more specifically to a concept called actualization.

Let's be honest here: during that decade, there was an explosion of self-improvement, self-discovery, self-reflection, self-realization, and self-exploration—ad infinitum. Previously confessed, by then I'd been reading self-help books for a couple decades in a secret search for the answer to life. I was Catholic, and that wasn't advised. And a little Italian boy in Lewistown, West Virginia, reading highfalutin self-help books might have been ridiculed. Surreptitiously, I kept them covered in brown paper bags fashioned from grocery pokes (pokes in West Virginia are generic paper grocery bags). Self-help books in plain brown paper wrappers. What a concept!

By the time I was in my thirties with a college degree and several credits to my name, I was no closer to the answers. But by this time, I was drowning in the above: (a) human-potential movement, (b) a hectic New York social life, (c) fine and cheap wine, (d) and a coterie of attractive women (one of the "beautiful people") on one arm and, for sure, a hard-liquor drink in the other.

One of the new theories making the rounds in the ripe 1970s was called self- actualization. It was OK in New York City to share your discoveries with your New York friends at cocktail parties (many used that as fodder for a joke, laughed up their sleeves—uncool in New York City—and/or in your face) and to say, "I want to be self-actualized."

Recently, from research, I revisited and paraphrased, from any source I could find, on the subject. Cut me some slack here, will ya?

Self-actualization was introduced by the organismic theorist Kurt Goldstein. He described its purpose was to motivate a student/fellow/person to realize his/her full potential. He explained his concept this way:

"Expressing one's creativity, quest for spiritual enlightenment, pursuit of knowledge, and the desire to give to and/or positively transform society are examples of self-actualization." Furthermore, "...the tendency to actualize oneself as fully as possible is the basic drive...of self-actualization."

Note: Self-actualization would soon encapsulate many "selves:" self-discovery, self-reflection, self-realization, and self-exploration.

The core: Kurt Goldstein's original theory in his weighty book with an even heavier title, *The Organism: A Holistic Approach to Biology Derived from Pathological Data in Man* (1939), presented self-actualization as "the tendency to actualize, as much as possible, [the organism's] individual capacities" in the world. The tendency toward self-actualization is "the only [true] drive by which the life of an organism is determined."

However for Goldstein, self-actualization was not a goal to be reached sometime in the future. No, it was for *now*, in the moment, any time the seeker has the fundamental inclination to actualize all his/her/their capacities, his/her whole potential, as it is present in exactly that moment, in precisely that situation, in contact with the world under the given circumstances. Hang in there with me. The convoluted concept had momentum.

Under the influence of Goldstein, Abraham Maslow would later develop his highly held hierarchical theory of human motivation, which he called "hierarchy of needs."

Motivation and Personality, Abraham Maslow, published by Harpers (1954).

Abraham Maslow's "hierarchy of needs" theory—he claimed *the next level* of psychological development popularly sought—states that the hierarchy of needs could be achieved when all basic and mental needs were fulfilled. Then "actualization" of the full personal potential could take place. Hallelujah!

Yes. When I read that, I said, "That's for me." (What exactly is it again?)

Abraham Maslow confirmed, first, that the basic needs of humans must be met (e.g., food, shelter, warmth, security, sense of belonging) before a person could achieve self-actualization, which he defined as the desire "to be good, to be fully alive and to find meaning in life." Sadly, Maslow admits "that reaching a state of true self-actualization in everyday society was fairly rare." Aha! For me, a further brass ring to reach for.

Further incentive and additional fodder:

TAKE IT TO THE BANK
Research confirmed that when people live lives that are different from their true nature and capabilities, they are less likely to be happy than those whose goals *and* lives match up—that is, a talent who has inherent potential to be a great artist or teacher may never realize his/her talents if his/her energy is focused on attaining the basic needs of water, bread, shelter. No starving artists in garrets, thank you very much.

SELF-ACTUALIZATION—SUCCINCTLY
Abraham Maslow describes "the good life" as one directed toward self-actualization, the pinnacle need.

Synopsis: Self-actualization occurs when you maximize your potential, doing the best that you are capable of doing. Maslow studied individuals who he believed to be self-actualized—Abraham Lincoln, Thomas Jefferson, and Albert Einstein—to find, to isolate, to get to the heart of the common characteristics that made up a self-actualized person.

From his book, Abraham Maslow, *Motivation and Personality*, Harpers, 1954.

All worth the time and the space. Monumental to me at the time, and the concept still haunts me. Here are the characteristics of a self-actualized individual, included with the express hope that the details may help some-one out there, and me, searching for answers, always on the lookout for solutions, and, I am quick to add, to stay clean and sober for the rest of my life:

1. Self-actualized people embrace the unknown and the ambiguous. Not threatened or afraid of it; instead, they accept it and are comfortable with the uncertain. Yours truly left West Virginia at eighteen, hardly having been anywhere much before that, with little money in my pocket. In hindsight, how did I do it?

2. They accept themselves, together with all their flaws.

   She perceives herself as she is and not as she would prefer herself to be. With a high level of self-acceptance.

   "They can accept their own human nature in the stoic style, with all its shortcomings, with all its discrepancies from the ideal image without feeling real concern…One does not complain about water because it is wet, or about rocks since they are hard…simply noting and observing what is the case, without either arguing the matter or demanding that it be otherwise." I went to a large university, got a full time job ten hours a day, and carried a full-time load. I didn't know any better. Later, I moved to New York City with little life experience under my belt. Periodically, I get on my knees and thank God I got out of West Virginia and for everything else. Don't fault me. Check the statistics in every category regarding West Virginia and you'll see why.

3. They prioritize and enjoy the journey, not just the destination.

   "[They] often [regard] as ends in themselves many experiences and activities that are, for other people, only means." That sounds nice. However, I was ill equipped to handle most New York realities. A new friend suggested therapy to help me in my "work-career" area. Therapy did that and more. I was not used to expressing how I felt or if anything hurt. Back home, there were too many of us clamoring for attention for adults to listen. I had learned to fend for myself. But by the time I stopped drinking, there were multiple layers in the onion of a human being that needed to be addressed. And they were looked at in therapy. Yes, there were many enjoyable moments, and I've listed some of them in other chapters in these pages, but the good news is not always the lead story of the day, is it?

4. While self-actualized people are inherently unconventional, they do not seek to shock or disturb.

Unlike the average rebel, the self-actualized person recognizes "the world of people in which he lives could not understand or accept [his unconventionality], and since he has no wish to hurt them or to fight with them over every triviality, he will go through the ceremonies and rituals of convention with a good-humored shrug and with the best possible grace." Oh, for sure, an ideal way to approach life, but how does one learn to do that? It's a process, Mr. Pino. Life's a process. As I've mentioned, I do not know how to measure "growth" and "grace," and maybe way back in there, I admit, there is a fear, a superstition, a fallacy to not let God know things are somewhat better, or then he will punish me, at the very least take them away. (I suspect that's not how it works.) However, in AA, someone got my attention with this, "If you want to make God laugh, say, 'I have a plan.'"

5. They are motivated by growth, not by the satisfaction of needs.

While most people are still struggling in the lower rungs of the hierarchy of needs, the self-actualized person is focused on personal growth. Growth is one of those intangible words that haunt me. Growth, grace—how do you know? How do you measure? Do the next right thing. How can you tell?

6. Self-actualized people have purpose.

"[They have] some mission in life, some task to fulfill, some problem outside themselves, which enlists much of their energies...not necessarily a task that they would prefer, or choose for themselves, it may be a task that they feel is their responsibility, duty, or obligation." Yes, yes, yes. I always wanted to be a writer and didn't even acknowledge that fact until I was in a session with Dr. German Accent. "You're a writer, Mr. Pino; you're a writer." And now, years later, I realize I wanted to write to express myself, to be heard; possibly no one was listening during my childhood. It was too chaotic, too loud, too filled with superstition, rife with untried theories and generations of misconception—all OK, but none of that sustained me. I wanted to know the answer to life. And still do.

7. They are not troubled by the small things.

Instead, they focus on the bigger picture. "They seem never to get so close to the trees that they fail to see the forest. They work within a framework of values that are broad and not petty, universal and not local, and in terms of a century rather than the moment." Easy for you to say. I was overwhelmed with small things, minutiae, details—some of which sustained me. The therapist said, "You care a lot about little things; you wrote an article about pennies, for God's sake." Guilty.

8. Self-actualized people are grateful.

They do not take their blessings for granted, and by doing that, they maintain a natural sense of wonder.

"Self-actualizing people have the wonderful capacity to appreciate again and again, freshly and naïvely, the basic goods of life, with awe, pleasure, wonder, and even ecstasy...Thus for such a person, any sunset may be as beautiful as the first one, any flower may be of breath-taking loveliness, even after he has seen a million flowers...For such people, even the casual worka-day, moment-to-moment business of living can be thrilling." Or what's a heaven for? A high, heady place to which to aspire. But from time to time, fleetingly, true in my life, I do try hard, but then in the 1970s, the metaphysicians used to say, "'Trying' is a low space." And as for grateful, as I mentioned a hundred times, I express gratitude every day, every evening, and even collect quotes on the subject. *Piglet noticed that even though he had a Very*

Small Heart, it could hold a rather large amount of Gratitude"—A. A. Milne.

9. They share deep relationships with a few but also feel identification and affection toward the entire human race.

"Self-actualizing people have deeper and more profound interpersonal relations than any other adults...They are capable of more fusion, greater love, more perfect identification, more obliteration of the ego boundaries than other people would consider possible...side by side with...benevolence, affection, and friendliness." Wouldn't that be nice? Maybe Gandhi and Jesus Christ or Thomas Merton, but I will keep that in mind. Who among us?

10. Self-actualized people are humble.

"They are all quite well aware of how little they know in comparison with what could be known and what is known by others. Because of this it is possible for them without pose to be honestly respectful and even humble before people who can teach them something." Wow. Yes. Humble gets a bad rap. I remember the word frequently spoken in the Catholic Church and echoed in Alcoholics Anonymous and other 12 step programs. I suspect it will take years of further study to truly, fully grasp humility—humility as a virtue. The Greeks didn't think it was one. Aristotle does not list humility among his list of virtues. The New Testament does use the word multiple times. Saint Thomas Aquinas categorizes Christian humility as a by-product of the virtue of temperance, which comes in handy for anyone trying to shake an addition. All I can say for now: humility is a difficult one for twenty-first-century man, but we can, along with many other areas, keep searching.

11. Self-actualized people resist enculturation.

Nix to fads. "They do not allow themselves to be passively molded by culture—they deliberate and make their own decisions...neither accept all, like a sheep, nor reject all, like the average rebel."

Self-actualized people "make up their own minds, come to their own decisions, are self-starters, are responsible for themselves and their own destinies.

"They are the most ethical of people even though their ethics are not necessarily the same as those of the people around them... the ordinary ethical behavior of the average person is largely conventional behavior rather than truly ethical behavior." I keep bumping into reality. AA suggests we practice their high-level principles in all our affairs/behavior. It's a worthy height to which to aspire but daunting and sometimes exhausting. And I think most people, including myself, have built-in resistance. I have to constantly guard against resisting, to get out of my own way, but then that may be an entire other subject.

12. Despite all this, self-actualized people are not perfect.

"There are no perfect human beings! Persons can be found who are good, very good indeed, in fact, great...And yet these very same people can at times be boring, irritating, petulant, selfish, angry, or depressed. To avoid disillusionment with human nature, we must first give up our illusions about it." Ah, it keeps coming up: we are human beings. I've been over this territory a million or more times. Heaven will forgive us our indiscretions if we ask for forgiveness and then forgive ourselves. (The most difficult part here: to forgive ourselves.) There's more: heaven then does not keep track up there; heaven forgets our "sins" at this point, I'm told (there is no longer a list in the Ethernet; the error of our ways has been erased). So then, I ask, if God forgives me, why is it so hard to forgive myself? I now evoke my Aunt Maria, who used to say to me as a child, "Forgive and forget, forgive and forget..." *Gracia tutti*, Zia Maria; she nearly lived to be a hundred.

One of the few images of running in the Bible is in the parable of the prodigal son. The father rushes to the returning, uncertain, insecure son, who has failed. Maybe, just maybe, God will not only forgive us for our indiscretions but also with any luck, forget them too.

If you want more information, get the tell-all book (ditto, from): *Motivation and Personality*, by Abraham Maslow, published by Harpers (1954). It's worth owning. All of this material is online and in print. I pay tribute to Maslow and his work with a prayer that the words help someone heal, whatever his or her affliction may be—including myself.

And now, after all that, there's this to consider:

Not the Last Word

As my not-well-educated Italian father customarily, sarcastically, snarled when I expressed an opinion about anything, "Another country heard from." Well, the following is another country heard from and a worn paperback I pored over and highly recommended to anyone who can read or will listen: *The Psychology of Romantic Love*, by Nathaniel Branden, Bantam Books, (1980).

"What is unfortunate is that many exponents of the human-potential movement have adopted increasingly apologetic and defensive postures in response to accusations of 'selfishness.' Of *course*, the pursuit of self-actualization is selfish. So is the pursuit of physical health. So is the pursuit of sanity. So is the pursuit of happiness. So is the pursuit of your next breath of air." *Yes, Mr. Branden! And thank you.*

From *The Psychology of Romantic Love*, by Nathaniel Branden, Bantam Books (1980).

May I please go out of this detailed chapter with a song? There's a wonderful cut on an early 1960 Jack Jones album called "Nina Never Knew"*: "Nina never knew till now," he sang. Well, *Nino* never knew, still doesn't know, and he's still looking.

*"Nina Never Knew" was a 1952 chart hit for crooner Johnny Desmond and was then picked up a decade later by Jack Jones, Kapp Records, and released on two Jack Jones albums: *Wives and Lovers* as well as *Gift of Love*, 1962. One of those albums won a Grammy.

At the end of chapter 17, lyrics/words running through my mind: "She was just seventeen, do you know what I mean?" What is that *song*? No such title. "She was just seventeen..." I've been humming it all day long.

CHAPTER 18

The Middle Period

*   *   *

A READER'S REVIEW...

In front of Bloomingdale's, I ran into a friend from way back. Excitedly, she said, "I read your book. I *love* reading about your family." (It's a novel, my love, a *novel!*) I said thank you and moved on.

I bumped into this same friend-now-fan again after my second outing, this time near Lincoln Center. She was even more effusive. "I love both your books! I would like to meet your family." (Silence. Should I remind her the novels are novels?) Before I could say, she said, "And I want to know more about *you* in your work."

I hugged her, thanked her, kissed her check and got on the bus.

I ruminated all afternoon. What more could I tell her?

1. Somewhere along 1943, 1944, 1945 (age three, four, five), my father, then "Daddy," took me to see the showy Harlem Globetrotters jokesters at the Carmichael Auditorium in white uniforms. I was transfixed, wide-eyed; my jaw might have dropped. Here was live entertainment like I'd never seen it before. What a joy for a kid to watch basketball antics from bold, splashy, dazzling, professional players-experts goofing around up and down the wide rectangular court in the flesh. I recall unusually nondescript uniforms, not the red, white, and blue the flamboyant jokesters wear these days. (Maybe white was for out-of-town gigs.) Then on another afternoon, another local basketball game: from the Carmichael's balcony (always from the balcony), we watched as, at game's end,

some dude handed out trophies. From then on, at every game, I wanted to know, "When they were going to hand out the trophies?" *Naaaw.*

Most important to note here, after that, Father/Dad/Paw had little time for me. The siblings begin popping out one a year. Later, he was less interested in entertaining me and more prone to belittling me. That's fodder for another time, a separate issue, a different chapter? *And more of a guy's story, don't ya think?*

2. What about that early visit to the funeral home? Somewhere along about 1945, (age five, six), my father, my Uncle Pete, and I went to Wheeling for an afternoon visit to what Grandmaw Pino would call "the undertaker." It was my great-grandfather on her (Grandmaw Pino's) side who'd passed. Laid out, hands folded over himself, there was this old gentleman I'd never seen before, the subject of the afternoon, my dead great-granddad— and another first, it was the initial initiation seeing a dead person. Most of the folks milling around/circling the funeral parlor viewing area I'd never met either. Mercifully, we didn't stay long. The three of us went to a diner. I found it hard to eat. Late that afternoon, we had an uneventful drive back to Lewistown. *Nino, that's not very interesting. She's not going to care about that.*

3. Hey, what about World War II? I remember a multitude of details about World War II: air-raid rehearsals; chewing-gum rationing; strapping, young uncles—one on each side—marching off and then returning home in uniforms. (Only one *zia* saw battle and came back shell-shocked. For the longest time, he had disturbing early-morning nightmares. During the loud episodes, he'd get hugged by a saint of an angel of a wife and soon got over the yelling spells. Thank God, the screams in the night stopped). *No! For sure, she won't want me to rehash that, will she?*

4. What else I could tell her, my avid reader, my new best fan? True confession here: I scanned my brain; when I evoke the past, most often what comes up are popular songs. I revert to hit records in

my mind. Big bands blast trumpets in my head. Glenn Miller's unmistakable sound takes over. Artie Shaw's mesmerizing Artie Shaw clarinet solo interrupts. The Dorsey Brothers' "So Rare"— the melody, the arrangement, the words as alive in my mind as Beyoncé's bounce. And if the truth be tolerated here, *fact*, I remembered every popular song that came on the radio from infancy on. Not news. *Biggest Fan/Friend/Reader knows all that, Nino. You already told those tales; move on.*

5.   I got it! By Jove, I think I got it. *How about the middle period? Those middle years! My biggest fan could respond to the mid-1950s. It's worth a shot. She just might be endeared.* After the stint on the North Side with my grandparents, Mother and Dad located a three-story, a not-too-expensive fixer-upper on Dennison Run. The tireless-workers-in-every-area parents set out to do just that and did, fast, with the help of friends and relatives. Mom and Dad made over what I called "The Cat House" as fast and as fine as a Quaker house hoedown. (The previous owners had a shitload of cats, and the faint aroma of performing seals still hung around in some parts of the house, hence, The Cat House.)

By that time, some of us were in our teens. It wasn't long before we all seemed to be the same age. We were one year apart and, to a stranger, could have been the same age. After the paper route, I had a shoe store job that paid more, and I began to spend way too much money on 45 rpms. (Grandmaw Pino used to sneer, "You gonna eat those records when you're hungry?") Day and night, rock 'n' roll spun out from a tiny turntable in the downstairs hall, yes, at all hours. Soon, Toni blossomed into a classic beauty, a real knockout, in the mode of an Italian Brigitte Bardot, a twenty-four-carat Marilyn Monroe. (We have snapshots.) Not long after, Pina, Pietro, and Leonardo followed suit—an attractive lot we were.

"The House of Adventure" one second cousin renamed our home. It rocked: young friends and teenage cousins dropped in unannounced any time they felt inclined. Rock-'n'-roll music.

Button-down Oxford shirts. Khaki trousers. Penny loafers. Blue suede shoes. Acne. And for me, two girlfriends, one at the local high school, the other way across town in the Catholic area. (The distance and the different crowd of friends, disparate enough for me to get away with it.) Laugher, jokes, food, fun. We had great times because we were congenial-natured kids. Yet Mother never liked for us to be too holy and instilled a touch of "orneriness," as she called it, in each one of us. She even verbalized, "I like for my kids to be a little bit ornery." I loved making my siblings laugh and for my antics was dubbed Felix the Cat.

So the whirlwind middle period, the mid-1950s, between 1954 and 1958 (and one half), as a family unit, were the happiest for us.

I was to graduate from high school on top. June 1958: sports editor of the weekly newspaper, secret *The Hilltopper* columnist for that rag, called "The Hallwalker" (but everyone knew). Not to mention the ubiquitous class photographer for the weekly *Hilltopper* in both junior and senior years. Then, ta da, sports editor for the 1958 high school annual, where the editors put all the writer-reporter's photographs on page one. When he saw my picture in the 1958 yearbook's front section, the usual distant dad said, "You must be proud of that." Faint praise but a pat anyway.

Then I went to Miami early, late summer 1958, to get the jump on things. I didn't have much money. It was imperative that I get work, that I, come September, be ahead from the start at a major university—prejitters about freshman subjects had set in—and to be ready when cousin Robbie met up. (He was to arrive after Labor Day to be a roommate, to share expenses and my company). Right off, I got a job at the behemoth, and a bit overwhelming, supermarket within walking distance of the college campus's edge. (It goes without saying that small-town West Virginia boy was forced to grow up pronto.) Bummer of all bummers, instead of showing up, Rob got married and packed off to Las Vegas without so much as a postcard with an "oops, change of plans.".

Every time I visit a supermarket today, I'm reminded at checkout what it was like yesterday at Coral Gables, Steven's Market in 1958-1959. You wheeled your cart up to a chatty cashier, placed the groceries to their left, then that clerk punched in every item, one digit at a time: 50 cent tissues: Five. Zero. Click. Eggs 60 cents. Six. Zero. Click. Then, he/she placed them on a conveyer belt. A young gent, called a bag boy, (usually a guy back then), at the end of the conveyer's end, would place the groceries in the brown paper bags. Afterward, if you preferred, for a small tip, he would chat you up (hoping a bigger tip) and wheel your purchases out to your car and place them in the trunk for you. (You do know that (tip) stands for To Insure Promptness?) Times have changed...

Soon after, one of my girlfriends got married. The following year, the other one followed suit. Do you suppose they were cheating on me?

I survived two years, four semesters at the University of Miami, Coral Gables, Florida, USA, and then transferred back to West Virginia and earned an English degree (no journalism school there) at a local Lewistown college. After that, it was New York City for me, and I've written about that ad infinitum. It's a helluva town.

Next!

6. Here's something I find an enigma. I recently skimmed several hit-song lists of the 1950s—rock 'n' roll, rhythm and blues, and other tunes—and I swear on my mother's chicken soup recipe I knew every cut on those lengthy rosters. One hundred, two hundred songs I'm familiar with. [Serious question here: I now ask—it's academic—*why was I not studying Shakespeare?* Conversely, let's see if you believe this one. I am grateful to have heard passages read aloud from the King James Version of the Bible every Sunday (and I mean *every* Sunday) at the High Mass at St. John the Baptist's Catholic Church. The Bible is rich literature, and to this day, those words serve me as a writer.]

(The editor weighed in: you should spend more time on plot and less time on popular music. My answer to her: there is no plot. Many readers see a "story line," but I don't want a conventional narrative. The simple secret of the plot is there is no plot. There is, however, this rigorous, trying triathlon: a solid beginning, a strong middle and an energizing-bunny ending.)

And a message to my biggest fan/old friend, thank you for triggering this chapter with your support and your comments. These words are dedicated to you.

Caveat: Chapter Nineteen, a Spiritual Section, Is an Option for You. Read It, or Jump to the Eclectic Mixed Appendix. However, there is an *answer* here that stopped me in my tracks. You just might embrace it, too.

A prayer to begin:

Dear God, I've saved you for last, and I pray You are not offended. Mea culpa. Mea culpa. Mea culpa.

Dear Reader, if you find this chapter *troppo-sigh* (Calabrian dialect for "too, too much"), keep your pants on. I've saved dish, dirt, and divineness (divinity?) for you in the appendix—some naughty, other not so nice. GIGO, as the computer geeks say: "garbage in, garbage out." You may be shocked in the appendix, so hang on in there with me. Signed, Mr. Nino X. Pino.

I gush: In my ongoing search for the answers to life, I found a few bold, workable answers here. I experienced these revelations, thought provoking, inspirational, sometimes riveting.

CHAPTER 19

Is That All There Is?

* * *

*"Something more, I need something more. Nothing is enough."** *

Do I DARE? Do I have the chutzpah to even attempt to distill the answer to life (in my ongoing search) according to the twentieth century's monumentally distinguished educator, existentialist philosopher, political activist, Jewish, religious thinker Martin Buber after reading his slim but weighty volume of aphorisms, *I and Thou*, a compendium of complex messages? I have to confess it was so exciting for this almost-jaded, overworked, human-potential junkie to find a philosophy/concept/idea I hadn't heard before. It bears a taste of.

A detour, disclaimer, caveat, query. Before going on, I'd like to admit, in the 1970s, I was aware and privy to all that was going on in and around New York City and Los Angeles, especially of the burgeoning human-potential movement: books, magazine articles, newspapers, programs, seminars, classes, ad infinitum—I couldn't get enough. Now I question and wonder if Werner Erhard, Louise Hay, and all the others—those ad hoc gurus who sprung up and got rich—read the 1970s retranslation of Martin Buber's groundbreaking work *I and Thou* (smartly transcribed by Walter Kaufman and published by Scribners) and then incorporated (appropriated?) into the 1970s then-burgeoning human-potential movement Martin Buber's philosophies in their works as their own original thoughts. Merely speculating.

Buber's impressive background, briefly: Martin Buber considered himself a "philosophical anthropologist." He spoke multiple languages:

English, French, German, Italian, Hebrew (and Yiddish), Polish, Spanish, Greek, and Dutch. Buber studied Hegel, Marx, Kierkegaard, Nietzsche, Dilthey, Simmel, Heidegger, Socrates, Aristotle, Goethe, Kant, Hegel, and Jesus and was well versed not only in Hasidic Judaism (the Talmud) but also in Christianity and the Bible. Therefore, I trust Martin Buber.

A predominant theme in his work: Human life finds its meaning in relationships. And, accordingly, *all* of our alliances ultimately bring us into alliance with God, which/who Buber calls "the Eternal Thou." Thus, and I liked this, if God is the universal relation to all relations, then He is everpresent in human consciousness *and* is manifest in *all* forms of culture/self-expression: music, song, dance, all kinds of writing, gaming, blogging, etc.

"One who truly meets the world goes out also to God," wrote Buber.

(Reminder here: Martin Buber was Jewish.) In essence, Buber says one's goal should be to study the wholeness of man. He did not believe that Jesus Christ took himself to be divine. Buber thought Jesus's form of faith corresponds to what he called *emunah*—faith in God's continual presence in the life of each and every individual. For this reason, Buber reasons from the beliefs of Apostles Paul and John (labeled *pistis*), God does exist in Jesus.

At the same time, man's task is not to eradicate the evil urge but to reunite it with the good in order to become a whole being, and he maintains that creative power, in conjunction with will, is wholeness. Buber upholds that "the good urge" in the imagination limits possibility by saying *no* to innumerable, distracting possibilities—and, seriously, you/one/I must *direct passion* in order to decisively realize his/her/their/our potential. "In so doing one redeems evil by transforming it from anxious possibility into creativity"—commonly, the above listed: music, song, dance, writing, gaming, blogging.

And I restate for your and *my* benefit: "...in *all* forms of cultural self-expression."

(All unfamiliar, new to me, a self-improvement aficionado, this *"something more" theory encompassed so much more).

Existential angst, worries of meaninglessness, and the impending sense of doom that we modern human beings feel often lead, "in the dead of night when one can't sleep," are (all?) the result of our reliance on *experience* to the exclusion of encounter. (Hang in there, Nino: I kept reading and studying.)

Buber's solution to our/yours/mine/modern man's woes?

All encounters, he says, in effect are fleeting. For that reason, it is only matter of time before any "you" dissolves into an "it" (that is, as soon as one/we begin(s) to reflect on the "you," it becomes an "it.") Let that sink in, Nino…we're near the punch line.

Hang on, hang in: "Love, then, is a constant oscillation between encounter and experience."

Subsequently, every/any human encounter we live through does <u>not</u> wholly fulfill our yearning for relation. (A ring of truth here—I white knuckled tight with the concept.)

Thus, we eternally feel that there could be *something more out there*—something more lasting, something more fulfilling. This "more" is encounter with God. But according to Buber, we cannot seek our encounter with God; we can only *ready* ourselves for it by concentrating both aspects of our self—that "I" he spoke of, of experience, and the "I" of encounter—in our very soul(s).

Ultimately, Martin Buber succinctly concludes: The human being is not he, she, it and/or bound by anything. For that reason, our relationship with God cannot be explained; it simply is. Aha! The human-potential gurus of the 1970s kept professing (knocking off?) that specific theory as if they dreamed it in the middle of the night—one of the reasons I became suspicious of the originality of the human-potential cohorts.

Again, to state for emphasis: if God is the universal relation to all relations, then He is ever-present in human consciousness *and* is manifest in *all* forms of culture/self-expression—let me state again: music, song, dance, all kinds of writing, gaming, blogging, etc. Amen. This clean, original concept enables me every morning at eight, when I sit down to write in the unsteady, four-wheeled computer chair, to focus 110 percent.

And the above concept may be the answer to life; at least, one of them.

At this time in my life, it takes a great deal of effort to keep me productive and focused. Maybe I've read too much, too many, for too long. But now Martin Buber's words work for me. All of my life I've run into people who were ultimately unsatisfied. They don't start out that way, but eventually they express how unfulfilled they become. They actually say there has to be "something more." Why, even Miss Peggy Lee asks us, "Is that all there is?"**

*Opening quote:"*Something more, I need something more. Nothing is enough.*" from Martin Buber.

The German I and Thou, *first published in 1923, was translated from German to English in 1937 by Ronald Gregor Smith. Then again, in 1970, transcribed by Walter Kaufman; Kaufman's version was published by Scribners.*

And, to me, it is all as fresh and as beautiful as tomorrow's daisies.

Apropos of everything

Writer G. K. Chesterton said, *"You say grace before meals. All right. But I say grace before the concert and the opera, and grace before the play and pantomime, and grace before I open a book, and grace before sketching, painting, swimming, fencing, boxing, walking, playing, dancing and grace before I dip the pen in the ink."*

Damn, I'd like to invite both G. K. Chesterton *and* Martin Buber to dinner some evening soon, at 7.

And, if you need more fodder--geez, you're tough—Mr. Homer began both *The Odyssey* and *The Iliad* with a prayer to Ms. Muse. For years I've been trying to locate Homer's first name. It's now where to be found. And, The Muse? The Muse was/were actually nine goddesses. Who knew?

Riders to Chapter Nineteen

Gautama Buddha: The first of Buddha's Four Noble Truths, "Life is suffering."

God: (1) "God's dream for your life—that you always have a smile, that you're always in peace, that you're always excited about your future...

God wants you to have an abundance, so you can be a blessing to those around you."

From *Think Better, Live Better*, by Joel Osteen, pages 76 and 128, FaithWords, Hachette Books.

God: (2) "God's dream for your life is that you would be blessed in such a way that you could be a blessing to others."

From the uplifting *Power of I Am*, by Joel Osteen, page 145, FaithWords, Hachette Books.

P.S. to *all* that. I will use any and all I can find to help me get (and to keep) my mojo (back). It takes monumental amounts of reading, praying, dancing, self-talk, and strong coffee to get me in that swivel chair in front of the typewriter, the computer, IBM Selectric, yellow pads, Post-it notes, 3 x 5 index cards—not to mention an enormous amount of energy (and coffee) to write. I found Martin Buber's new-to-me-philosophy a mind boggler. And every morning, Mr. Buber keeps me in that squeaky computer chair. No small thing, *paesano*.

***The song "Is that All There Is?," written by Jerry Leiber and Mike Stoller was a big hit for Peggy Lee in 1969, and is published by Sony/ATV Music/Warner/Chappell Music. There is a rumor that Donald Trump has gone on record to say "Is That All There Is?" is his favorite song. I've not seen that Tweet, but wouldn't be a bit surprised.*

Coda

* * *

Is THERE TROUBLE IN RIVER City? Naw. Poetic, energetic, copasetic, but as they say on the street, no problem. I wonder just how seventy-six trombones, playing in unison, would sound. Awesome, I suspect.

76 Trombones, by Meredith Willson*
Seventy-six trombones led me to you
With a hundred and ten cornets close at hand.
They were followed by rows and rows of the finest virtuosos,
The cream of ev'ry famous band.
Seventy-six trombones caught the morning sun,
With a hundred and ten cornets right behind.
There were more than a thousand reeds springing up like weeds,
There were horns of ev'ry shape and kind.
There were copper-bottom tympani in horse platoons,
Thundering, thundering, all along the way.
Double-bell euphoniums and big bassoons,
Each bassoon having his big, fat say.
There were fifty mounted cannon in the battery,
Thundering, thundering, louder than before.
Clarinets of ev'ry size and trumpeters who'd improvise
A full octave higher than the score.
Seventy-six trombones led the big parade,
When the order to march rang out loud and clear.
Starting off with a big bang bong on a Chinese gong,

By a big bang bonger at the rear.
Seventy-six trombones hit the counterpoint,
While a hundred and ten cornets played the air.
Then I modestly took my place as the one and only bass,
And I oom-pahed up and down the square.

*From the *best* Broadway musical ever (and I missed it), *The Music Man* (book, lyrics, and music by Meredith Willson), which opened on Broadway on December 19, 1957, and starred Robert Preston, Barbara Cook, David Burns, and Pert Kelton and then went on to win five Tony Awards as well as a Grammy. Music publisher: Frank Music and Meredith Willson Music.

Before my time, I have a list of things I missed. *Music Man* tops that list. Second on the roster, legendary musical *Gypsy*. I'd visited New York during the last days of its run and skipped *Gypsy*. I thought it was about fortunetellers. (Honest. Remember, I was from Lewistown, West Virginia.) I've been kicking myself ever since about both.

"So be it."—KING JAMES BIBLE

With the above words, and all other direct and indirect quotes, in awe, I pay homage; I give tribute. And in the process of perusing these pages, I pray that some readers were able to shake off an addiction or three.

Aspiring to heal you, heals me.

The Afterword

*   *   *

THE MISTAKE WE MAKE IS to turn upon our past with angry wholesale negation... The way of wisdom is to treat it airily, lightly, wantonly, and in a spirit of poetry; and above all—to use its symbols, which are its spiritual essence, giving them a new connotation, a fresh meaning.

From *The Spirituality of Imperfection, Storytelling and the Journey to Wholeness*, by Ernest Kurtz and Katherine Ketcham, Bantam Books, 1992, on page 227, and attributed to one John Cowper Powys. I highly recommend this book to everyone with an addiction or any problem that makes them antsy.

END PRAYER

King James, Luke 12:48, "For unto whomsoever much is given, of him shall much be required." I am humongously grateful, and these pages were written, once more, to say thank you and to give back.

After twenty-five years of drinking; after nearly twenty-*nine* years and thousands of 12 step meetings; with approximately $11,000 cash dropped into those baskets (a dollar or two at a time) passing by me--more I cannot give you than the aforementioned sentiments, experience, and quotes. Will you please use my hard fought, hard won bodhi to your ultimate advantage, benefit, and good?

Mr. Nino Pino

The End, the Bittersweet End

You can overcome your addiction(s)—anything you're hooked on—simply by ___?____ . I *do* know one thing for sure: Addiction? Using? Drinking? Sobriety? Sober is preferable. I read somewhere in order to recover you have to throw everything you can find at your addiction: support groups, psychotherapy, medication, and the newest approach (from Padua, Italy, no less), electromagnetic zaps to the head. *Benedica, paesano.*

Pox vobiscum.

Appendix feedback one from my second novel, *F.U.! (Follow Up)! The Answer to Life Revisited:* Reader A J S, who has a master's degree and loads of life experience, e-mailed this, "I liked your second novel. My favorite section was the appendix."

Additional appendix feedback on *F.U.! (Follow Up)! The Answer to Life Revisited:* Signore F, an avid reader, "I enjoyed the 12 step take in your second book, but I skipped the appendix." Too bad—it might just be the best part.

Appendix to *Seventy-Six Trombones*

AAA

Aging

From yours truly: "It's a good day when nothing hurts."

Queer aging: John Reichy quote cited in Ramirez-Valles's *Queer Aging:* "I became obsessed with age. At 17, I dreaded growing old...Old age is something that must never happen to me...The image of myself in the mirror must never fade into someone I cant [sic] look at...I know—and the face knows—that I am no longer a 'boy.' I appear Young, yes—but, inside, it's as if miles of years have stretched since I left that window in El Paso."

From *City of Night*, John Reichy's landmark novel about male hustling and a lot more. Grove Press, 1963. e-Reader, 2013.

Jesus Ramirez-Valles, PhD, wrote a 248-page riveting praxis called *Queer Aging, The Gayby Boomers and a New Frontier for Gerontology*, which was published in 2016 by prestigious Oxford Press, which encompassed the fields of sociology, history, cultural studies, and social work. The nonfiction work may be an invaluable resource for grad students as well as for serious, special-interest health pros.

Baby boomers are those born between 1946 and 1964.

Queer defines the multiple ways in which "people can find themselves at odds" with white heterosexual culture.

The book: As eleven men enter their autumn years, their responses to the physical and emotional tolls of aging, documented in detail; their advances in AIDS; their strides in civil rights activism; their personal lives and responses to friendship, caregiving, romance, sex, and the biggies: their handling of illness and grief.

The author: Mexican-born scholar Jesus Ramirez-Valles details conversations with the eleven racially and economically diverse gay men he's dubbed "the gayby boomers." The probing first-person accounts give insights into their lives (career professionals, retirees, AIDS survivors, caregivers for ailing partners), backdropped by recent social as well as cultural changes.

Ramirez-Valles's opening question: "What is it like to be an older gay man?" And then: "How do homosexual men experience old age? How does *race* mold such experience? If at all, how does HIV make a difference in aging?"

He claims gay men are at elevated risk for mental health disorders such as depression and substance and alcohol abuse. As many as one-third of older gay men report depressive symptoms, more than double the rate in the general older male population. The "mental health disorders" could be higher among those with HIV.

Queer Aging counterview: Crisis competency indicates that gay men are actually better equipped to face aging due to the skills they have acquired through confronting marginalization and the AIDS epidemic. Their age clock might also extend their youth or adulthood and even blur those age distinctions since gay men for the most part do not live the normative milestones such as marriage and parenthood.

Short arm and other inspections: Ramirez-Valles distills other studies that purport that today, most (all?) older people can create a sense of themselves—called "technologies of the self"—by these means: good health (diet and exercise), counseling (therapy and support groups), physical alterations, and finances (independency retirement) as in the successful aging creed. (Hurrah).

Space does not permit the entire story here, and for me, it got more complicated as Ramirez-Valles moves toward the end. Near the close, he opens up a new can of snakes: shame. (In fact, he focused on three joined themes: identity, shame, and the friendships and associations of gay men.)

In that process, he leaned on a couple of scholars, experts on homosexual sociology, Michael Warner and Michel Foucault. (The two scholars dealt with aging and race only tangentially and dismiss social class systems.) So Ramirez-Valles was able to use their found work useful in digesting the gay men's stories of aging gay men and then to do his construction of a queer gerontology.

Conversely, Ramirez-Valles admits that the lives of the men he interviewed and the course they took cannot be condensed to sex and sexuality. (Isn't that what he just did?) And he quotes Michael Warner: "identity and shame are tied together." (And subsequently, Mr. Warner's advice to gay men: "embrace the shame not to treat it…experience freedom.")

Near the end, Mr. Ramirez-Valles quotes one of the eleven men he interviewed and pored over: "Sex does not define me…sex is only one part of me."

A resounding conclusion: Ramirez-Valles says aging gay men are dealing with losing their sex appeal, the grief of AIDS, melancholia of a better and happier life behind them, and the loneliness that comes with age in general.

I found this book both riveting and exasperating. I was led to wonder: *Sure, I agree, these reflections provide a context and a clear picture as well as an ideal understanding of the aging arc and the moving experiences of the eleven well-chosen, diverse, older gay men.* But—the big but here: this alternative study leads one to suspect that their concerns as well as the author's deductions are not so far different from the concerns of many mainstream heterosexual men—perhaps of the entire male population.

Upshot, and don't shoot me: After all is said and read, as you too might have suspected, homosexual male aging is not so far different from heterosexual male aging. Even with all that, this enlightening book is well worth the read.

Queer Aging, The Gayby Boomers and a New Frontier for Gerontology, by Jesus Ramirez-Valles, from presidios Oxford University Press, a department of the University of Oxford, 2016.

Ancient Chinese Curse?

Not! "May you live in interesting times" is an English expression, supposedly a translation of a traditional Chinese curse. Seemingly a blessing, the expression is usually used ironically—with clear implication that "uninteresting times" of peace and tranquility are more life-enhancing than stimulating ones, which from a historical perspective included disorder and conflict. Hence, the so-called "Chinese curse" is not only apocryphal, Wikipedia tells me, but also not Chinese. The Chinese claim there is no equivalent expression in Chinese. They don't want it.

Addiction and Copious Coping Components – "Addiction Reflexes"

Attend AA and other 12 step Meetings

Have dinner with other 12 steppers, or supportive friends, or professionals. Avoid jokesters and putdown artists.

Suck on crushed ice, especially in the evening while reading the papers, and/or watching television. Hard candy helps, too. Lifesavers?

Avoid/stay away from *and out of* bars and clubs. Anonymous quote: "The best side of a saloon is the outside."

Nix specific drinking partners/buddies (the ever present *workable* "avoid people, places and things").

Telephone another 12 step/sober person, preferable those with long term sobriety; or a supportive friend, or a professional. Again, no jokesters nor putdown artists at this time.

The gym, the gym, the gym.

Read something, or skim AA literature. Don't be afraid of "pedestrian" outings. You can be highbrow later.*

Actually *turn off* the cellphone and/or other devices to which you're attached for certain periods during the day; and, at night–just do it. Yes, video games, iPads, computers, etc.

Mute the news (I admit, I'm addicted). Instead, watch comedies, or outrageous television fare: *TOSH. O* or *Ridiculousness.*

Do the dishes, by hand—using *Brillo* on anything pesky. If you're worried about hand wrinkles, wear rubber gloves. I read somewhere doing the deed by hand is a "loving task." I can't remember where. Maybe I read too much.

Shave. Shave your face. Under your arms. Your legs. Clip your nails.

Making a gratitude list – just do it. Volumes have been written about the value of.

A short nap in the middle of the day.

Soak in a warm—hot—bath, with a book or magazine. When you've had enough, pull the stopper and let the water drain out, while you're sitting there, until it's all gone letting all your pain, sadness, and urges go with the it.

Because. Ask for help. Because Albert Einstein said it: "The significant problems we face cannot be solved at the same level of thinking we were at when we created them." And because, you must " ... be brave enough to accept the help of others."*

*From *How to Survive the Loss of Love* by McWilliams, Bloomfield and Colgrove (Bantam Books).

Get outside yourself. Do something for someone else. Call it what you want: help, assistance, kindness, *service*. R. A. Torrey said, "There is not one single passage in the Old Testament or the New Testament where the filling with the Holy Spirit is spoken of and not connected with the testimony of service."

If it's not too late, avoid getting angry, sad, lonely, tired, and hungry. When you find yourself "restless, irritable and discontent," have a cheeseburger with a milkshake, it works miracles. (Hold the mayo). Worry about your diet some other time. I confirm: no one ever got arrested for fat driving.

Pray not to just any God, petition the "God of your understanding." *Or,* better yet, investigate other disciplines: medication, chanting, cycling classes, therapy, (a shrink is considered a discipline), etc. If there's an "easier, softer way," I don't know it.

*Leaf through uplifting books. Some suggestions:

Anything by Joel Osteen, Bruce Wilkinson's *Prayer of Jabez* (Multnomah Publishers), *The Language of Letting Go* and *Journey to the Heart*, Melody Beattie (HarperCollins and Hazelden Publishers), *New Testament Psalms and Proverbs*, (Gideons International), *The Secret* and *The Magic*-- both by Rhoda Byrne (Atria Books, Simon & Schuster: New York; Beyond Words Publishing: Oregon), *What You Think of Me is None of My Business*, by Terry Cole-Whittaker (Berkeley, 1979); skim any volume of affirmations, aphorisms, mantras, pep talks: try Shakti Gawain's work. It's been reported that aging Catholic crones who incessantly recite the rosary attain the same mental state as Zen masters.

MORE, IF YOU CAN STAND IT: Let go of Arrogance, Fear(s), Obsessions, Perfectionism, Procrastination, Resistance to doing what you want and/or *need* to do; Self-censorship, Self-doubts, Self-judgment, Self-loathing(s)—any form of Self-sabotage—subtle but a real syndrome; and, for sure, make a stab at turning off/silencing your Inner Critic.

Reverse idea for the t-shirt "Just Do It" -- "I Did It."

ARTISTS—AGING ARTISTS, A LIST OF

Successful, aging artists: John Baldessari, 85. Chuck Close, 77. Jim Dine, 82. William Eggleson, 77. Eric Fischl, 68. Brett Gorvy, 53. Brise Marden, 78. Carol Massa, 71. Claes Olderburg, 88. Lee Seung-taek (sculptor), 85. Kiki Smith, 63. Pat Steir, 74. Frank Stella, 80. Gerhard Richter, 84. Ed Ruscha, 79. Angela Valeria, 60.

ANGER

In his guttural, grating, pronounced, annoyingly off-putting German accent, the therapist asked me one afternoon, "Mr. Pino, do you know how angry you are?" And then in a slightly lower tone, he added, "You are boiling inside." Wow. I did not know. I really was not aware. But I asked myself, in flashback, *Why didn't you/he tell me before? Why have you waited? Why couldn't you have let me know sooner?* Knowing that early on, would it have changed anything? Probably not.

May I please reintroduce a telling "anger" quote from an early page in this effort: "Loathing and self-hatred are always very good for writers…A degree of anger at oneself makes you better at something you're doing."

Author Aravind Adiga on National Public Radio, January 8, 2017, promoting his coming-of-age novel about fathers, sons, brothers, and the butch game of cricket, *Selection Day*, Simon & Schuster (2017).

BBB
James Baldwin

When being interviewed by a British journalist, James Baldwin was asked what it was like to be born poor, black, and homosexual. Without skipping a heartbeat, Baldwin answered he felt as if he had "hit the jackpot."

Breaking news—Finally, someone snagged the rights to a James Baldwin novel to make a feature film: a big win. Working alongside the

Baldwin estate, writer-director Barry Jenkins, whose *Moonlight* won the Academy Award for best picture in 2017, has an adaptation of Baldwin's 1974 *If Beale Street Could Talk*. Barry Jenkins received critical acclaim for tackling the touchy subject of gay black youths living in Miami in the trailblazing tale, written by "out" playwright Tarell Alvin McCraney (who adapted from his play *Moonlight Black Boys Look Blue)* and sensitively directed by Barry Jenkins, who is straight.

Yes, during Black History Month, the pundits trotted out all the big names to tout: a huge one—double-point win, gay *and* black—James Baldwin. We all know there was a documentary/movie,"* a lengthy piece in the *New Yorker,*** and that December church production up in Harlem.*** But did anyone notice or say there has never been a feature film of any of James Baldwin's books/novels? Baldwin distinctively stipulated in his will that no motion picture be made of his work, and his heirs complied, granting that wish—until now. (A name producer told me that again and again he offered huge sums to the heirs, but so far they won't allow a feature.) You didn't read that anywhere, especially not in the productions out there that skirt the issue and do stagings on James Baldwin, not on the novels themselves. And now there will be a feature film of a James Baldwin novel in the masterful hands of Barry Jenkins.

The three productions mentioned above: *I Am Not Your Negro*, Raoul Peck's documentary-like film; **New Yorker Magazine*, February 13 and 20, 2017, issue; and, "Can I Get a Witness?"—the Harlem Stage's December 2016's "The Gospel of James Baldwin." Nary a one from James Baldwin's books so far.

James Baldwin's novels: *Giovanni's Room*, 1956; *The First Next Time*, 1963; *The Devil Finds Work*, 1976; *If Beale Street Could Talk*, 1974.

BLUE DOG

I've been accused of being a Blue Dog Democrat. (I had to look it up.) The Blue Dog Coalition, commonly known as the Blue Dogs or Blue Dog Democrats, is a caucus of US congressional representatives from the Democratic Party who identify with conservative Democrats.

Formed in 1995 during the 104th Congress, the movement gave the more conservative Democratic Party members a unified voice after the last Congress in the US congressional elections of 1994. Losing ground, Blue Dog Coalition membership experienced a rapid decline in the 2010s, holding fourteen seats in the 114th Congress. I consider myself an independent. And, I hiccup, it's hard to stay independent—of anything.

CCC
Cocktail Parties

British actress Gladys Cooper was continually rattled every time she went on stage. She claimed she'd hear this hissing sound, *s-s-s-s-s*, from the audience. Cooper would cry to fellow cast members, "They hate me; they hate me." Finally, one wag took her aside and said, "The audience doesn't hate you, Gladys. They're whispering to one another, 'Sybil Thorndike's sister; she's Sybil Thorndike's sister.'"

New York adman Joe Africano typically told this at every Manhattan cocktail party, every chance he had.

How I learned to survive upscale cocktail parties in New York City—I often retell this: Fresh from West Virginia, I was invited to a lot of events: cocktail parties, art openings, real estate closings—everywhere. New Yorkers perpetually need a new audience. I'd suit up and show up so nervous my palms dripped with perspiration (hyperhidrosis is the technical term). I soon learned all I had to do was to bring up the subject of real estate—moving, finding a place, redoing an apartment, buying or selling a flat—for God's sake, *cleaning* an apartment—and I was home free. New Yorkers monotonously jumped in and grabbed the limelight, launching into their own real estate story. I then became a relieved listener.

Consciousness

A big idea (?) re: **"Conscious," a quote within a quote within a quote:
If you'll allow me, from my first novel, *The Answer to Life* (Amazon.com), on page 456, I pored over these words that, at the time, sounded a gong in

my head. I included them then, and I quote myself here. I had never heard such a concept.

"Coda Seven: The Aim. The aim of all religions is consciousness, said Robert S. De Ropp in his oft-quoted tome *The Master Game* (Delacorte), 1968. Direct quote: 'See, above all, for a game worth playing…the aim of which is the attainment of full consciousness…the most difficult game of all…man is asleep, that he lives amid dreams and delusions, that he cuts himself off from the universal consciousness…to crawl into the narrow shell of a personal ego…the aim of which is the attainment of full consciousness or real awakening.'" Note: he wrote this back the 1960s.

At the time I read the above quote, the theory struck me as monumental, especially when Robert S. De Ropp emphasizes "all"—all religions. When I was young, one of my father's putdowns was: "You and your big ideas!" Well, Daddy dear, the above concept strikes me as a humongously big idea.

Robert S. De Ropp, *The Master Game* (Delacorte). This concept haunts me: The aim of all religions is consciousness. I think maybe I take too many naps. Wake up, Nino; get conscious!

Confession

"Open confession is good for the soul" (Psalm 119:25). Since childhood, I've heard over and over again that confession was good for the soul. I didn't buy it. For those of you who read my previous work, you might remember an anxious episode in the confessional box when a priest was a tad too breathlessly interested in my masturbatory habits. Even as a young man, I knew there was something off about that soul-cleansing session. (I never went back. Oddly enough, in keeping with my zipped lips, I did not share the specifics of that disturbing episode at the time it happened.) Now decades later, I ran across another account/ an opposing point of view/a fresh voice that claimed in these words: when we confess our sins, God not only forgives us but also chooses not to remember those indiscretions. Wow. So if the Lord God chooses to not remember, to actually forget what we confess, then why can't we?

Why can't I? To this onetime Catholic child: revolutionary. (And how freeing is that?)

Some research:

Acts 3:19, ESV Version: "Repent therefore, and then again, that your sins be blotted out."

Acts 3:19, New International Version (NIV): "Repent, then, and turn to God, so that your sins may be wiped out, that times of refreshing may come from the Lord..."

To reminisce: One of the few guileless souls in my childhood—in my life actually—Zia Maria Bruno, used to say to me, "forgive and forget, forgive and forget." Let me ask myself here: If God has let go of my sins, then why can't I?

While we're in a forgiving mood, I'd like to take this opportunity to apologize to the Catholic Church for my previous criticism from my first novel, *The Answer to Life*, of confession. Sorry. Conversely, I sure wish those catechism educators [(in the form of teachers, priests, and nuns (in their oppressive black habits)] had laid it out a little more clearly if they themselves had any clue at all.

California Ca-ca? Maybe not.
A few years back, a phrase popped up out west: "It's all good. It's all good." I would cynically reply back, "No, it's not." And, "It's all good" is part of the vernacular. Recently, I ran across these quote from you-know-where: James 1:2: "Count it all joy when you fall into various trials." And, 1 Thessalonians 5:18: "In everything, give thanks." Possibly, after all, they may be right about something in California. Maybe it *Is* all good.

Cell Phone Contumacy–Non Rebels Without Any Cause–"*Whatever*"
Psychologist Jean M. Twenge, San Diego State University professor, and author of a new book, reports that smartphones may have destroyed an entire generation of young people. Cell craziness has "radically changed every aspect of teenagers' lives from the nature of their social interactions to their mental health," says Twenge in her new-long-titled-nonfiction, *iGen: Why Today's Super-Connected Kids Are Growing Up Less Rebellious, More Tolerant, Less Happy—and Completely Unprepared for Adulthood—and What That Means for the Rest of Us.* Psew. (An excerpt also appeared and

in my favorite magazine *The Atlantic*, September 2017.) Within a range of misc. behaviors, 18-year-olds now act more like 15-year-olds, and 15-year-olds more like 13-year olds. The "iGen is on the brink of the worst mental-health crisis in decades," Twenge emphasized. These young folks are "… on their phone, in their room, alone and often distressed." Parents try to talk to them and get a cell conniption: "Okay, Okay, whatever." Yep, when you try to engage a teenage, they'll roll their eyes, look at their Apple Watch, and not you. You are more likely to get the standard, "Un-huh, yeah, whatever." Whatever.

*iGen: Why … by Jean M. Twenge, Simon & Schuster, August 2017

DDD
Drugs
State with highest drug use: Ohio. Second: Virginia, and they say it was for lovers.

Specific drugs mentioned along the way. Adderall, Ambien, Antibuse, Concerta, crystal meth, crystal meth, crystal meth, Cymbalta, Effexor, Lexapro, Lunesta, LSD, Prozac, Seroquel, Strattera, Valium, Wilburton, Zanax, Zoloft. I might have missed a few.

Dessert Tip
When my good friend, lifestyle-cookbook editor Lee Bailey, made a cake and it cracked, he would leave it that way and then ice the dessert and serve as is, crack and all. He didn't like for his food to look too perfect, even in photographs. LLB often quoted Ralph Waldo Emerson, "There is a crack in everything God has made."

Drunks, Old Drunks, New Drunks
Foreshadowing—or is Mercury retrograding? I dreaded being an older man in New York City. I'd seen far too many mature gents at social events who'd thrown cocktail parties, invited "people over for drinks," and then got sloppy drunk as the evening progressed, in front of our very eyes.

Note to self: older, sloppy drunk is unattractive, unappealing, unacceptable, and I vow never to do it—all this as the bartender made me another Dewar's and soda with a twist. Fast forward: Thank the Lord I was able to avoid that pitfall with a little help from my friends or at least some AA buddies. And while we're on the subject of older guys, I'd like to slip in here (while no one's looking): it's surprising and pleasing to me that there is an audience for older men out there, older men who are sought and coveted in the romantic-sex department. Who would have thought that silver hair was appealing?

Dreams

Frederick Perls* once said the dream is "the royal road to integration... That all the different parts of the dream are fragments of our personalities." He advised us to put together the disparate fragments of the dream. His theory: *All* of the dream, each part, is some aspect of the dreamer. Example: one man had a recurring dream in which there was always a desk. The dreamer's summation: "I am a big desk. I'm stuffed full of other people's things. People pile things on me, write on me, poke me with pens. They just use me, and I can't move. That's me, all right. Just like a desk. I let everybody use me, and I just sit there."

Perls further described dreams as "the most spontaneous expression of the existence of the human being." and suggests integrating dreams rather than analyzing them. He says to tell the dreams or to write them down or recount them as a story happening in the now. Each part of the dream is likely to disguise a message about the dreamer. He also says to speak out loud** and then to ask each person, object, and event in the dream: "What are you doing in my dream?" When that message comes through, the dreamer is likely to say and feel, "Aha. That's the way I am." Ask further questions. Ask yourself: Was I avoiding something in the dream? Was I running away? Hiding? Was it similar to my real-life avoidance patterns?

Culled from *Born to Win*, by Muriel James and Dorothy Jongeward, Addison-Wesley Publishing, 1971.

*Frederick (Fritz) Perls, German-born psychiatrist who coined the term Gestalt therapy, became world famous and spent a lot of time at infamous Esalen.*** He lived to be seventy-six (1893–1970).

**See my chapter 8, "I Confess I Talk to Myself" as well as the appendix "Alternative-Medicine Exercise."

***Esalen, an alternate philosophy spawned by the 1960s human-potential movement.

Devil, the—He Made Them Do It

The devil's old clothes: At this typing, there's an in-the-works musical adaptation of Lauren Weisberger's *The Devil Wears Prada*; Miranda Priestly's to sing. Pop star Elton John and playwright Paul Rudnick are to write. And Kevin McCollum's to produce. Hold on here. With all the advanced press and impressive credits, no one's mentioned the most important fact of all—to me, anyway.

In the late 1990s and early 2000s, the novel's author, Lauren Weisberger, took classes at the West Side YMCA's well-respected, long-standing Writer's Voice seminars. That program, The Writer's Voice, was founded in 1982 at that Y, and one of the founders was Charles Salzberg. To this day, the school is one of the longest-running and highly esteemed creative writing programs in town. Lo and behold, Ms. Weisberger created and honed in those classes what was to become her published first novel, in 2003, *The Devil Wears Prada*, which was to become not only a bestseller but an even more successful Meryl Streep feature film in 2006.

Educator Charles Salzberg calls his program at the West Side YMCA "works in progress" and he himself an author. (His novel *Swann's Last Song* was nominated for a Shamus Award.) As a freelancer, Charles Salzberg's work has appeared in *Esquire, New York Magazine, Elle, New York Times Book Review,* and *GQ.*

Why am I making such a fuss about all this? As Fanny's mother (Kay Medford) sang out in *Funny Girl,* "They all forget ya when it comes to credit." Not one promotional piece on the upcoming Broadway musical mentioned Charlie's contributions. To this fellow writer, that's an oversight. P.S.—Memoirist James (*Lucky Jim*) Hart said in his book that he also took classes at the West Side YMCA's Writer's Voice. There are some people out there left with a little class.

Didion, Joan

One of our most highly esteemed writers, Joan Didion, at this typing eighty-two, has recently released sections of her journals in *South and West: from a Notebook* (with a snappy introduction by Frank Rich's son Nathaniel). It seems in the 1970s, Didion and her late husband, John (Gregory) Dunne, took a motor trip to the Deep South, and, as is her wont, she kept a detailed journal. Those notes are now part of this offbeat, unorthodox, ghostly, uncanny, eerie effort. Why is it being released now? Ms. Didion was prophetic forty years ago with an anticipation of the changes that led to the election of Donald Trump: her prognostications and opinions that the Deep South—not Southern California, as many thought—would exert influence over the rest of the country. Ominously, Didion groused about the growing gap between the elaborate and political elites as well as the sway, the change, the upheaval of the entire system. She chronicled some of the very attitudes about race and outsiders—foretelling then and surfacing now—in this new book that sound suspiciously like the very attitudes expressed by Trump supporters during the 2016 campaign. Space permits only one telling quote. On the Deep Down South "time warp," she observed (remember, this was the 1970s): "The Civil War was yesterday but 1960 is spoken of as if it were about 300 years ago." Knopf.

Dinner with... and keep in mind where I came from

Elaine Stritch, or Lee Bailey, or Lorraine Serabian, or Margaret Whiting, or Gordon Weaver, or Tom McBride, or John Berendt, or Michael Balaban, or Rosalind Zimm, or Terrence Kelleher, or John Metz, or Holland Taylor, or Richard Poirier, or Jim Elson, or John (director, not the singer) Desmond, or Gloria Safier, or Arthur Laurents, or Bobby Livingston, or Cyril Brosnan, or Jimmy Kirkwood, or Charlotte Rae, or Murray Salem, or Jerry Herman, or Mark O'Donnell, or Stewart Weiner, or Lily Tomlin, or Jane Wagner, or Ellen Violet, or Liz Smith, or Grover Dale, or

Lou Christie, or Edmund White, or Sam Whyte, or (sic) Beverely Brown, or Sam Bonasso, or Bill Bourke, or Dick Huebner, or Andy Tobias, or Herb Martin, or Jack Molthen, or Jim Shields, or Bill Bourke, or Charlie Calello, or David Rosner.

EEE
Let Me Entertain You. Failing That, Let Me Encourage You

While reading this, you might consider humming the strip number from Broadway musical *Gypsy*, "Let Me Entertain You." Here's the poop: Big-data analysis of scientific careers appearing in the journal *Science* found a host of factors that have nothing to do with age or early stardom. They suggest a combination of personality, persistence, and pure luck, as well as intelligence, leads to high-impact success at any age, and they added this bottom line: never give up. "When you give up that's when your creativity ends," according to Albert-Laszlo Barabasi, with Roberta Sinatra, who led a team of researchers at the Northeastern University of Boston. The fresh study illustrates "that the same forces are at play at all levels of discipline: the student, the young professional, the mid-career striver and beyond, to those old enough to wonder if their hand is played out…the scientists were as likely to score a hit at age 50 as well at 25. The distribution was random: choosing the right project to pursue at the right time was a matter of luck." The researchers suggest to make the most of the work (mundane or significant) at hand and find some relevance in a humdrum experiment; make an elegant idea glow. Why are we telling you all this? To encourage you, late bloomer; to encourage me, in my seventies, to keep this in mind.

"'Never Give up': Young Seize Success, But It's Not Because of Their Age," from Benedict Carey's November 4, 2016, *New York Times* article.

Encouragement

… or, hope for the procrastinator or, the methodical or, the slow worker or, the melancholy," Leonardo da Vinci spent a decade perfecting his portrait of Lisa Gherardini—Mona Lisa. When da Vinci died in 1519, the painting remained unfinished; and, it was not even exhibited during the his lifetime. The Lady with the Giaconda smile didn't become an icon until some hundred of years later, rescued by... Now, behind bullet proof glass, the painting is the most valued work of art in the world. Eighty percent of Louvre visitors want to see her. And, that's all I'm going to tell you. You *have* to read this book.

Mona Lisa: The People and The Painting, by Martin Kemp and Giuseppe Pallanti, Oxford University Press, 2017.

FFF
Friends
See previous chapter, "My Huckleberry Friends and Me."

Factoids
New study out of China: three thousand adults over the age of sixty-five who took an hour nap after lunch had better cognitive skills than those who took a shorter nap, longer nap, or no nap at all.

From the *Journal of the American Geriatrics Society*, January, 2017.

Feelings
What are you feeling, Mr. Pino? What are you feeling, Mr. Pino? What are you feeling, Mr. Pino? The therapist with the thick German accent would ask me every visit. I tried to answer and many times began my reply with "I think..." Since I exhausted the subject of feelings in *F.U.! (Follow Up)! The Answer to Life Revisited*, I'll be brief here. Quandary: What comes first, feelings or thoughts? I was never sure, and does it matter, and if so, why? Let me evoke an enormously popular, world-widely famous source, *The Secret*,* page 30:

"The importance of feelings cannot be overstated. Your feelings are your greatest tool to help you create your life. Your thoughts are the primary cause of everything. Everything else you see and experience in this world is effect, and that includes your feelings. The cause is always your thoughts...

"Your feelings tell you very quickly what you're thinking. Think about when your feelings suddenly took a dive—maybe when you heard some bad news. That feeling in your stomach or solar plexus was instant. So your feelings are an immediate signal for you to know what you are thinking.

"You want to become *aware* of how you're feeling, and get in tune with how you're feeling, because it is the fastest way for you to know what you're thinking."

*The Secret is a bestselling, highly controversial, self-help, educational book written by Rhonda Byrne, based on her film of the same name, which sold more than nineteen million copies worldwide and was translated into forty-six languages. For no other reason than its popularity, one should know this book. It's a quick read, easy on the eye, and if nothing else, makes you feel good. You may even want to pore over its universal philosophies and underline as you go. I received two copies as gifts in 2006 and still refer to it. I invariably find the sections I underlined uplifting.

Atria Books, Simon & Schuster: New York; Beyond Words Publishing: Oregon, 2006.

Footnote: One of the most valuable pieces of information I received from mentor/sponsor Stiletto Constance is worth nailing down here. "There are only a few basic feelings. Get in touch with them often. Mad. Sad. Glad. Lonely. Tired. Hungry." When I'm feeling squirrely, I take inventory of my feelings and then make an adjustment. Too simplistic? The price is manageable. Therapists are performing the same exercise for hundreds of dollars an hour. It's free here.

Feelings, better known as Emotions

And now, a walloping reward for those who bother to read the Appendix from Vivek Murphy, U.S. Surgeon General, from 2014 to 2017.

"I think emotional well-being as a resource with in each of us that allows us to do more and to perform better. That doesn't mean just the absence of mental illness. It's the presence of positive emotions that allow us to be resilient in the face of adversity. How do we fix that? The first thing is that we to change how we think about emotions. ***Emotions are a source of power, and that's what science tells us***. But many people I encounter have been led to think of emotions as a source of weakness. The second thing we have to do is cultivate emotional well-being." Tools? "… include sleep, physical activity, contemplative practices like gratitude and medication, and social connect as well."

From *National Geographic*, "The Science of Addition," issue, September 2017. Beg, borrow, or appropriate this issue and read it from cover to coverlet; from façade to front.

Forgiveness

Matthew 6, verse 12: Jesus says: "Forgive us out debts, as we forgive our debtors." The Lord's Prayer.

From uplifting Joel Osteen's* *Everyday A Friday*, (FaithWorks/Hachette): "Forgiveness is not about being nice and kind; it's about letting go … so you can claim the amazing future that awaits you. … Forgiving doesn't mean your excusing anything or anyone. It doesn't mean you're lessening the offense. … let it go for your own sake. … It will help you to forgive if you'll realize that the people who hurt you have problems. *Hurting people hurt others.*" Joel Osteen goes on to say: "Forgiveness is a process. It doesn't happen overnight. You don't snap your fingers and make a hurt go away. … if you'll continue to have the desire to forgive and ask God to help you, then little by little those negative feelings will fade away one day they won't affect you at all." Joel Osteen's wonderful wrap on Forgiveness, and I reread it daily: "You have to forgive so that you can be free to live each day with happiness in your heart. If you will let go of the hurts and pains and get on God's payroll, God will settle your case. He will make your wrongs right. He will bring justice into your life. You will get what you deserve, and God will pay you back with double the joy, double the peace, double the favor, and double the victory."

*Joel Osteen, senior pastor of Lakewood Church, Houston, Texas, America's largest, *fastest* growing congregation with more than 45,000 attendees every week–not to mention the millions who watch (his talks/sermons/inspiration) on television. Earlier, I recommended all of Osteen's twenty-plus books to anyone with an addiction of any kind from video games to a game anther person might play. Osteen's particularly prayerful, sometimes playful, if you merely need something to help you get through the night. More, I could not offer you. The above forgiveness paragraph is from *Everyday A Friday* (FaithWorks/Hachette). Obviously, I highly recommend the book and emphasize: savor all of Joel Osteen's efforts.

Family, Family, Family
Dateline: Lewistown, West Virginia.

Two of my *zias* (aunts) relocated to Detroit, Michigan. Two other aunts, on both sides, went to Baltimore, Maryland. Two uncles, on Maw's side, ended up in California. Oh, yes, one other aunt, Maw's sister, after marrying the aforementioned gravedigger, landed in Wheeling, West Virginia. (I'm reserving comment.)

Six first cousins, about my age, some younger, went on to their reward too soon. May they RIP: MVMR, CESS, PP, JSD, JCJR, and EBB.

Fortuneteller
Somewhere in the very early 1960s, a friend recommended a palm reader to me, Mrs. Frum. For a few bucks, she would read your beads. I was apprehensive. But at this time, I'd already spent two hard years at the University of Miami (Florida), where I was overwhelmed with ten-hour shifts at a supermarket while carrying a full college credit load—for two full years. Forward: I came back home to Lewistown to attend a local college and worked at a local Kinney's Shoe Store. I was apprehensive. I was acquainted with two of the soothsayer's teenage children; would they be there in her house for my "reading"? They weren't. Alas, the stars, dear Brutus: I can only recall two things she said. (1) "You will be standing at the church with tears. Mary will die." Not long after, longtime family friend Mary Basile passed away, *and* my paternal grandmother, Mary Peno, unexpectedly moved on. (2) Mrs. Frum added, "You will be well known and considered successful by the time you are thirty." At twenty-nine, I was receiving reflected glory in the music-record business, and the

world at large, for being the producer for a name musical-actress-singer. I rarely tell my New York friends about my visit or two to Mrs. Frum. I admit I'm still perplexed. Who wants to believe a fortuneteller? Are we underlings, dear Brutus?

GGG
Godmother

My mother had the most colorful, expressive godmother—let's call her Josephina Martina—who chattered in half English and half Italian and continually peppered her speech with spirited, vivid, Calabrian-dialect expressions. I can still hear her voice to this day, tossing off dialectisms such as "*uuuu-fah!*" to underscore something *you* just said. And "*ah-you-yah*" to mean, "sure, yeah, not on your life, sometime in the twelfth of never." Josephina was quite generous to her godchild, my mother, and I'm happy to say always kind to me. Mrs. Martina (we called her *parhena*), too, like Mom, was an exceptional cook, and it was her good fortune to have the resources to make elaborate gourmet Italian dinners for family and friends. I, personally, was always impressed by her upscale home, high on a hill with a view of Lewistown below, which was eternally pristine, downright shiny clean. Her housekeeper waxed floors and furniture, which at all times shined, sometimes reflected, picked up the light that shone in from the sparkling-clean plate-glass windows. One just knew the furnishings, down to the most casual throwaway throw pillow, knickknacks, and froufrou, were the best to be had anywhere. Summing up, I'm enormously grateful she was there for us and was quite fond of her. She often said to me, "Nino, God helps those who help themselves," which was ironic since she had tireless assistance around her home from her brood as well as hired help. She liked to shout out orders, and we all hopped to. Josephina Martina was an ostentatious original. *Gracia tutti, *parhena.*

Parhena is Calabrian dialect for "godmother."

Grant Study, the. Oh, How I Love George E. Vaillant's Grant Study
Notes: Between 1939 and 1942, one of America's leading universities, Harvard, recruited 268 of its healthiest and most promising undergraduates to participate in a revolutionary new study of the human life cycle. The originators of the program, which came to be known as the Grant Study, felt medical research was too heavily weighted in the direction of disease. Their intent was to chart, over the course of many years, the ways in which a group of promising, Ivy League individuals coped with their lives.

Nearly forty years later, George E. Vaillant, the study's director, took the measure of the Grant Study men. The result was the compelling, evocative, provocative, classic book, *Adaptation to Life*.

After years of study, George Vaillant's key insights:

Alcoholism is a disorder of great destructive power.

Alcoholism was the main cause of divorce between the Grant Study men and their wives.

Strongly correlates with neurosis and depression, which tended to follow alcohol abuse rather than precede it.

Together with associated cigarette smoking, alcohol was the single greatest contributor to their early morbidity and death.

Financial success depends on warmth of relationships and, above a certain level, not on intelligence.

Those who scored highest on measurements of "warm relationships" earned an average of $141,000 a year more at their peak salaries (between ages fifty-five and sixty).

No significant difference in maximum income earned by men with IQs in the 110–115 range and men with IQs higher than 150.

Political mindedness correlates with intimacy: aging liberals have way more sex.

The most conservative men ceased sexual relations at an average age of sixty-eight.

The most liberal men had active sex lives into their eighties.

The warmth of childhood relationship with mothers matters long into adulthood:

Men who had "warm" childhood relationships with their mothers earned an average of eighty-seven thousand dollars more a year than men whose mothers were uncaring.

Men who had poor childhood relationships with their mothers were much more likely to develop dementia when old.

Late in their professional lives, the men's boyhood relationships with their mothers—but not with their fathers—were associated with effectiveness at work.

The warmth of childhood relationships with mothers had no significant bearing on "life satisfaction" at seventy-five.

The warmth of childhood relationship with fathers correlated with:

Lower rates of adult anxiety

Greater enjoyment of vacations

Increased "life satisfaction" at age seventy-five

To wrap, Vaillant's main conclusion was that "warmth of relationships throughout life have the greatest positive impact on 'life satisfaction.'" Succinctly, Vaillant says his study showed: "Happiness is love. Full stop." You can't get more basic than that. I suspect most parents knew that already. Merely speculating.

For greater detailed and for more information, get George Eman Vaillant's *Adaptation to Life*, originally published in 1977 by Little, Brown, and then Lippincott Williams & Wilkins, and finally Harvard Press. I trust some of this will help you distance yourself from your addictions.

God

If most (every?) culture since the beginning of recorded time has believed in some form of a Higher Power, how could little ole Nino Pino poo-poo Her existence today? I would have to, at the very least, entertain a faith in a Supreme Being like the Lord the 12 step program suggests: One "… of my understanding." I cry *uncle*! I did *not* let *Time* magazine convince me God was dead, but I am still asking a lot of questions.

HHH
Hacked, Hacker, Hacking

Numerous attempts have been made to hack me, and I've been hacked twice (that I'm aware of), not to mention daily hits to my e-mail account, which I delete with a simple click. First time, a former employer got into my e-mail account, and I was frozen out for half a day. (I won't tell you how I know it was a Mickey Mouse operation that did this.) Second time, a large message came up on the screen that said I'd been compromised and to telephone a number immediately. I did. A gentleman answered, who said I needed to send him $149 to protect my computer *and* cell phone. I told him I didn't have $149 to give him and that I would go to the Apple store down the block. He said, "Hold a moment" and came right back with this: "I can do it for you for forty-nine dollars." I hung up, shut down the computer, and went to the gym. Two hours later, when I came back home and turned the computer back on, he was gone. However, frequently I get telephone calls from a blocked number and gentlemen with Indian accents, who inform they've called to help me with my computer. I hang up.

Two staggering quotes from "The Hackers," *Time Magazine*.* I'm still a subscriber after all these years.

Who are the hackers? "There are freedom fighters, the truth campaigners, the anarchists, the tinkerers. There are criminal kingpins and, yes, even working stiffs. A recent survey of 10,000 hackers in the US, UK, and Germany found that on average the annual salary for hacking was $28,744.

"Where does that leave the rest of us? Grappling with an acutely modern form of disquiet—the suspicion that the information we have become used to creating in mass quantities, almost constantly, may come to light, out of context and as destructive payload."

*From *Time Magazine*, by Matt Vella, page 104, December 19, 2016. I still subscribe to and read *Time Magazine* and have all of my adult life.

Happiness

a) Judith Newman in the Help Desk column in the *New York Times* Book Review (section), November 6, 2016, reports that when you Google "happiness" on Amazon.com, you get seventeen thousand results.

b) "If you want to be happy for the rest of your life, new books suggest working hard and playing nice; taking it a few steps at a time; watching your pocketbook; and just not trying so much." Judith Newman, *New York Times*, November 6, 2016.

c) Happiest people in America, Gallop poll findings: Provo, Utah—the happiest town in America. How can that be when Mormon Utah has twice the national average—the highest rate—of antidepressant use in the United States? Texas is twenty-ninth. West Virginia at the bottom, 51. New York: 26. I have been flip on previous pages here about West Virginia being near the bottom of many lists/surveys. That does not give me joy. I guess I could let it go, but on the other hand, maybe someone somewhere, sometime, will do something for my home state.

Happiness (cont.)

To me, "happiness" is one of the most misused, perverted words in the English language. Across the board, I have inevitably found it puzzling when the term is trotted out every time folks mention marriage and/or a relationship. Let me try to understand where they're coming from, to follow their thought process. When you get married or meet up with a love interest—as a rule, a new mate of some kind—you are or will be happy. Poppycock. I suspect and welcome the challenge that there are plenty of souls out there who have a working relationship and a solid sex life, who enjoy the union but are not "happy." And it's presumptuous of those wordsmiths out there to distort the word "happiness." We all have pockets of happiness and with any luck, a good *shtup** from time to time; some couples have several great kids even (or not so great), but why do they use the catchall word "happiness" to describe what's going on when we have a relationship and/or marriage? Am I off base?

*Yiddish. Thank you, Mel Brooks.

New York City's Rank Rankings

Wallethub's Annual Happiest Places in the United States to Live put New York at seventieth. (We New Yorkers complain about lack of sleep and exercise.) TripAdvisor, on the other hand, scored us at the top of their list with our multitude of "attractions." (New York City has 750 museums and galleries that showcase paintings, dinosaurs, ships, fire trucks, and gangsters.) Happiest place in the United States of America? Fremont, California. Last: Detroit, Michigan. Give me Gotham or give me death.

Hungers

Once more, the innovative Eric Berne nails it with something obvious and basic yet eluded by most of us. Berne calls our biological and psychological needs "hungers." Every person, he says, needs to be touched as well as to be recognized. What's more, every human being has to do something with his or her time between birth and death. (Hang in there with me for a minute.) The hungers, he points out, for touch and recognition can be appeased with what he dubs "strokes," and those so-called strokes include "*any* act that implies recognition of another's presence." Hunger-stroke actions take the form of physical touching and/or some symbolic syndrome of recognition—a look, a word, a gesture—*any* act that says, "I know you're there." Consequently, a human being's hunger for *strokes* often determines what he or she does with the aforementioned time. He/she/we may well spend minutes, hours, *a lifetime* trying to get strokes in a myriad, a multitude of ways, some of which include playing complicated psychological games. (Conversely, by withdrawing, we might also spend minutes, hours, a lifetime *avoiding* the hunger/strokes.) All that Eric Berne spells out in his groundbreaking, life-changing work.* *I hear you. I hear you. I hear you.*

From *Born to Win*, by Muriel James and Dorothy Jongeward, Addison-Wesly Publishing, 1971, and from *Games People Play*, Grove Press and Dell Publishers, 1964—five million-plus copies sold; on bestseller lists for two years—by Canadian-born psychiatrist Eric Berne (1910–1970). I'm reminded: Eric Berne is credited with creating the theory of transactional analysis as a way of explaining human behavior. Another Berne bestseller: *What Are You Saying After You Say Hello*, Grove Press, 1973.

Hygge, Hygge (Pronounced Like the Sound of Antique Car Horns: *Uuu-Gah, Uuu-Gay*)

If you like language and come upon a new word, it makes you feel good. New to me but common to old Danes—they have a word for it—hygge, which to them means everyday togetherness, coziness, warmth, well-being, charm, conviviality. They want us to turn off the cell phones, come on over, light some scented candles, to chat about issues, important or not, over fresh-brewed coffee and scrumptious, namesake Danish pastries. Those Nordics...

Hutton, Betty, See below under: "Mean."

III

Mambo Italiano—Or Is That a Tarantella?

My writing is mostly about being Italian. My effort, I've been told, is a little different from what most people know about Calabrians, and that's good for me (and I trust my work is pleasurable enough to take up your time). Its unusualness gives me a fresh audience, especially in New York City. And right on cue, I get a call from a surprised New York reader who pays me a mixed compliment: "Nino, this is really good." The fan bought the novel, is reading the effort, and didn't expect the work to be good. End of subject. All that—and then I run across a solid and thorough work by writer Helen Stapinski, *Murder in Matera: A True Story of Passion, Family and Forgiveness in Southern Italy*, which she researched to the max and gift-edly tells terrific, *horrific* tales in—nitty-gritty, teeth-grinding stories from the lower section of that fascinating country shaped like a boot. Dey Street Books.

JJJ

John's Pizza

One late evening, near closing time, a friend and I were the only customers left at famous John's Pizza, 278 Bleecker, seated in a booth, not far from the fire-breathing oven itself. Directly in front of the gaping flames was an oversized round table. Suddenly, all the employees (even manager and busboys) sat at that large table. Someone placed two loaves of Wonder Bread on the table's top alongside a large jar of peanut butter and strawberry jelly. The staff proceeded to dive in to make peanut butter and jelly sandwiches after a hard evening's work. My date and I were amazed as we scarfed up the last of the world's best thin-crusted pepperoni pizza with extra sauce.

Job Interview à la LA

During one of my frequent trips to Los Angeles, which I often took to sample writing classes and pitch screenplay ideas for a feature film, I thought maybe I could get a job out there and possibly stay in the sun for a while. After all, the weather was nice. I sent out a dozen résumés. Right off, I got a call from a gent on Sunset Boulevard. We set up an interview.

I wore a freshly pressed white button-down, donned my favorite Brooks Brothers tie, and even showed up early. A middle-aged man, casually dressed, ushered me into his high-windowed, good-view office. After talking for about five minutes, he leaned forward and said, "I have to be honest. I really don't have a job vacancy. I thought with your extensive résumé, you might be able to help some of my clients." (To have the chutzpah to do that, and to admit it, is the height of something unquotable.) I excused myself and immediately booked a flight back to New York. The temperature might be lower here in NYC, but it's much easier to deal with the higher-minded and quite possibly higher-IQed. Jeez.

My Favorite Joke

The late puppeteer genius Wayland Flowers had an "outrageous old broad" character puppet he called Madame. One of her cohorts, maybe crotchety Macklehoney, once asked dirty old dame Madame, "Madame, you're dating an eighteen-year-old. Aren't you afraid of death?" Madame's reply? "No. Not at all. If he dies, he dies."

KKK
"K"—a Puzzling Text under the Category of Keeping Abreast

I try to keep up and confess I'm not doing a perfect job of it. Prime example: I was confused by a text to me from an underthirty person that read "K." Just plain K. (I was to learn that K was short for OK.) Well, did you ever? K. So I'm slipping this next tidbit under the Ks. I don't know where else to put it. And, frankly, I don't know if it's OK, K, or not. So:

Thirty or so years ago, D. J. T. was having fights with the New York press. He threatened to sue and may have actually taken the Grand Dame of Dish,* much-loved Liz Smith, to court. (Note: At this typing, Liz Smith's outlet these days is online *New York Social Diary*, and she has no print bylines that I know of.) Anyway, in 1991, Smith got an exclusive with then D. J. T.'s wife, Ivana Trump, during their divorce debacle, which ended up a big plus for Ms. Liz Smith: it led to Smith's getting yet another column in her long line of syndicated outlets—in *Newsday*! It's fun to note: there was a point during all that when D. J. T.'s photo was in the *New York Post* eight days in a row—eight days in a row, thirty years ago: unheard of. One of the players, a Miss Marla Maples (now fifty-four or so) met D. J. T. in 1989, and they had a widely reported whirlwind relationship. She was to gush she had "the best sex I've ever had" with D. J. T. All that led to their marriage in 1993, their separation in 1997, and their divorce in 1999. Whew. (Maples went on to dance with the stars on TV in 2016.) This little tale is *not* meant to do anyone any harm; it's merely a series of facts that made and makes for obviously fine press and a pleasing (and/or "K") paragraph. How I know all this? I read it in the papers. I perused Liz Smith's column daily as she spelled out in detail the donnybrook as it unfolded. (In fact, I read three New York dailies daily. I don't know if that's an admirable trait or a bad one, and, yes, there are worse ways to spend one's time. I happen to like information in newspapers I can hold in my hand and not on a device.) Still turning it out: *Liz Smith turned ninety-four years old on

February 2, 2017. And it's astonishing to note that the Grand Dame of… has been at it since the 1950s: as journalist, *Cosmopolitan Magazine* movie reviewer, philanthropist, and widely syndicated columnist (*New York Daily News, the New York Post*, NBC's "Live at Five," *Newsday*, and multiple *Chicago Tribune* syndicated outlets). As I recall, and it wasn't mentioned in either of the two recent long articles on Smith: Liz got her start as traveling secretary to comic-actress Kay Ballard. (I love Kay Ballard. Google her.) Once, when I introduced Kay to my parents at an off Broadway production (Cole Porter?), she was nice, kind, and warm to them. They never forgot it; I never forgot it. Cheers to Kay. Cheers to Liz. Cheers to us. Cheers to longevity. And, I echo: Now Smith can be read regularly online on *New York Social Diary.*

Postscript to all that: Long after typing the above (I swear on my mother's spice cake recipe), I ran across a piece in the *New Yorker Magazine* by wonderful writer-commentator (a favorite of mine) Jeffrey Toobin, an author and articulate legal authority: "Liz Smith's Trump Memories," dated September 5, 2016. The ample article doesn't line up the way I remembered and read the situation. I'm tempted to cliché the situation with "that's what makes horse races" if it weren't so troubling to me. I'm not questioning Smith. I'm questioning *me* and how I recall events. I'm reminded of a Dorothy Canfield Fisher short story where the narrator remembers a story over the years, and every time in the retelling the tale gets more salacious. Since Dorothy Canfield was assigned to us: maybe, in an ongoing reevaluation, I have to wonder once more if my West Virginia education was better than I thought.

At press time, another article appeared in the *New York Times* with three different headlines, even went out in syndication, that made me sad. I wish Liz had never granted the interview. In syndication: "Liz Smith could turn anyone into a star, until she couldn't." Online, with this headline: "The Rise and Fall of Liz Smith, Celebrity Accomplice," by John Leland, July 30, 2017. In the Sunday, *New York Times*, Metropolitan section cover story with large photo, lots of space, and the jump to a full page on five, with four more photographs. July 30, 2017, with yet another headline: "Life Among the Boldface Names." All depressing.

Kennedy, Patrick

...is the youngest son of Edward M. Kennedy and the nephew of President John F. Kennedy, as well as the author of a brave, bestselling memoir, *A Common Struggle* (2015, Penguin/Random House). In his confession, Patrick Kennedy tells the world his father, Ted, suggested he play down a DC car crash he'd caused as "a fender bender," asking him to not speak out about it. Young Patrick knew he was intoxicated and addicted to drugs. Thus, instead, he went to the Mayo Clinic (for a second time) to peel away the onion's layers, to deal head on with the underlying problems of his addiction, which played out in a deadly combination of cocaine, stimulants, and alcohol, and also to deal with the "huge mood disorder" that ran in his family. To this lightweight writer, being as high profile as he is, I think it took a lot of guts for Patrick Kennedy to come clean. How much easier it would have been to once more sweep it under the wall to wall. I tip my baseball cap to him.

LLL

Love

There are 7.5 billion people on this earth. Surely there is one to love you.

Love Thy Patient—Love Thy Neighbor, but Love Thy Patient?

Not what you think. As you might have heard so far, ad infinitum, *Seventy-Six Trombones* is my third novel. Since writing the first one, I've been looking everywhere I could (aka ask experts) for an elusive quote, and I finally found the words that haunted me as I neared the end of *Seventy-Six Trombones*.

"...there is nothing at all inappropriate in the feelings of love that a therapist develops for his or her patient when the patient submits to the discipline of psychotherapy, cooperates in the treatment, is willing to learn from the therapist, and successfully begins to grow through the relationship. Intensive psychotherapy in many ways is a process of re-parenting. It is no more inappropriate for a psychotherapist to have feelings of love for a patient than it is for a good parent to have feelings of love for a child. To the contrary, it is essential for a therapist to love a patient for the therapy to be successful, and if the therapy does become successful, then the therapeutic relationship will become a mutually loving one. It is inevitable that the therapist will experience loving feelings coincident with the genuine love he or she has demonstrated toward the patient."

As for me, I've had many years of analysis and openly admit I never questioned whether my therapist liked me, let alone loved me. I looked at the work/discipline as a laboratory situation—a place you went to "get your head examined," to use a sarcastic phrase my father often tossed out back home—an office/lab much like a dentist's office, a place you go when you need your teeth cleaned. So when I read the theory years ago, it haunted me; I needed to read it again to understand the concept. Issue: I still haven't figured why the man in the chair across from me shrinking my problems had to like me.

From *The Road Less Traveled*, by M. Scott Peck, continually on bestselling lists for four years! A Touchtone Book/Simon & Schuster, pages 174 and 175.

MMM
Minutiae
I'm drowning in minutiae. At least I'm having trouble keeping up with it. Coupons, rewards, beginning dates, end dates, expiration dates, renewals, hash tags, passwords, tracking numbers, call waiting, redial, barcodes, apps—goddamn apps—spoiled milk, *spilled* milk, birthdays, anniversaries, milestones, and, new to me, no-cash businesses, especially restaurants, that accept only barcode scans or iPad clicks or credit cards but no cash. That one's hard to believe. To do business and not accept cash—who would have thought that? Etc., etc., etc. More on that later, I suspect.

Mother Merde
Mother didn't like for people to pay her a compliment. She would yawn and wave her hand in front of her face with a "Psew. I've been *fasha-ed*, I've been *fasha-ed*." Fasha was the evil eye and a double superstition. I hear there are like superstitions in Jewish/Hebrew/Yiddish. I don't want to know; I'm too susceptible.

One more Mother hang-up I don't exactly know where to put: mother disliked talcum power; she didn't want talc, *talco*, or talcum around, and often claimed she was allergic to it. I don't know if she was, but I do wonder how she could have known, decades ago, that talc was not good for you. If she would have only warned the drug companies, she might have saved them millions in ovarian cancer lawsuits. Allegedly, 417 million. 110 million. 72 million 70 million. 55 million. Allegedly.

Mean

Mean, as promised above. Mirror, mirror, on the wall, who is the meanest of them all? Hollywood? Ethel Merman? MGM? There's a funny story I used to tell, passed on to me at Joe Allen's by one of the big name "swells" I used to hang out with when I first came New York City. (I have vowed to myself to never bring up the mean tale again.)* Since, I've learned some facts about the life of comic, singer, actress, and blond bombshell of 1940s/1950s Hollywood musicals and comedies Betty Hutton that make me sad. Betty Hutton never knew her father. To support them, her mother (an alcoholic) bootlegged. Young Hutton, as young as three, used to sing on street corners for loose change to help out at home. On opening day night of the Cole Porter musical *Panama Hattie* on Broadway (1940), the star Ethel Merman cut/deleted/scrapped the brassy, energetic performer's only number. But Hutton was to go to Hollywood and there, worked hard *and* often to become a star. Every time at the mike, she gave her all and I think, in reconsideration, was a joy to watch—always enjoyable. (*Panama Hattie* was made into a Hollywood film, 1942, without Hutton, but one suspects she was otherwise engaged with bigger fish. Ann Sothern played Hattie, and Virginia O'Brien, not Ethel Merman, played Flo.) Forward: In the middle of production, Judy Garland was fired from the lead in *Annie Get Your Gun* (a role played on Broadway by Miss Ethel Merman), and Betty Hutton was given the part (1950). I remember as a kid seeing that movie and loving Betty Hutton, an actress I don't think I'd seen before on film. I'm not quite sure. I was taken to movies when I was a small child, three, four, by aunts and cousins and don't always know what I did or did not see back then. Moving along. I became aware of Betty Hutton in 1950 (at ten years old) as Annie in *Annie Get Your Gun*. And, again at twelve, in *The Greatest Show on Earth* (1952). (She *had* appeared in films prior to that even if I wasn't aware of her.) Hard to fathom, Betty claims, during the filming of *Annie Get Your Gun*, no one on the set spoke to her. After all, she wasn't Judy Garland, and they wanted and expected Judy Garland. Further claims of abuse: her costar, Howard Keel, if we are to believe Hutton, tried to upstage her. Maybe. With scared, insecure divas, one never knows what is real and what is temperament. If we're to be a tad empathetic here with millions at stake, a performer has to get up and out there every day in front of the cameras and dance as fast as she can. You might say your ass is on the line. Either way, she was an ideal Annie in *Annie Get your Gun*—some thought even better and more suited than Broadway's Ethel Merman. Duck when you say that; Ethel Merman's not to be tangled with. Personally, I can't imagine a better actress as Annie. When the film came to New York City, Betty Hutton was not invited to the premiere, she says. The MGM studio was not so hot on her. And, let's face it, New York was Ethel Merman territory…hi-ho, alas, and lackaday.* After all that, what are we left with? Some wonderful performances on film that still play and speak for themselves. Why, she was even in a film with the legendary Preston Sturges that most actresses would kill to have on their résumés. OK. OK. If you haven't noticed, the Betty Hutton story gets to me. Because it's really sad? Because I identify? Because…because… for example, late in life, when Hutton moved from the East Coast to Palm Springs, California, she hoped to reconnect with her children. (She had three daughters, products of three marriages. I assumed they lived with their dads. Don't know for sure.) Not one of the three wanted anything to do with her. Why? I speculate. She hadn't been a good mother? Wasn't she childlike herself, ill prepared for life, having only gone to the ninth grade? Hence, Hutton bequeathed her royalties to the Catholic Church and not to her daughters. (After all, there has to be some income from her many film performances that still play here and around the world nonstop. Who gets that money—the Catholic Church?) Case in point: Betty Hutton's version of standard song "Hit the Road to Dreamland" was a standout in the 1997 feature film *L.A. Confidential*. I don't know, I just don't know, but it all makes me sad.

And now for that all-around mean-spirited story/joke* I will no longer tell, told to me, I think, by stage director Burt Shevelove at Joe Allen's Restaurant, circa 1969:

When Walter Matthau and Barbra Streisand were filming *Hello, Dolly* and at one another's throats, the story goes that Walter Matthau looked Streisand in the eyes and said, "I was on this set when Betty Hutton was a star."

"Hi-ho, alas, and lackaday," words from Gershwin/Gershwin song "But Not for Me," Warner/Chappell.

And while we're at it—separately, another Ethel Merman story:

A New York gent had his apartment completely redone at great expense. When it was finished, he invited some friends over to show his pride, joy, and showplace. When all the guests were there, he assembled them for a tour through his new palace: the lushly carpeted hallway, the marble guest bath, and a froufrou powder room, the elaborate mahogany library/work...halfway through the walk, we hear this loud, signature voice of Miss Ethel Merman say, in her unmistakable voice, "What does all this have to do with me?"

The Mayo Clinic

"Hold the Mayo"—so goes an old Dorothy Parker punch line. Let's face it, growing older is no picnic. I read everything that comes my way on the subject and sometimes want to bury my head in the sandbox. I've run across some truly helpful advice, some of which makes me want to run for the West Virginia hills, how majestic and how grand. I do suggest if you are strong enough to read The Mayo Clinic's online "Aging: What to expect," the blog includes gobs of up-to-the-minute advice, some of which you know and other tidbits you may need to be reminded of. Merely a suggestion. To be honest, I felt uncomfortable perusing some of them.

Medicine, Alternative Medicine—Unscientific Exercise

From the Bible, Mark 11:23, King James 2000 Version: "For verily I say unto you, That whosoever shall say unto this mountain, Be removed, and be cast into the sea; and shall not doubt in his heart, but shall believe that those things which he said shall come to pass; he shall have whatsoever he said."

OK now:

1. Substitute any affliction you have for the word "mountain."
2. Talk to the mountain that plagues you (hurt/ache/wound/affliction/condition). For example: "Left knee, *heal*." "Respiratory system, *heal*." "Rectum, *heal*."
3. Rephrasing the above exercise: "Lower-back pain, *I'm telling you to leave*." Or, "Depression, *I'm commanding you to go*." Or, "Right-hand pain, *beat it*." Another one: "Sinus condition, *remove yourself*." Or, "Cancer, *I serve you notice—out*." Or, "Carpal tunnel, *go away*." More specifically, "Right-hand carpal tunnel pain/condition, *be gone*."

This simple exercise is not for everyone. I tried it on a longtime friend in Washington, DC, plagued with multiple medical problems, who said to me, "Oh, I don't believe that." (She's entitled.) Of course, on the other hand, she won't experiment outside the test tube, Petri dish, or clichéd box; she's allowed to hold on to her aches and pains for dear life, dearly. I say be somewhat open; be more playful. It has come to light over and over again that there are some transactions in heaven and on earth beyond circumstance, and in this case, the price is right.

The best footnote in the world about now: all of my life I've been ambivalent about religion, spiritualties, God, and all that heaven allows. (After my first year of college, I announced, "I don't believe in God anymore.") Over the years (decades), I've read and studied and meditated and experimented and hunted—and finally, recently, in a simple way, I have learned, quietly, to live with, to softly accept the ambiguities, the contradictions of faith. (Example: in the AA program, members suggest that you get sober and "pray for God's will." And then other times, they're keen to remind: "You have free will.") I won't even broach the subject of predestination.

Back to the front: It's OK to talk to your affliction and ask it to go away.

Masturbation on the Rise

Self-love for men and women is up some, and it's attributed to readily-available pornographic material. A 1992 study revealed, the willing did the deed once a week. Today, it's once every six days. Well, a solid stat is a solid stat. What a difference a day makes. Attention must be paid.

NNN

New York, New York, It's a Helluva Town, And…

Only the Dead Know Manhattan

One of my favorite short stories is Thomas Wolfe's classic "Only the Dead Know Brooklyn."* (Not the Tom Wolfe of *Bonfires of the Vanities*.) I'm appropriating the title to read Manhattan, "Only the Dead Know Manhattan." I find the city changes faster than a New York minute. Just today I subwayed down to Twenty-Third Street and Broadway and then tried to hop on a cross-town bus. I was stopped by the driver and told to get off and to insert my Metro card in a slot in the blue box outside that wasn't there yesterday, embedded in the cement at the bus stop. When did they start that? My point: it's hard to keep up. Only the dead know Manhattan. (The rider gets a little slip of paper he keeps, and if an inspector comes on the bus and you don't have proof you paid, you're fined $120.)

*The required-reading Thomas Wolfe short story "Only the Dead Know Brooklyn," written in Brooklynese, appeared in the June 15, 1935, *New Yorker* and was assigned to us in high school back in Lewistown. In re-re-re-review, maybe my West Virginia education wasn't so bad after all.

Cash Only

Maybe this is old news to you, but it's new to me: one store I visited will only take credit cards—"no cash, thank you very much." And recently someone ran an advertisement for a multimillion-dollar apartment in New York City with this caveat: "Cash only." Hold on, let me check the safe. (After that, the new Amazon bookstores in New York City accept no cash. Credit cards only.) The world of this new generation, as I wrote above under "K," I find dizzy-making.

OOO
Old
Favorite movie about old folks: *Grumpy Old Men*, Jack Lemmon, Walter Matthau, Ann-Margaret, Warner Brothers, 1993, written by Mark Steven Johnson.

Favorite play about getting older: *Driving Miss Daisy*, by Alfred Ulhry, which got its start off Broadway in 1987 starring Dana Ivey, Morgan Freeman, and Ray Gill and then went on and on and on…

Seventy-year-old Glenn Close on reopening night in the Broadway musical *Sunset Boulevard*, on the show's theme, aging: "I work pretty steadily but the quality of the parts for somebody my age is not streaming out of Hollywood. You look at cable, you look at independent films."

Obsolete
Whatever happened to biorhythms, oleo margarine, pressure cookers,* gay "camp," original Herbal Essence Shampoo, dodo birds, and the Golden Rule? (I suspect you have your own list.)

PPP
Porn Star
When writing the two other novels, it didn't come to my mind that I once had dinner with Harry (*Deep Throat*, 1972) Reems, prolific pornographic actor. After dinner, we went to hear the esteemed singer-interpreter of American popular standards, phrasing expert Miss Mabel Mercer. Reems wasn't familiar with her work and was not too impressed by one of the most iconic singers of all time. (Even Frank Sinatra was in

awe of her impeccable phrasing.) Possibly, Reems's mind was on other things. (His court case.) If you're curious: the *Deep Throat* "porn star" didn't think he had a particularly large member and was annoyed when people brought up the subject. (I once interviewed Harry Reems for a *Playboy Magazine* spinoff, *OUI*, for an article called "Do Large Genitals Improve Your Sex Life?" I was instantly paid. I needed the money. He was pissed I asked.)

Pepperoni Rolls Reheated
Back in the early 1950s, my mother, Louise, passed her pepperoni roll recipe on to Zia Maria for her local restaurant, Ritzy Lunch. Immediately, Zia Maria and Uncle Bruno (yes, *that* Uncle Bruno) began selling pepperoni rolls for pennies a piece. It took the world years to catch on to the delight coal miners had been enjoying in underground West Virginia caverns tucked in their black tin lunch boxes for years. I was reminded once more in July 2017, when *Oprah* magazine highlighted neighboring-town, neighboring competition for scrumptious pepperoni rolls, Country Club Bakery, Fairmont, West Virginia, where the million-dollar delicacies go for a mere $1.50. If only they'd had recipe royalties back then, originator Mama Lou would have died a millionaire by the time she passed in July 1981. I wonder if her grandniece Antonia, who now runs still-bustling Ritzy Lunch, knows the real story. History perpetually fascinates, particularly when it pertains to food.

Pennies
Superstition: Demons and dreams. My therapist once told me in his thick German accent, "I'd never bend over to pick up a penny." I replied to him, "I do." And every time I say—out loud, eyes heavenward, with my superstition, when the humble coin is heads *up*—"An angel is watching me." If it's *tails* up, I assert with confidence, "A *choir* of angels is watching me."

Jock Talk
Most folks know baseball players' takes on off-base, oddball rituals they believe can help them to win. After each success, Daytona Beach Islanders

pitcher Jim Ohms added a penny to his jock strap. At a successful season's end, his every run, infield and out, was supported by a jolly jingle-jangle.

Penmanship
In 2013, President Obama required New Yorker Jack Lew, upon his appointment to treasury secretary, to learn to make his signature (more) legible. His name was going to appear on US currency. In grade school, back home in West Virginia, a matronly, professionally nice woman/teacher came by our classroom regularly to teach us how to write long-hand. She would place on the blackboard large examples of the alphabet, lowercase and uppercase, perfectly shaped. We were asked to emulate these letters as closely as we could. What's more, we were even required, periodically, to turn in pages of the best script we could produce—and those assignments were critiqued with a grade letter, A to F. To this day, when I write out something, I attempt to make my words look as close to Mrs. Shakelford's as possible.

Good news for modern man: New York State is going back to basics and bringing back classes on what they call "cursive instruction." Future New Yorkers who become treasury secretary will now automatically know how to make a legible signature. Even better, both scientific research and name psychologists have confirmed that learning how to write cursively helps the development of not only improved motor skills but also brain development.

QQQ
Quotes, Quotes, Quotes

1. Till death do us part? "When the marriage ritual that included the formula 'till death do us part' was developed, few people could hope to survive their twenties. By the time a man died at the age of twenty-six he may easily have had three wives, two of whom died in childbirth. 'Forever' had a different meaning in that context

than it has today for us who can look forward to living into our seventies or eighties." Nineties?

Most of us resist change, but maybe we might consider eliminating that from any wedding ceremony for a multitude of reasons. No?

From *The Psychology of Romantic Love*, by Nathaniel Branden, PhD, Bantam Books (1980). I sure liked this book and wish Bantam would reissue it.

2. "I am so impatient with conservative ideas about how language is supposed to be. I love old books and the ancient prose. It's cute like old perfume or looking at a silent movie. But really, you should be able to write more like you talk than we're often told."

John McWhorter from *Salon*, San Francisco, progressive/liberal website owned by David Talbot.

Controversial quote that still has me in a quandary. And then:

3. "Very often the best fiction employs language...just like the language we use every day, only better."

Wrote Charles McGrath in the *New York Times*.

4. "Nearly half of all meals are eaten alone in America," said 2014 Food Marketing Institute Report. May I hazard a theory: ask someone to dinner, and your sexual batting average will skyrocket. Merely a thought and not a scientific study. I really can't take credit. Didn't *Cosmopolitan Magazine* invent this theory?

5. "More Americans than ever are taking antidepressants. The prevalence nearly doubled between 1999 and 2012, increased to 13 percent from 6.9 percent...Antidepressant use increases with age, with more than one in six of those over 60 taking a drug for depression...Is it risky to have a drink or two if you're taking drugs for depression?" A word from the wiser—author Steven Petrow concludes: Yes, it is.

From Steven Petrow, the *New York Times* citing the Mayo Clinic and JAMA. Dec. 20, 2016.

6. One of the most controversial subjects in Alcoholics Anonymous: Is it cheating to take antidepressants? The unprofessionals are not doctors and might keep their opinions to themselves. So there.

7. "You owe reality nothing and the truth about your feelings everything," so wrote poet, essayist, inspiring teacher Richard Hugo in *The Triggering Town*, W. W. Norton.

8. Five quotes (5) from my hero, Daniel G. Amen, MD*:

   a. "How your brain works determines how happy you are, how effective you feel, and how well you interact with others" (page 3).

   b. "Stressful early beginnings could set up lifelong problems" (page 4).

   c. "The brain is the seat of feelings and behavior" (page 35).

   d. "People who are depressed have one dispiriting thought following another. When they look at the past, they feel regret. When they look at the future, they feel anxiety and pessimism. In the present moment, they're bound to find something unsatisfactory. The lens through which they see themselves, others, and the world has a dim grayness. They are suffering from automatic negative thoughts...cynical, gloomy, and complaining thoughts that just seem to keep marching in all by themselves" (page 56).

   e. "Thoughts have actual physical properties. They are real! They have significant influence on every cell in your body...Teaching yourself to control and direct thoughts in a positive way is one of the most effective ways to feel better" (page 57).

   From *Change Your Brain, Change Your Life*, Daniel G. Amen, MD. Three Rivers Press, 1998. This book should be required college freshman reading.

9. Quote from Apostle Paul, the New Testament: "I run with purpose in every step." My mother was not an educated woman, and yet she had the instincts of a PhD. Mom instilled a work ethic in each one of us that has served us—me, all of my life. At home, we needed to be doing something constructive at all times. And when we did something wasteful, she would ask with a tone you didn't

question, "Now what did you get out of that?" Her words haunt but serve me well.

10. **All Day, All Night Marianne.** New quote from new ager: "You there, standing in the station of relationships and perfect jobs... the trains keep going by, going by, not stopping, and they keep going by, and keep going by, never stopping: Why? *It isn't your train!*"

    New-age self-help guru/bestselling author, Marianne Williamson, in one of her sold-out Los Angeles lectures. I was there. She now does her thing in New York City.

11. **Personal:** I, Nino Pino, ran into Charles Nelson Reilly in Los Angeles and reminded the *Hello, Dolly* stage actor and Tony winner we once had drinks at Elaine Stritch's apartment in New York. He said, "Yes, yes, yes, I remember you. They kept sending you out for the ice."

12. T. S. Eliot reportedly said, "Bad poets imitate. Good poets steal." Didn't one of the Beatles once say that it was smart to know from whom to appropriate? I think so.

13. Two more quotes from an underrated, (paperback version) of *The Psychology of Romantic Love**

    "Perhaps the essence of our evolution as human beings is to keep answering, on deeper and deeper levels, the basic question: 'Who am I?' We answer that question, we define ourselves, through the acts of thinking, of feeling, and of doing—of learning to take more and more responsibility for our existence and well-being—and of expressing through our work and through our relationships more and more of who we are. This is the wider meaning of the concept of *individuation*; it represents a lifelong task."

    From **The Psychology of Romantic Love*, by Nathaniel Branden, Bantam Books (1980). I was lucky enough to find this book in a dusty, used book bin somewhere offbeat. Published nearly forty years ago, I think it deserves a reprinting, Mr. Bantam.

14. "Innovators and creators are persons who can to a higher degree than average accept the condition of aloneness. They are more

willing to follow their own vision, even when it takes them far from the mainland of the human community. Unexplored spaces do not frighten them—or not, at any rate, as much as they frighten those around them. This is one of the secrets of their power. That which we call 'genius' has a great deal to do with courage and daring, a great deal to do with *nerve*."

From **The Psychology of Romantic Love*, by Nathaniel Branden, Bantam Books (1980). Ditto the above sentiment to Bantam Books.

15. Three quotes from one of my favorite actresses, Ruth Gordon:

"Courage is very important. Like a muscle, it is strengthened by use."

"Never give up. And never, under any circumstances, face the facts."

"To be somebody, you must last."

Ruth Gordon gave one of the most touching Academy Award-winning speeches ever.

16. From *Literary Hub:*

"I think almost every fiction writer I know would say you don't want to start out writing something if you think you can do it...If you know you can write it, it's not worth writing in some way."

Author Katie Kitamura in *Literary Hub*.

Do you care that every time I sit down at the typewriter or computer or 8.5 x 11 yellow pad (my mother called them "tablets"), I feel insecure to a high-decibel degree? But I do it anyway. As a mentor Barbara Wycoff Haines used to say to me, "Don't despair, Nino, and if you do, write anyway."

17. Controversial quote (?):

"The secret is the answer to all that has been, all that is, and all that will ever be."

Rhonda Byrne used the above words in her ubiquitous blockbuster *The Secret* to support her theory that the past's great minds—Newton, Plato, etc.— also believed in "The Law of Attraction" and attributed the words to Ralph Waldo Emerson. The quote may have been misattributed or actually made up.

There's no record of Emerson penning that sentence. Either way, I like it. Right on, Rhonda. I go back to *The Secret* periodically and, without fail, feel uplifted.

18. Liz Smith quote:

Syndicated columnist and writer Liz Smith once said to me, "It's good to do nice things for people, but when you do, do not expect to be paid back in kind." I think most of us like to be rewarded, paid back in some way, when we do an estimable deed. (Even with a thank-you.) It's worth getting over, at least for me. The septuagenarian speaks! The two words I use more and more the older I get are "thank you."

During the frightening blackout of 1977, I was at Liz Smith's office-apartment on a high floor at Thirty-Eighth Street and Third Avenue when the lights went out. I had to stay there the night to take care of her cats. Honest.

19. Sarah Manguso quote:

In an interview with *Hazlitt* on writing and getting paid for it, Sarah Manguso said, "So, clearly, this is not a job. Writing these books is not a job. And I guess I'm lucky in that I never assumed it would be, so I made other plans." Amen. I am grateful I never set out to get rich. I wanted to write because I wanted to write. I saw those around me getting successful and amassing big and bright, shiny things, but I continued to write, not resenting them. Sure, a house in the Hamptons would have been nice, but a job on Wall Street, to me, would have been hell on earth.

Check out Manguso's work *300 Arguments: essays; The Two Kinds of Decay, a memoir; Ongoingness: The End of a Decade.*

20. That subject again: A tall order and my life's work in this quote (also used in my second novel). I favor it so much, the words of W. Somerset Maugham from *Of Human Bondage*: "The secret to life is meaningless unless you discover it yourself."

21. "It takes the same amount of energy to be negative as it does to be positive."*

Oh God, I need to remember that sentiment every moment of every day. Negativity to me is a constant battle, a war to stop the cacophonic committees in my head, from all those noisy (sometimes screaming) words I heard as a small child back in Lewistown. You might say that was a long time ago. Or get over it! Sure. However, the criticisms that began as a kid for me—piercing putdowns, vociferous voices, jarring judgments—I now find difficult to shake: those remarks from the adults in power, the mean-spirited, off-base cousins, the boundaryless grade-school teachers. Now I seek out new terms to still (*to quiet*) the negative thoughts in my head, in my heart, in my mind, in my brain the millisecond they come up and, in the reversing process (thank you, Johnny Mercer), "accentuate the positive." If you think this is all too hokey, you're fortunate. Midlife, I confronted one of those older, putdown-artist cousins about her attacks. Her response? "*You* were too sensitive." Perfect. The ball thrown right back into my court. No, I wasn't too sensitive. You, tootsie, were too mean.

   *Wise words to remember from *BREAKOUT!* by Joel Osteen, FaithWords Publishing. If you're not aware of his work and need a pep talk, there are moral- and morale-boosting words on every page.

22. "You can find art and beauty in imperfection, and true art is from your soul."
    From neurologist Jay Lombard, *The Mind of God*, Penguin/Random House 2017.

23. James 4:14: "Our lives are like a mist. We're here for a moment and then we're gone."

24. "Life is what happens while you are busy making other plans." John Lennon and similar words from writer Thomas LaMance.

25. "The longer I live the more beautiful life becomes." Frank Lloyd Wright

26. "Youth is happy because it has the ability to see beauty. Anyone who keeps the ability to see beauty never grows old." Franz Kafka

27. "We never thought we could get old." Bob Dylan

28. "Life is short: life it up." Nikita Khrushchev

29. The most profound and powerful quote of all time: "Oh Lord - thou givest us everything, at the price of an effort." Leonardo da Vinci

30. Proverbs 17:27: "A wise man is known by his few words." Ooooopppps! *Few* words?

Footnote on quotes: (1) I collect/save quotes to which I responded. I need all the fortification (dancing) I can find to stay positive. It's an ongoing, constant, continual enterprise. (2) And if that's not enough, I want to inspire other people with like problems—those who need a little help from their friend—as often and as best I can. (Folks respond more to a solid source than to my experience, though I pray that even my colloquial experience might help another soul.) (3) What else is there? I've discovered this late in life—what the frig else is there than helping someone else? Ultimately, all those fleeting pursuits I found dire and desperate when I was young no longer apply.

RRR
Radio

It was so important to me as a young child that I could write a volume on radio. We had a five-foot console that sat next to Dad's recliner in the living room, an area Mother called "the parlor." I spent much of the time right next to that lumbering piece of furniture. Dramas, mysteries, comedies, music, news ("Pauline Fredericks and the News")—I ate it up. Fred Allen, Baby Snooks (the product of comedic actress Fanny Brice. When Fanny Brice died, I asked Dad who was going to replace Fanny Brice); *Amos n' Andy, Duffy's Tavern*, Bing Crosby (I recall distinctly when it was announced that Crosby's first wife, Dixie, died). Our grade school was directly across the street, and I'd run home at lunch, grab a sandwich, and plop down next to the Philco. I threw a fit when Daylight Saving Time came to our parts, and my noontime programs were shuffled around.

Imagine that: I suspect when you have to listen and not see the programs, your imagination is stretched. Merely guessing here. *You*, the listener, have to invent what you're hearing in your mind—not bad training for a writer. Editor's note to me: "Nino, I totally agree."

Radio today: when I'm shaving, I tune in to 1010 WINS Radio, which they tout as the most listened-to radio station in the nation. 1010 WINS reports new stories before most other outlets and many times puts me ahead of the crowd. I often get asked, "Now where did you hear that?" The answer is, "1010 WINS Radio." As for music, I'm sheepish to say, I tune in to free computer "stations" Pandora or Accu-radio. I used to like MySpace. MySpace let me select what I wanted to hear from an infinite list and then remembered those songs. Then the next time I logged on, the sequence was still there. That was my favorite, and one day it went away. (Hint: Somebody, somewhere reinstitute that approach to listening: We select; you remember the songs in sequence. You'd have me faithful for life.) So now it's Pandora and Accu-radio from the computer. Mostly I select American popular standards. Sinatra, Streisand, Peggy Lee, Margaret Whiting, Jo Stafford, Matt Munro. Occasionally 1950s rock 'n' roll: Four Aces, Como, the Platters, etc. Occasionally, big bands—love them with all my soul: Artie Shaw, Glenn Miller...

Recipes

In *F.U.! (Follow Up)! The Answer to Life Revisited*, I included fifty of my mother's precious recipes in her own words. I was reminded recently that when we were small children and Mother had eight to cook for, for expediency and tenderizer, she used the then-popular pressure cooker. As we grew older and there was less *pressure* on her, she became a great cook, and that apparatus/appliance was neither used nor mentioned again.

After this was locked in, an article appeared in one of the dailies, touting something called the Instant Pot, a new kitchen gadget that resembles a pressure cooker, only this one is electric. [Coincidentally, one of the recipes The Instant Pot People endorsed was polenta, a recipe of my mother's included in *F.U.! (Follow Up)*!] More user friendly, the advantage of the new gadget over the old-fashioned pressure cooker that operated on a stove's flame—that hissed and that made some cooks nervous—was that this update has self-regulating safety features, including temperature sensors that monitor amount of pressure. (More superb recipes presently. See recipes at the end of this volume.)

Roseto, Pennsylvania—Examined and Reexamined

The town of Roseto, Pennsylvania, was named for the Italian village of Roseto Valfortore. Our Roseto was largely settled by German, Dutch, and Italian Americans employed at the numerous local slate quarries. Our interest here: Roseto is known in the fields of sociology and cardiology for "the Roseto Effect"—a close-knit community that exhibited *half*, in the midtwentieth century, the national average rate of heart disease. This finding helped to establish the theory that stress might contribute to heart disease. Subsequently, Roseto, Pennsylvania, was dissected, studied, examined, and profusely profiled.

The Roseto Effect phenomenon was first noticed in 1961, when the local Roseto doctor encountered Dr. Stewart Wolf, then head of Medicine of the University of Oklahoma, and they discussed, over a couple of beers, the unusually low rate of myocardial infarction in Roseto compared with other locations around the country.

Multiple studies followed. From 1954 to 1961, Roseto had nearly no heart attacks for the otherwise high-risk group of men fifty-five to sixty-four, and men over sixty-five enjoyed a death rate of 1 percent while the national average was 2 percent. Widowers outnumbered widows too.

These statistics were incongruous with a number of contradictory factors. The locals smoked unfiltered stogies, drank wine "with seeming abandon" in lieu of milk and soft drinks, and skipped the Mediterranean diet in favor of meatballs and sausages fried in lard as well as hard and soft cheeses. Roseto also had no crime and very few applications for public assistance.

Dr. Wolf attributed Rosentorians' lower heart disease rate to lower stress. "The community," he said, "was very cohesive. There was no keeping up with the Joneses. Houses were very close together, and everyone lived more or less alike." Elders were revered and incorporated into community life. Housewives were respected, and fathers ran the families.

Sum and substance: As the original authors had predicted, in the years following the initial study, as the locals shed their Italian social structure and became more Americanized, heart disease rose.

On the other continent, Roseta, Italy, a beach resort on the Adriatic Sea, is in the Abruzzo region of central Italy.

Rader, Dotson—A Writer

My running joke: "Don't let your daughters be writers," summarizing how demanding a profession writing is. Journeyman Dotson Rader, seventy-five, was the only contributor to *Parade Magazine* that landed on his feet after the longtime, widely circulated Sunday supplement was sold to Althon Media in September 2014. Rader still does profiles for the pint-sized weekly that really gets around: (a) *Parade* is the most widely read magazine in the country, with a circulation of 32 million weekly and readership of 54.1 million. (b) The 8 x 9½ (but mighty) periodical used to be inserted in the Sunday *New York Post* and these days in the *New York Daily News*. (c) Tomorrow, who knows? On some days, Rader is in London working on rewrites of his play after its successful run at the Pasadena Playhouse; *God Looked Away*, starring Al Pacino and Judith Light, is about one of our most esteemed playwrights, Tennessee Williams. Other weeks, he's in Hollywood beating the bushes, trying to get a feature film made. Some of us are young enough to remember when Dotson Rader squired alluring (not to mention wealthy) model/stage and film actress Ruth Ford* around town. *People Magazine* wrote the couple up in 1975. Ruth Ford was once married to smoldering actor Zachary Scott,* who had not long before divorced his first wife, Elaine. [Elaine Scott went on to marry American author John (*Of Mice and Men*) Steinbeck to become Mrs. Steinbeck. Psew!] Recent events for Dotson Rader: Not too long ago, he sold the Dakota apartment he shared with aforementioned beauty Ruth Ford to Yoko Ono. (Ruth Ford owned several coveted flats in the Dakota. Egad: When Ruth Ford passed, she had $8+ million in her checking account.) Now for Dotson Rader, it's the play *God Looked Away* and a movie script or two. In a recent e-mail to yours truly, he wrote:

> *I flew from London to L.A. I just got back. I'll probably be returning to the Coast shortly. I'm waiting to hear what is next for my play. It is very time-consuming.*
>
> *I have never really understood why it takes so many years to get a play on or a movie produced. I trust things going well for you. It is increasingly tough to make a living as a writer. That's my experience, anyway.*

We know. We know.

Zachary Scott feature films: Mildred Pierce, Flamingo Road, The Unfaithful, Born to Be Bad, and more. Scott was also a Texas friend of Liz Smith who claims he got the columnist her first magazine job on Modern Screen.

ROCK
Is rock and roll unraveling? Gulp.

At press time, this came in. Let me begin by referencing a hit song from 1958. I was a senior in high school back in Lewistown when Danny ("At the Hop") & the Juniors assured me "Rock and Roll Is Here to Stay."* I not only believed them; I agreed whole heartedly—100 percent. Surprise! A new report was released Fourth of July week 2017 from highly regarded Nielsen, the music industry's leading source for record data and insights. The Nielsen Music US Mid-Year Report announced streaming is on the rise. And the turntables have turned: now hip/hop and R&B claim 25 percent of the market. And rock? Twenty-three percent. Not in my house. With Accu-radio, Pandora, Spotify, and the like, the hits keep smoking out of my computer monitor.

This Nielsen Music Mid-Year Report revealed, for the first time, weekly on-demand audio streams surpassed 7 billion. What's more, on-demand audio streams were a whopping 184 billion so far in 2017—62.4 increase of the same 2016 time period. (Overall on-demand streams, including video, have gone up 284 billion so far this year, an increase of 36.4 percent from last year.) Sadly? There was a decrease in album sales: digital down 19.9 percent and physical album sales down 17 percent.

"Rock and Roll Is Here to Stay," was a 1958 doo-wop hit out of Philadelphia by Danny & the Juniors, BMI, with four publishers listed: ARC Music, Carlou Music, BMG Bumblebee, One Song.

SSS

Sex and the County

A nursing home in the Bronx has a dating service called Grandparent Date (G-Date for short). Forty of their 870 residents are involved in relationships. Last spring, the Hebrew Home at Riverdale even held a senior prom. Most evenings, the house also has a heavily attended happy hour. One eighty-five-year-old hopeful reported, without shyness, that she found "the love of her life" at the Hebrew Home. What's more, the staff nurses encourage the patients to "take a chance on love." All this from a full-page-plus July 13, 2016, article in the *New York Times*, by Winnie Hu, with a long headline worth recounting. This *New York Times* piece and Winnie Hu give me hope. I will soon be an octogenarian and look forward, if you will, to a senior prom.

"Too Old for Sex? A Nursing Home in the Bronx Says No Such Thing." Subheading: "Aiding Residents Seeking Love." There's hope for all of us.

SEX AND THE SINGLE MAN

"Internet porn,…" according to savvy, prolific novelist Tom Perrotta in a *Time* magazine interview promoting his latest effort about the "complex," *Mrs. Fletcher* "… has become a democratizing force…real people are not as sexually picky as American commercial culture might lead us to believe. 'There's a place in porn for older people, people of different races.'"

From August 21, 2017 issue of *TIME* magazine, touting Tom Perrotta's smart seventh novel *Mrs. Fletcher*, Scribner.

Self-Actualization

Further considered: more on a subject I can't get enough of. I find it healing, hopeful, and habit forming.

"Looked at on its plus side, the human potential movement has helped to create a fresh intellectual climate in which to approach the subject of romantic love."

I liked this book and prevail upon the publishers once more to reissue the work. From *The Psychology of Romantic Love*, by Nathaniel Branden, Bantam Books (1980).

If nothing else, I say to supporters, or detractors, that self-actualization has brought back into psychology a renewed respect for and interest in (no small feat) mind, consciousness, choice, purpose, wholeness, self-development, and self-fulfillment. A 1970s creation that helped me a great deal, I want to share it with the world to help you heal, to help you shake any kind of addiction. I am not a professional; I attempt to speak about self-actualization in simple, straight- forward language in an effort to help you and to remind myself.

From a yellowing paperback* over which I poured until it was worn, and I pray it plays out of context, "Self-realization is not complete until it lives as action."

From *Loving What is, by Byron Katie (a woman, by the way). Three Rivers Press, 2002.

Scripture Quotes—Inspiration or Warnings?

1. Proverbs 18:20–21 (NIV): "From the fruit of their mouth a person's stomach is filled; with the harvest of their lips they are satisfied…The tongue has the power of life and death, and those who love it will eat its fruit." Do we figuratively eat the fruit of our phrases? Gulp.
2. Proverbs 22:29: "Do you see a person skilled in their work? They will stand before kings and great men." Also, Proverbs 18:15: "A man's gift makes room for him and brings him before great men."
3. Ecclesiastes: "Whatever your hands find to do, do it with all your heart."

4. And now an ardent argument for prayer: "Delight yourself also in the Lord, and He will give you the desires and secret petitions of your heart," from Psalm 37:4, the AMPC (Amplified Bible, Classic Edition). Yes, the secret petitions of your heart; I like the sound of that. Your deepest dreams. Your hidden hopes. The planned and unplanned innermost promises. If you haven't noticed, at seventy-six, I still have a trunkful of ideas and hopes and dreams. I thank my mother for instilling in me the habit of always being productive, of not wasting time and energy, to "go on Johnny Carson when you want to sell something." My mother's belief in her son/child still serves me nearly eighty years later—no small present. Psychologists have spoken volumes about how a mother's belief in her child sustains him/her for life. At least they're right about something.

Staff /Rod/Battery Not Included

When Moses parted the Red Sea in a victory gesture, he held up his walking branch. In Old Testament times, it seems, most folks carried a five- or six-foot-long twig—called a staff, a rod, or a walking stick—for protection, for power, and for authority even, much like a today's policeman's club, not to mention to keep the wild animals at bay. Enterprising ones etched events such as important dates and personal records on their walking branches. No need to worry the battery might give out. I include this simply; I like it.

Sad, Very Sad

I begin this sad memory of my maternal grandmother, a five-foot-two, older Italian woman with white hair pulled back in a bun and oversized blue eyes, throwing herself on a casket at the graveyard in Bridgeport, West Virginia. One of her daughters, my aunt, a tall, thin, svelte Anna Marie "BeeBee" Pino Lee, had passed away in December 1953 at a way-too-young twenty-six. Aunt BeeBee was the first woman in the area to wear men's gray dress slacks like in the movies a la Katharine Hepburn and Marlene Dietrich and could carry it off since she was tall, trim, striking, seductive. (We had recently been evicted, and now I was witness to the first close family death.) Succinctly, BeeBee Lee had had scarlet fever, which led to rheumatic heart disease (and this was long before antibiotics, decades before streptococcus vaccines). My Aunt BeeBee's scarlet bout left her with a scarred heart valve, which led to one of the early experimental Cleveland Clinic heart operations (to repair the damaged heart valves). (Note: the residual effect of scarlet fever often led to rheumatic hearts.) Since then, experts have learned streptococcus might cause infections that lead to defective valves and a vaccine might suppress the problem. Fast forward to 2016, there is now a vaccine available to those with the funds to finance a treatment. Oversimplification ahead: in poor countries where doctors and diagnostic kits are scarce (and cardiac surgery even more rare), many victims die of rheumatic heart disease—mostly children and young adults (the South Pacific, Fiji, New Caledonia, Africa). We trust the new vaccine will somehow soon find its way there and here, to the poor.

Although I was only thirteen years old, Aunt BeeBee's death, the funeral, and the out-loud sobs (even from BeeBee's young husband) were etched in my mind forever. For God's sake, I recall, not long before, we'd been evicted, and by thirteen I'd gotten used to the idea of the eviction and the torture laid on me from my grade-school principal*—and then a close family member's death presented itself. As they like to say in AA, that's life on life's terms. I say, "Life."

*Detailed previously, I was called into the principal's office daily, shivering in my skivvies, and told we had to move to another school.

Studio 54—An Addendum

Friends and acquaintances never tire of asking me about Studio 54. The New York dailies continue to often write it up. And, randomly, young people ask me about it today.

As I've shared before, in the 1970s, I sometimes went to exclusive, debauched Studio 54, infamous for only letting cool people in. And I got in easily. At the door, I was privy to name and face recognition. That's important to note. Out front, there was a long line, a denizen of noisy drunk and drugged-up club goers clamoring to get in with yells like

"Mark! Mark! Over here" to the doorman with power, Mark Benecker. (Rumor has it Frank Sinatra was turned away. A rich restaurant owner shared with me he'd tried to bribe his way in with a folded hundred-dollar bill and was rebuffed.) Yes, Studio 54 was all they said and more. But for me, it was a mixed emotion among the mixed drinks. I was part of it, but there was a bigger part of *me* that was "square." On any given evening, Studio 54 could easily hold two thousand, and yet the hoi polloi, the common folks, could not get in. So who *was* in there?* (Later on that.)

On the one hand, I enjoyed my infrequent trips to the world-famous disco. But then I liked being at home by midnight. Most of the excitement at 54 happened after twelve. I used to share my philosophy on nightlife to my buddy Lloyd Lee, "Nothing much happens after midnight." Maybe in *some* places but not Studio 54. Good news for me: Occasionally the club/disco hosted by-invitation-only early evening special events. I preferred those. They were not only fun, but they also afforded me early exit. I could be home by what I considered a decent hour to turn off the light at the stroke of.

To quote Duran, Duran and multiple other pop songs, it "come undone." By the end of the decade, owners Steven Rubell and Ian Schrager** were in prison for tax evasion, or so they said; henceforth, by the first stroke of 1980, it was all over. I suspect we'll never see the likes of Studio 54 at least in New York City ever again.

*Asterisk: If the place could hold two thousand-plus and most ordinary people were turned away, who *was* in there? Vladimir Horowitz, Jimmy Connors, Bianca and Mick Jagger, Halston, Deborah Harry, Alfred Hitchcock, Truman Capote, Calvin Klein, John McEnroe, Liza Minnelli, Jack Nicholson, Dolly Parton, David Bowie, Pele, Paloma Picasso, O. J. Simpson, Michael Jackson, Tennessee Williams, Richard Pryor, Jerry Hall, Roy Cohn, with or without his driver, Andy Warhol (obsessively taking Polaroids), and the best and hunkiest bartender this side of the Mississippi, Skip Odeck, a good friend, who was able to retire young. I suspect the tips were ample.

**Ian Schrager went on to thrive as a successful hotelier, and his pardon was to become President Barack Obama's last official act. Yeah. In 2017, he opened a dazzling, 370 room, Lower East Side hotel with glowing escalators, he called Public. Check-in desks have been replaced with roaming attendants toting iPads, who will program in your phone to act as your room key. Who said there were no third acts in American lives ...?

***Steve Rubell, the other Studio 54 cofounder, also had success in the hotel business but passed away of a bacterial infection in 1989 at forty-five.

SPAN, PAULA – Who is Paula Span and why do we need to pay attention

Earlier, I had the chutzpah to quote Ms. Paula Span. Paula Span is a relatively new addition to the *New York Times* who writes a twice-monthly online blog called "The New Old Age" and weighs in alternate Tuesdays in the Science Section. Attention must to be paid because the Census Bureau predicted twenty percent of America's population will be over sixty-five by 2030. Succinctly, Ms. Span is covering the asses of folks of a certain age exhausting subjects from senior care to colonoscopies. A couple of her other concerns 1) senior citizens are not going to the dentist often enough anymore. 2) If the elderly enters the hospital in the "under observation" category, and then later needs help, Medicare will __not__ cover rehab costs. *World*, we're drowning in minutiae out here. Who needs more technicalities to deal with? Thank you, Paula Span for being there. We're happy to have you in the bull pin. Give 'em hell.

TTT

Toilet Training

When I was a child myself, I witnessed my mother toilet training my younger siblings. (We're all one year apart.) She would lean over them while they were on the potty, chiding, "Shame. Shame. Shame." I assume I was subject to the same approach to instruction process. I don't claim to know a lot about all this and that. I do know I have felt a great deal of secret shame and embarrassment most of my life. I'll pull out one example: when I urinated into a toilet, I tried very hard not to make the sound of the piss hitting the water in the bowl. If there were others outside the door waiting to use the lavatory, for sure I was careful not to let them hear me urinating. I don't know if this is not normal.

Also, my mother and my maternal grandmother frequently used several Italian as well as English phrases at every opportunity. "What a shame," my mother often said in English, with a *tsh, tsh* after it. And (dialect) *key-ver-gonia*, which meant "what a shame." And "extreme shame" (more dialect): *tech-a tend-too-da*. So we can assume shame was around the house and ingrained in all six of us.

Later, that always-lurking adult mentor, Stiletto Constance, gave me a copy of John Bradshaw's *Healing the Shame That Binds You*.* At first I found it hard to read but then later embraced the theories of basic shame as well as toxic shame. Who knew?

"I used to drink," writes John Bradshaw, "to solve the problems caused by drinking. The more I drank to relieve my shame-based loneliness and hurt, the more I felt ashamed."

Bradshaw's theory, succinctly: Shame is the motivator behind our toxic behaviors: the compulsion, codependency, addiction and drive to superachieve that breaks down the family and destroys personal lives. His work on shame has helped millions identify their personal shame, understand the underlying reasons for it, address these root causes, and release themselves from the shame that binds them to their failures.

Healing the Shame That Binds You, by John Bradshaw, Heath Communications, 1988. Bradshaw, an active presence in self-help, was frequently on PBS, speaking and espousing on addiction, recovery, codependency, and spirituality. Though Bradshaw passed away not long ago, he and his work are always present.

Things I'd Never Seen before--AKA Chutzpah or Just Plain Cuckoo

In the locker room at the gym, an Asian gentleman washing his hand (washing just *one* hand) in a drinking fountain. I pointed to the restroom; he ignored me.

In the center of an AA meeting, a woman named Beck takes out a computer and begins to type.

Heavyset black youth, eighteen or so, standing in the middle of Broadway and Sixty-Seventh Street, texting on a cell phone as cars dangerously maneuvered around him. "Get outta the way, ya bum."

Some gent put a fifty-dollar bill in the basket and made change in a downtown AA meeting. The fifty was counterfeit.

Time

Oversimplified and not easy to grasp, Mr. Einstein's theory: Our perception of time, according to Albert Einstein, is not accurate. Events do not occur in a sequence, one after the other. Einstein (and fellow quantum physicists) theorized "time" this way: Everything is happening at the same time. And if that's true, then all is going on simultaneously, and our perception of time (as we experience it) does not exist. He opines: everything is going on at the same time. My question: how does that change things as they are? At this period in my life, I use time more effectively, more efficiently, and make an effort not to waste it. I've always wanted to be productive and now I *need* to be productive. Maybe it's part of the biological ticking clock—either way, I try not to fritter time away.

The New York Minute

A common expression meaning an instant or a flash, an extremely short time, defined by the fast pace characterizing New York City. And now: "the unforgiving minute," by Rudyard Kipling.

The Rudyard Kipling poem "If" is filled with suggestions on how to best spend your time, better ways to react in every situation presented to you despite their triviality. When Kipling states, "If you can fill the unforgiving minute/With sixty seconds' worth of distance run," he might be saying with every minute, make the absolute most of that "unforgiving minute." Every single minute is sixty seconds long, no more, no less; when that sixty seconds is up, it's gone. You can't call it back to use that time in some other way. It's unmerciful, that minute; it will not slow itself down. It is unforgiving, invariably elusive. From *New York Review of Books*: "We know, much better than our ancestors, the exact lineaments of what

Kipling called 'the unforgiving minute.' Our time is more universal and more precise than ever, and we're more than ever aware of the fact: it's no wonder that we dream so much and think so fervently of ways in which time might be bent, stretched, reversed, made less unyielding and less unforgiving. All prisoners dream of freedom, perhaps never more so when they know there isn't, and will never be, any possibility of escape."

From *New York Review of Books*, "Can We Escape from Time?" by John Lanchester, November 24, 2016.

Thought—I Don't Know *What* to Think

How and what to think: If you're uncertain of how and what to let go through your mind all day long, consider this: There is *not* one example/ incident in the holy scriptures where a person is advised to remember our defeats, to recall the times we failed, to take inventory of the bad breaks. The Bible (and every self-help book worth its pepper) suggests that to change and to change situations, we need to begin to remember our vic- tories—no matter how small or big. We have to actually take stock of and actually list our successes—those times we won, those times we excelled, the times we were healed, the time we got that promotion, those the time(s) we snagged the girl/guy, the times when our prayers were answered. Don't make a roster of your sins (sins in archery is when you miss the mark); make a list of your *wins*. There are worse ways to spend your time.

Footnote: I rarely write about or utter the word "sin." I heard it too often and too cavalierly spoken as a kid. However, I'm not above trotting out an evocative quote on the subject from scripture. "To him that knows what's right and doesn't do it, then it's sin" (Matt. 22:39).

Trump

I've saved this for the appendix. Folks tend to think I made it up. I promise you I didn't. The year was circa 1986–1987. I was visiting Dad, who lived alone in the family home in Lewistown. (Mother passed in 1981.) It's early evening. I'm dressed to go out, waiting for cousin Shirley Lorraine to pick me up to take us to dinner. Dad is watching the *second* go-round of "Jeopardy," his favorite, which he can view back to back on a neighboring channel. Why anyone would watch the identical "Jeopardy" twice in a row escapes me, but ours is not to reason why. ("I might have missed something," he explained.) In the sitting room, Dad has back issues of *Sports Illustrated* piled halfway to the ceiling, and I'm leafing through an old issue while waiting.

Out of the blue—and this is the mid-1980s since Dad passed away in 1989—as I was reading, out of left field he asked me, "Do you know Donald Trump?" Absently, I answered, "No, not really. I've heard of him, but I can't say I know who he is." While I was leafing the next issue of *Sports Illustrated*, his reply to that was an emphatic, "Stay away from him." I think I said, "OK." At that time, I hardly knew who Donald Trump was. Most likely, I suspect, I could not pick him out in a lineup. Without any effort, I stayed away from him. Possibly, my father saw Donald Trump on one of the thirty times he appeared on "The David Letterman Show," I don't know. I *do* know I wasn't watching late night television back then. In afterthought, if I had made a move to meet him then, I could now say (at cocktail parties), "Oh, Donald Trump...I met him in the eighties." Darn. I missed the boat.

As we speak, the editor is waiting with a red pencil to make a note. I reread this and the earlier paragraph to see if I said anything distasteful about D. T. I affirm: I'm pulling for Donald Trump. I'm pulling for the United States of America. I'm pulling for his not dickering with my "entitlements." I had nothing against him personally, but it was my experience that presidents were articulate, not fast-talking agitators. And I pray he doesn't have an enemies list a la Richard Nixon. Amen.

In 2016

Ali, Muhammad, passed
Dylan, Bob, won Nobel Prize for Literature
Bowie, David, passed
Brexit
Castro, Fidel, passed
Chicago Cubs overcame curse to win World Series
Clinton, Hillary, won popular vote by 3 million ballots but lost the presidency due to Electoral College

Cohen, Leonard, passed

Depp, Johnny, accused of spousal abuse

Dow soared 800 points

Jolie, Angelina, and Pitt, Brad, separated

Lee, Harper, passed

NFL viewership fell 27 percent

Prince passed

Rickman, Alan, passed

"Rigged," the most overworked word of the year; the most spoken? "Trump."

Scalia, Antonin, passed

Shandling, Garry, passed

Simpson, O. J., trial made into two TV series

Summer Olympics twelve-time winner Ryan Lochte concocted phony story about being robbed in Rio

Trump

Trump, Donald, talked about his penis and grabbing women by the privates and became president of the United States of America to the chagrin of many

Wilder, Gene, passed

Television—A Cool Medium

In 1954, Mother packed me off to Wheeling, West Virginia, to spend a month with Uncle and Aunt Tocci. Aunt Lizzie was her sister, and Uncle Manfredi, Aunt Lizzie's second husband, was a graveyard maintainer and digger of in Wheeling's Catholic Cemetery. More to the point, the Toccis had television in Wheeling. (Television had not reached Lewistown or at least our house.) More pressing here, summer of 1954, every afternoon in black and white, something called the Army-McCarthy hearings were on the Stromberg-Carlson. Since the medium was new to me, I would have watched paint applied and dry. But what fortuitous programming as an introduction for me to the new (to me) medium: the history-making, still-relevant Army-McCarthy hearings. This was a decade before Marshall McLuhan dubbed television "a cool medium." McLuhan might have meant an unemotional, cold medium. But I like to think the opposite. If he were still around, he might have to reconsider.

The Army-McCarthy hearings were a series of sessions held by the US Senate's Subcommittee on Investigations between April 1954 and June 1954. Their purpose: the investigation of conflicting accusations between the US Army and unappetizing Senator Joseph McCarthy. The army was accusing chief committee counsel, Attorney Roy Cohn, of pressuring it to give preferential treatment to a former McCarthy aide, G. David Schine, "a friend" of Cohn's. McCarthy countercharged that that accusation was made in bad faith as well as retaliation for his recent aggressive investigations of suspected communists/security risks in the US Army. (The term "communist" was pejoratively thrown around in almost every sentence spoken.)

Chaired by Senator Karl Mundt, the hearings began on March 16, 1954, and received considerable press attention, including gavel-to-gavel live television coverage on ABC Network from April 22 to June 17. The media coverage, particularly television, greatly contributed to McCarthy's decline in popularity and his eventual December 1954 censure by the US Senate. All of this smack-dab in the middle of my coincidental 1954 summer vacation in Wheeling, West Virginia. What a lucky break that was for me. When I got back to Lewistown and junior high school, I was able to give a rousing "what I did on my summer vacation": help to dig graves in the mornings and watch the Army-McCarthy hearings on television in the afternoons.

Even more curious to me, I not only was later to work for ABC Television Network but also to become a close friend of a future Roy Cohn chauffeur, David T. What's the old joke about a brush with greatness? In this case, maybe more of a bump into a great mess.

If we may make a fast twenty-eight-year forward to the early 1970s, when Watergate began with the 1972 break-in discovery, which led to the resignation of President Richard Nixon on August 9, 1974: Between May to August of 1973, the TV networks aired Watergate hearings, breaking scandal news, cover-up talk. In contrast, I watched sporadically. I saw, listened, and read with less rapture, but I was aware of what was going on, yet my concentration in the early 1970s was on other fish to fry and eat in New York. Coincidentally, and it was a genuine coincidence, I made one of my frequent train trips to Washington, DC to visit a friend in Georgetown on August 9, 1974. I arrived midday to his painted gray brownstone, and fortuitously (again by coincidence) my friend Michael Gambaro had the television on. Together we watched and heard Richard Nixon resign on that day.

Which brings me to today. At this typing, I'm watching CNN for an update on Donald J. Trump, Jr. May I say as little as possible about this latest television obsession. From the election 2016, I haven't felt my usual self, not 100 percent well, and some of that blame goes to the outcome of that election and the dizzy-making, upsetting, distracting, jaw-dropping daily newscasts and now US Senate hearings. God in heaven, spare me.

Tomorrow and Tomorrow and Tomorrow

After seeing a movie with my younger sister Toni, when we were children, subsequently she would say, "I want to see 'the tomorrow'. What happened after the end?" Back then, I had no answer and would say, *I don't know!* Today, I find that question endearing.

ANOTHER EDITOR QUERY: Tomorrow for *you*, Nino?

I started *Seventy-Six Trombones* early 2016, at 76, and I am now pushing 78. In fact, I am also at times asked by friends: what next for you? I answer, not sure. I *do* know I recently jotted these words on an unlined 3 x 5 card "Eighty! X8@#& Eighty!" Maybe, in the future, I pray before the 2020 election, I might begin a new effort--since you ask: possibly a new novel in 2020.

Meanwhile, a word from our sponsor:

"Tomorrow, and tomorrow, and tomorrow"
By William Shakespeare
(from Macbeth, spoken by Macbeth, Act 5, Scene 5)

Tomorrow, and tomorrow, and tomorrow,
Creeps in this petty pace from day to day,
To the last syllable of recorded time;
And all our yesterdays have lighted fools

The way to dusty death. Out, out, brief candle!
Life's but a walking shadow, a poor player,
That struts and frets his hour upon the stage,
And then is heard no more. It is a tale
Told by an idiot, full of sound and fury,
Signifying nothing.

UUU

VVV

Victimhood: Do I Perceive Myself As a "Victim"?

Psychologists call the everyday occurrences "adverse childhood experiences" (ACEs). ACEs include traumatic childhood events and their consequences that we can assume extend far beyond and into adulthood. The trauma need not be physical. The following events and feelings are some of the most common adverse childhood evidence and victim experiences:

Being sworn at, insulted, or humiliated by parents
Being pushed, grabbed, or having something thrown at you
Feeling that your family didn't support each other
Having parents who were separated or divorced
Living with an alcoholic or drug user
Living with someone who was depressed or attempted suicide
Watching a loved one be physically abused

I can attest to six of the above. I do not feel sorry for myself. On the contrary, I'm trying to be a whole, well, sober, and productive human being. I've been told the unexamined life is not worth living. As you can see in the pages before, I have been ad infinitum poring over my time on this planet. (1) I have been belittled by my family, especially my father. (2) I have been slapped around some by my parents. (3) I did not always feel my family could or would support me, so I learned to fend for myself. (4) There were several good boozers on my father's side—a couple I witnessed daily. (5) I suspect there was a line of depression that went through my father's side of the family and possibly the generation before his. 6) One of the most horrific scenes I've ever witnessed was my two younger brothers (at four and five) being beaten repeatedly with a barber's razor strap as they squirmed on the floor like injured praying mantises. Therapists had a field day with that last one and my denial about of any kind of abuse.

Video Games

A new study reports twenty-something men work fewer hours than they did a decade and a half ago—the biggest reason is they prefer to play video games. "Men aged 21–30 worked 12% fewer hours in 2015 than they did in 2000," according to the study published by the National Bureau of Economic Research, and about half the reason is the time they spend gaming. In fact, "in 2015, roughly 15% of young men worked zero weeks over the year, nearly double the rate in 2000." In the *New York Times*, Jane McGonigal, a video game scholar, suggested that games offer these young cohorts something lacking in available jobs—a meaning to life, specifically that "I'm trying to improve this skill, teammates are counting on me, and my online community is relying on me." More men in this age group are living with their parents, "35% of them in 2015, compared with 23% in 2000." According to Erik Hurst, one of the paper's authors, "Their attitude," he tells the *New York Times*, may be "why not have a little fun in your 20s and work in your 80s?" On July 9, 2017, the insightful Kyle Smith of the *New York Post* weighed in with additional wisdom and understanding, using the same sources. "The problem is that for many young men, video games have become a substitute for living. They're so addictive and soul consuming that they're unlike other leisure activities...Video-game addicts are engaged in a mass retreat from life...simply dropping out of the workforce and becoming PlayStation willing slaves...Happiness is not to be confused with fleeing pleasures delivered by artificial drug-like stimulants. Genuine life satisfaction is closely linked to the feeling of productivity we derive from doing jobs well and to the security of enduring close relationships, especially marriage." Remember *that?*

From Christopher Matthews at *Axios* online and the National Bureau of Economic Research, Cambridge, Massachusetts, 2017. And from Kyle Smith, July 9, 2017, the *New York Post*. Gracia.

Isn't it great, consistently, there is a contrarian. You can count on it. On the other foot, writer *Allegra Goodman, said this in **Commonweal*, June 8, 2017: "I do not think novels are necessarily more worthwhile than games. A novel can be trivial waste of time, and a game can teach…At their best, novels and games serve as vehicles for discovery." I loved this quote. Life is damn interesting.

American author *Allegra Goodman, won the National Book Award for *Kaaterskill Falls* and Best American Short Story, 2011, for "La Vita Nuova." **Commonweal Magazine* is a Roman Catholic literal journal of opinion(s).

WWW
Writers/Writers on Other Writers

"It is not enough to succeed; one's best friend must fail." Source: Gore Vidal? La Rochefoucauld? Somerset Maugham? Wilfrid Sheed? Iris Murdoch? David Merrick? Genghis Khan? Larry Ellison? All of the above.

How to Write

I, Nino Pino, admit I'm small potatoes. Nonetheless, I'm often asked "How to write? What can I do to become a writer?" By that time, the aspiring author, should have read and studied and absorbed a Pike's Peak of material. Though I have a couple credits in several fields, I honestly don't consider my self very successful. But, I answer the aspirant this way: Read all three of the blocked writer's best friend, Steven Pressfield's, books in the order published: *The War of Art, Turning Pro,* and *Do the Work.* Coincidentally, while we're at it, here is a relevant, masterfully profound, powerful, insightful, (cherished by me) quote from Pressfield's *Turning Pro,** in a chapter he called "Beautiful Losers":

"Addiction itself is excruciatingly boring. It's boring because it's predictable—the lies, the evasions, the transparent self-justifications and self-exonerations. But the addict himself is often a colorful and fascinating person." Please note the aforementioned books are kick-in-the-ass master classes on being productive--not solely about addiction?

*Black Irish Entertainment, 65 Central Park West, New York 10023

Writer Gary Lutz

"If I believe in anything when it comes to writing, and I can't stress enough that I detest writing, it's something that sticks with me not from any English class but from some awfully recondite driver's-ed seminars... It's the term 'right of way.' The writer, as I see it, has the right of way, so it's up to the reader to look out."

From writer-educator Gary Lutz in an interview in *The Rumpus.*

Writer Jack Kerouac, more on

American writer-poet, famous for his novel *On the Road*, Jack Kerouac (1922-1969) died too soon at 47 of internal bleeding due to alcoholic poisoning. The story goes, and I repeat, Kerouac would hook up a roll of paper to his typewriter which allowed him to continuously write without changing page after page and that approach prompted Truman Capote's *On the Road* review: "That's not writing, that's typing."

Words, Words, Words...as someone said in *My Fair Lady*

The bane of my existence is trying to find the right word, *le mot juste.* Occasionally, I consult Mr. Roget's thesaurus; sometimes even he fails me.

Workout Escape

Anytime anyone takes too long talking about his or her workout regimen, even me, I interrupt with this quote, which gets me off and out of there.

"Now, here, you see, it takes all the running you can do, to keep in the same place. If you want to get somewhere else, you must run at least twice as fast as that!" Works every time.

From *Alice Through the Looking Glass*, Lewis Carroll.

XXX

YYY
Young, Inside Tip on How to Stay
In a looong, puffed-up, well-written, twelve-page, multiple-word piece in the April 3, 2017, *New Yorker* that took place in Norman Lear's living room in Los Angeles's Mandeville Canyon, the article titled "The God Pill— Silicon Valley's quest for eternal life" (written by Tad Friend) gathered an impressive group of Silicon Valley venture capitalists, Hollywood celebrities, Harvard scientists, health spanners, so-called immoralists to mull over "the secrets of longevity": to be brought up to date on the new nitty-gritty of aging, staying young, living longer, and possibly existing forever, as well as to pore over experiments, medications, etc. What's more, big-money donations were revealed: Google gave a billion dollars, Larry Ellison, $300,700,000 for aging research. Psew.

One of the attendees of that March 2017 Norman-Lear-Los-Angeles-living-room, billion-dollar-plus, celebrity-peppered presentation/discussion/meeting to thrash out the solution to "eternal life" Was forty-nine-year-old biochemist Ned David of upstarter Unity Biotechnology. Youthful Ned David revealed (shared?) that he employs state-of-the-art, cutting-edge medications/treatments in his ongoing search for extended youth, *and* by his own admission "battles his own aging on multiple fronts, down to his choice of sneakers." And there he was, in Red. High-Top. Converse. Sneakers. I loved the article and coveted the sneakers. The *New Yorker* rarely does any wrong, don't you think?

From *New Yorker Magazine*, April 3, 2017, "The God Pill," by Tad Friend and worth a read.

ZZZ
Zzzz

Wake up. "I'm not asleep." Wake up. It's an inside job. "What do you mean it's an inside job?" How do you feel? "I feel fine." How do you really feel? "I'm not sure." OK, then, one can only have a few basic feelings. "Who says so?" Never mind; they are: Angry. Sad. Glad. Lonely. Tired. Hungry. That's about it. How do you feel? "Oh, inside job—feelings. I get it." Right. (Pause). Well. "I'm thinking." Don't think. Feel! "My wife—" Fuck your wife. "OK, then the kids—" The heck with the kids. And the mortgage and your goddamn boss. Keep the focus on yourself. Keep the focus on yourself. How do you feel? "I get it—I get it. I haven't eaten today. I'm hungry. That affects the blood sugar and moods, right? And I'm sad about—" *Now* you're getting it. Have something to eat and then check in with me later.

Recipes

THE FOLLOWING RECIPES WERE WRITTEN out, in long hand, by Mama Lou—an exceptional cook, to say the least—but they were not tested by yours truly. I'd like to add that the chicken soup recipe may just be for the best chicken soup you've ever had in your life.

For loyal fans:

My second Amazon.com novel, *F.U.! (Follow Up)! The Answer to Life Revisited*, contained fifty-plus (50+) original family recipes. Here are a few more. My favorite: the banana split cake. The most revered: my mother's chicken soup recipe. I have yet to taste chicken soup any better than my mother's. And I've been around the block and have done everything, twice.

Fruit Bars

2 EGGS
1½ cups granulated sugar
2½ cups flour
1-ounce can fruit cocktail, do not drain juice
1½ teaspoon baking soda
½ teaspoon salt
1 teaspoon vanilla extract
1½ cups flaked coconut
½ cup chopped nuts

In a large mixing bowl, at high speed, beat the two eggs. Then add the one-and-one-half cups granulated sugar.
Next add fruit cocktail with its own juice, the flour, baking soda, salt, and vanilla.

Beat this mixture at medium speed until blended.
Spread on a greased and floured pan.
Sprinkle top coconut and nuts on top.
Bake at 350 degrees for twenty-five or thirty minutes.

Applesauce Cake

(HERE AGAIN HERE DUE TO great response from Book Two)

Pre-recipe Prep for the Cake's Glazed Topping
In a pan, combine:
3 cups sugar
½ cup butter
¼ cup evaporated milk
½ teaspoon vanilla extract
Boil all the ingredients for two minutes, mixing often.
Remove from heat.
Stir in nuts.
Let the glaze cool.
Note: Meanwhile, thaw one can frozen orange-juice concentrate.
*Secure greased and floured ten-inch tube pan.

The Applesauce Cake Recipe

3¼ cups sifted all-purpose flour
2¼ cups sugar
2 teaspoons baking soda
1½ teaspoons salt
¼ teaspoon baking power
1 teaspoon cinnamon
½ teaspoon ground cloves
¾ teaspoon nutmeg
¾ cup shortening

6 tablespoons frozen orange juice concentrate—thawed, undiluted
6 tablespoons tap water
1 fifteen-ounce can of applesauce
3 eggs
1½ cups raisins
1 cup chopped nuts

In a large mixing bowl, sift in flour and then add the sugar, baking soda, salt, baking powder and spices.

Add shortening, undiluted orange juice concentrate, water, and applesauce. Beat for two minutes at medium speed.

Next, add eggs and beat two minutes longer.

Blend in raisins and nuts.

*Place in a greased and floured ten-inch tube pan. Bake in 350-degree oven for one hour and fifteen minutes—cake test. Cool in the pan for fifteen minutes.

Turn out of the pan onto cake dish and cool completely.

Then top with the glaze.

Serves at least twelve.

Raisin Cookies

(A LONGTIME BIAFORA FAMILY FAVORITE) Hundred were made during the holiday, any holiday, and passed out to friends.

1 cup water
2 cup raisins
1 cup shortening
2 cups sugar
3 eggs
1 teaspoon baking power
1 teaspoon baking soda
2 teaspoons salt
1 teaspoon vanilla extract
1½ teaspoons cinnamon
¼ teaspoon nutmeg
¼ teaspoon clove
4 cups flour

Cook 1 cup water and 2 cups raisins for five minutes.
Set aside and let it cool.
Cream one cup shortening, two cups sugar.

Then to shortening and sugar, mix in the rest: 3 eggs, 1 teaspoon baking powder, 1 teaspoon baking soda, 2 teaspoons salt, 1 teaspoon vanilla extract, 1½ teaspoons cinnamon, ¼ teaspoon nutmeg, ¼ teaspoon clove, and 4 cups of flour.

To the above, now add the water/raisins
Combine thoroughly.
Bake at 400 degrees for 12 to 14 minutes
Yields two dozen-plus cookies.

Anise Slices

7 EGGS, BEATEN
pinch of salt
1½ cups sugar
1 cup Wesson Oil
1 tablespoon anise extract
1 tablespoon vanilla extract
3 cups of flour
1½ tablespoon baking power
1 pound walnuts

Beat eggs.

Then add sugar, oil, anise extract, and vanilla extract.
Fold in flour and baking powder and continue to mix well.
Put the dough on a greased pan or glass baking dish.
Bake 25 to 30 minutes at 350 degrees.

Cut diagonally ½-inch thick.
Then put back in the oven and toast lightly.
Makes five or six dozen cookies.

Banana Split Cake

2 CUPS GRAHAM CRACKER CRUMBS
1 stick butter—melted
2 cups powdered sugar
2 eggs
1 teaspoon vanilla extract
1 can crushed pineapple—drained
1 layer of bananas
1 nine-ounce carton of Cool Whip
Crushed nuts of your choice: walnuts, pecans, almonds, etc.
Option: cherries

And Now Banana Cake As Easy As One, Two, Three: Here's How

1. Two cups graham cracker crumbs and one stick butter, melted. Mix well and put in a 9 x 12 x 2 pan.

2. One stick of butter, two cups of powdered sugar, two eggs, and one teaspoon vanilla extract. Spread this mixture on top of graham cracker crumbs.

3. One can crushed pineapple, drained. Add one layer of bananas and one 9-ounce carton of Cool Whip and then spread on top of the above. Next, sprinkle on nuts of your choice.

Note: Keep refrigerated.

If you'd prefer, put some maraschinos or other cherries on top of the pineapple. It couldn't hurt.

Feeds a dozen or so.

Fun Italian Wedding Cookies

10 EGGS
1½ cups granulated sugar
¾ cups shortening
10 teaspoons baking power
1 bottle orange extract
10 cups flour
Beat the ten eggs well, really well.
Add the sugar, the shortening, the baking powder, and then the bottle of orange extract.
Gradually add the ten cups of flour. You may find the recipe can't take all of the flour; use your baker's judgment when enough is enough.
After all is well mixed:
On greased cookie sheet, roll out pieces in thin snake form. Twist into different shapes; have fun with it.
This recipe feeds a small army.
Editor's note: This is fun.

Cranberry Salad

2 CUPS GROUND RAW CRANBERRIES
2 cups chopped fresh apples
½ cup ground walnuts
2 orange rinds
2 cups sugar (more or less, if you prefer)
2 packages of cherry gelatin
1½ cups hot water
2 cups orange juice—fresh or canned
Dissolve cherry gelatin in the cup and 1½ cup hot water.
Add the two cups orange juice.

Chill until gelatin begins to set/congeal.
Then add the other ingredients: ground cranberries, ground walnuts,
orange rinds, sugar, and chopped apples.
Mix well.
Pour into mold.
Refrigerate for one day.
The cranberry salad may be served with mayonnaise.
And note: the dish can be frozen.
Serves six to eight.

Italian Fruit Cake

(ALCOHOLICS BEWARE)
Prep
Heat in a pot and put aside:
1 quart wine
1 water glass of whiskey
1 pint of vegetable oil
½ pound shortening. Let this cool some. Also, put aside.

Filling:
8 pounds cleaned and chopped walnuts
8 pounds seedless raisins that were rinsed and strained before including
2 or 3 orange rinds
clove
cinnamon
nutmeg
2 pounds sugar
Mix all of the filling together, in that order, and also put aside.

Dough
8 pounds flour
salt
1 pound sugar
8 eggs

In a large pan: put the above prep, the warm wine mixture. Kneed—like dough—until elastic.

Roll out into balls as large as grapefruits and let them rest for about ten minutes, covered with cloth or towel.

After ten minutes, roll the above into long, thin strips.

Meantime: have above filling ready, with a few drops of oil.

Place the filling *onto* the thin dough stripes, moistening with a little oil.

Then on one side, roll some of the above filling—like jelly rolls—until you reach midway.

Then go to the other end and roll until you reach the center.

Meet the two halfway and then connect the ends together.

Put on a greased cookie sheet.

Bake for one hour at 350 degrees.

Serves a family of eight and some unexpected company.

Coconut Drop Cookies

1 CUP SOFT SHORTENING
2 cups brown sugar (tightly packed)
2 eggs
½ cup sour milk or buttermilk
3½ cups flour
1 teaspoon baking soda
1 teaspoon salt
1 cup coconut—finely shredded
Mix well: soft shortening, brown sugar, two eggs.
Next stir in ½ cup sour milk or buttermilk.
Mix together and then stir in 3½ cups flour, 1 teaspoon soda, 1 teaspoon salt, and 1 cup shredded coconut.
Blend all of the above.
Chill/refrigerate for one hour or more.
Preheat oven 400 degrees.
When ready, drop teaspoon two inches apart on greased pan.
Bake for eight to ten minutes.
Makes a dozen or so cookies.

And now, The Recipe I promised you at the end of my second novel, *F.U.!* *(The Follow Up)! The Answer to Life Revisited.* Another holiday favorite, thousands were made, packaged and passed along to friends, family, and an occasional foe.

Galette(s): A French Cookie

ITALIAN STYLE AND GRANDMAW PINO's favorite
Note: You need a waffle iron.
10 eggs
2 sticks of butter
1 cup granulated sugar
3½ cups brown sugar
2 teaspoons vanilla extract
4 or 5 cups flour
1 pound butter
1 teaspoon baking powder

Separately, separate egg yolks and egg whites and put aside.
Cream butter until fluffy.
Slowly add granulated sugar and brown sugar to fluffed butter.
Mix/combine well.
Then fold in flour and vanilla extract and baking powder into the sugars-butter mixture above.
Again, mix well. When well mixed, beat in egg whites—whites only.
Lastly, add egg yolks to the above; fold in and mix until you have a soft dough.
Use conventional waffle iron to make these galette cookies as you would make waffles.

Drop in mixture to preferred size: teacup size, the size of an orange, or large grapefruit sized.

Follow this recipe and you will out-French the French.

Makes and feeds dozens. You will want to give some away to the neighbors.

Louise's Exceptional, Exquisite Chicken Soup

WORTH THE PRICE OF ADMISSION Times Ten. Guaranteed to make you well made when you were ailing and usually supper every ten days for good measure.

Chicken Soup

1 chicken (4 or 5 pounds), preferably a stewing bird
1 large yellow onion (finely chopped)
4 carrots (peeled and finely diced)
4 celery ribs *with* leaves (finely chopped)
1 bay leaf (whole)
½ cup of parsley (Italian)
1 teaspoon of black pepper
2 teaspoons of salt (kosher)
3 teaspoons of butter
½ teaspoon of thyme
½ teaspoon of poultry seasoning

In large pot, over medium-low heat, sauté onions in the butter until the onions are clear and soft.

Rinse the chicken.

Cut the chicken into quarters and place in large pot on top of the onions/butter.

Add some water and the 2 teaspoons salt.

Cover the pot, heat, and bring to a boil.

Uncover and skim scum from the top.

Then cook for one hour.

After one hour, add the rest of the ingredients listed above.

Raise heat now up to medium.

Cook for one hour more.

Taste broth at this time.

Options: if broth is weak, can add one can of broth or 3 or 4 chicken bouillon cubes.

Take chicken out of soup; let cool.

Remove bay leaf.

Once chicken is cooled, take off all meat from bone and shred and then put *back* in soup.

Preference: use large egg noodles, cook and drain, and then combine with chicken and broth.

Sprinkle a little fresh parsley for color and taste.

Option: You may use white rice or pasta, as stated above; we preferred and had great success with half inch wide egg noodles. We've not seen chicken soup anywhere with lots of white meat chicken in it as well as made with wide egg noodles.

Hang in here for the West Virginian Italian Calabrian dialect, phonetically.

West Virginian Italian Calabrian Dialect

As I RECALL THEM; AS they spoke them…

As a young person, I would never have admitted I could speak Italian. After all, I knew a few words here and there; that's it. (I could make my Uncle Manfred* from Trieste smile when I spoke an occasional word in dialect.) The truth: I could not string an Italian sentence together. As an older person, I realize this: I know dozens of Italian words, and that means I *could* converse in Italian. I might say "wait," *aspeta*, and an Italian would understand me. I might accuse: "You're a royal pain in the ass" with *prima–cha cuolo*. So I realize I can speak a bastardized version of the Italian language: Calabrian dialect via the West Virginia hills. It affords me a small smile.

AAAA

a la vort-za—"You have to do that right now?" Implication: Can't you do that some other time? *Shouted at me when I insisted on something.*

ah-you-yah—A nonsensical phrase. What does it mean? Something like "the twelfth of never." (For example, "Wait. You'll get what you want *ah-you-yah*.")

You have permission to skip this one:

aa-kay-taa-we-a in-ess bot-ta—A nonsensical phrase of which no one knew the meaning. It was like an emphatic exclamation without meaning. If it was hurled your way, with a flip of a hand, to the air around you, you wouldn't be offended.

BBBB

bro-da—Broth, soup.

bee-AH-col—To be drunk.

bee-ah-cone-a—A drunk.

bella-too-cee-merde—To have a good bowel movement.

boo-fah—Angry, quietly stewing. (Italians are also known for high-decibel outbursts that dissipate in a few minutes, unlike the *boo-fah*, which can last for days.)

boom-aa—Loosely, "you bum you." Also an actual hobo. Not the British bum.

bruta-a-baastea—Mean bastard, mean beast.

bruta fach-a—Ugly. Ugly face.

botza or just plain *botz*—Crazy, touched, "titched" in the head

ben-a-dee-ca—A warm, sincere blessing. Tossed off, sarcastic blessing, *veec-cha viah-cha.*

baa-phone-tro guolo—Fuck you, up the ass.

CCCC

cop-pa-tol-sta—Hard headed. *Heard regularly around our house when you weren't paying attention or defied an adult.*

chee-cha-thaw—Dopey, dummy, not a smart person.

chee-kay-ta—A little drink, maybe in a shot glass. *Usually accompanied with a giggle.*

chew-ta-bock—Looking down one's nose at someone who chews tobacco.

cum-pah-ren-za—Not giving a person the attention he or she deserves or thinks he or she deserves; not paying them any mind. Ignoring someone who might want, expect, or deserve special attention.

cuut-son-ella—Ladies' underwear (more white cotton than sexy panties). Little rhyme: bella wella, cuut-son ella.

coo-ka-dah—Little nap. *Wah coo-ka-dah*—Sarcasm: Get out of here. Go take a nap. Go to sleep.

cannoli—Plural for that scrumptious, cone-shaped Italian dessert. If you're only having one, it's *cannolo*. Few adhere to the singular/plural pronunciations.

compare/compadre—A friend, a close friend, even a close family person, primarily male. Are you young enough to remember Julius LaRosa's novelty, number-one 1953 hit record "Eh, Cumpare!"? *Brothers-in-law even called one another compadre.*

DDDD

dough-dough-jud-da-dah—Nonsensical phrase, at times used as a put-down or criticism of a person you want to make fun of (for example, my ex-boss).

EEEE

e-cot-tee-scat-ta—I hope you explode (more like burst).

FFFF

fa-cal-do—It's hot. (The opposite: *key-kotz-aa-freeda*—it's fucking cold.)

farn-east-ta—Farmer, but more of a putdown of local country people; those who came into the County Seat to shop or visit the Court House. Read: hick, someone to look down on. We had to have someone to feel superior to.

GGGG

ga-vone—Phoney. Real fake.

gumba—Close friend; even family members can be *gumbas*.

HHHH

hurry-oop-pah—Pick up the pace. *When you were avoiding something, get crackin'.*

IIII

JJJJ

jake-katha-a—Shabby, turned-out, jerklike, an entire group of lower class.

jake—A prefix Mother used with various categories for multiple creative putdowns and criticisms.

jitty-jitty—Someone routinely on the move, a gadabout. Or merely running around; traveling a lot. A social butterfly.

joel-tool or *joel-taah*—Dumb, really stupid, and somewhat clueless.

KKKK

kotz—A putdown without a literal translation, but it was a catchall. Fuck, or little fuck, or damn fuck. My paternal grandpaw used that word at the end of every sentence, whether he'd just landed a fly with the swatter or with someone who just pissed him off, encompassing everyone from a family member to the president of the United States.

kotz! or key-kotz—That fuck.

key-ver-gon-ia—What a shame.

key-pay-cot-ta—What a pity. Also what a shame.

kee-sa cot-ta—Like elbowing someone with "will you look at that one!"

key-kotz-aa-fre-da—It's fucking cold.

LLLL

lupa, lupa-lea—Pig.

love-ul-tel-la—Literally, "little wash"—to us, an enema.

MMMM

more-ful—Mucus. Also *more-fuu-saa*—One with mucus running down his/her nose.

me no cosh-ka—I don't care. I don't give a shit.

moo-tha conten-ta—You might think "never contented," but it was more "mad at the world," never satisfied with anything. *If one, if I, was in a bad mood, I got* moo-tha conten-ta.

moo-sha morta (also *morte*)—A deadbeat; one who lacks energy without get up and go. *If I moved to slow for Mother, I heard it.*

mun-ee-cha-la—Undershirt, ordinarily a male's. Even the Italian-T.

mow-sas—Fake gestures. A faker. Faking it, the subject was not serious.

managia/managia America—An epitaph. An expletive. A cussword, sometimes cussing out the country.

merde, merda—Excrement.

minestra—A spinach soup dish that made the spinach palatable to me and to other spinach haters. *As an adult, minestra is now scrumptious to me.*

NNNN

nay-sha-cada—Get the fuck out of the way.

no ca-pece niente—I don't understand anything.

no re-cee-cha niente—"Don't say anything," almost always whispered.

nay-sha-kotta—Get out of the way.

nay-shoo-ta—Go out, go outside.

OOOO

oye, man—Stated putdown if a young girl behaves in a masculine way.

PPPP

pod-ella—"You poor thing" or merely "poor thing."

peed-a-tood-da—Breaking wind; a fart. Said in film *Goodfellas*.

pee-sha-coca—Piss-shit, an old-world expletive.

pee-shot-sa—To take a piss. Also just plain *pee-sha*.

pet-tro-zeen-ah—Parsley.

per-pet-ta—Meatballs.

pre-sto-pres-tol stamatina—Early this morning. Evening: *stazeta*

pes-cos-ca—Pretend, faking it, insincere.

pre-sap-pra cuolo—Someone with highbrow standards and first-class pain in the ass. A person who needs and gets special attention. *If I ask for something out of the ordinary, or too soft for their tastes, I heard it.*

pa-chun-na—Female genitals; a vagina.

Pee-sha-tood-a—Male genital; penis.

pro-pria—Tossed-off sarcasm like "Sure, soon, you'll get that," or "I'll do what you want, sure." (Similar to *as-PAA-ta*. "Wait, hold on a minute, and you'll get what you want." Also like nonsensical *ah-you-ya*. When you hear these phrases, you know you're not going to get what you want and you're being humored.)

prima–cha cuolo—First-class pain in the ass.

po–lee-ta—Clean. A word that was used frequently as they did laundries and house cleanings every day and made sure you were squeaky clean. No greasy wops here.

par-heen-na—Godmother.

phy-sick—Another term for laxative.

pate-za—Dollar. *Chinqua pate-za*—Five dollars.

pee-la-soon-na—A pinch of love, possibly a grandmother loving an attractive grandchild; an actual twist of two fingers on a check.

QQQQ

RRRR

re-crea niete—I don't remember, or I recall nothing.

re-crea—By itself, means you want to comfort yourself, lounge (a tad sarcastic). *I heard this from Mother when I tried to rest, relax myself.* **Work** *was the watchword in our household—not a bad legacy.*

SSSS

scaata or *e-cot-tee-scat-ta*—Bust. I hope you burst. Explode.

score-dot-da—I forgot.

sack-a-merd-da—Sack of shit—that is, a fat ass.

scut-ta-mut-ta—An ill-mannered person.

sha-baa-ta—Trailer trash. Someone terribly turned out.

snuffy—Looking down one's nose at someone who rubs snuff. (*Chew-ta-bock* and *snuffy* refer to an entire class of West Virginians that other West Virginians look down on.)

speeza or *make speeza*—To grocery shop.

squeech-cha-la—Short or small person, a pejorative term that also might mean little piece of shit. *Mother did not like for my sisters to date short guys and when they did, the objection of their affections were referred to as squeech-cha-la.*

sta-zeta—Evening.

strun-za—Also little piece of shit.

stuu-fot-ta—Stupefied.

stun-cot-ta—Tired, exhausted.

sotch-uu-ee-uu—I don't know.

staa-taa-chew-tool—Shut up. Be quiet.

staa-taa-quit-ul—Stop it.

see-taa or *zee-tah*—New squeeze, new boyfriend or girlfriend, new relationship.

TTTT

tech-a-ten-too-da—What a shame, a variation on *key-ver-gon-ia*.

toast-sta—Limp—not your noodle; more likely an out-of-shape garment.

tu-zee-brute-ta—Unattractive, ugly, mean.

trop-po sigh—Too much, too damn much!

UUUU

uuu-fah—Emphatic expression, sometimes in answer to something said, that's more of a sound than a word.

VVVV

vee-cha vee-ahh-cha—A sarcastic Italian "good luck." A "God bless" with a touch of sarcasm, a sardonic term. *Grandparents used this one often to remind you, you're not going to get what you want.*

vor-ba—A wise person, many times a smart, "on-to-you" one, as a young person says.

vergonia—Shame, yet another word for shame. For emphasis, *key vergonia, yoy, yoy, yoy.*

WWWW

way-cha haa-jot-ta—Witch, haggard witch; an unattractive woman, more often than not an old one. Mother was observant and judgmental, and used it regularly.

ward-da kee-sa (also *ward-da kee-sa cot-ta*)—"Look at that one," observing someone with a critical eye. (Also just a brief look: *warda*.) Elbowing someone you're with: "look at that one."

wuu-ca-pert-ta—A stupid person, mainly one with a dumb expression on his or her face. Dopey with a lazy streak.

XXXX

YYYY

ZZZZ

zord-da and/or *zord-deez*—Money, scratch, filthy lucre.

zia—Aunt.

za-chu-eo-I don't know. I don't have a clue.

"Poke"—Poke has a multitude of meanings: (1) Back home in West Virginia, a shopping bag is referred to as a poke. (2) A jab with a finger anywhere is a poke. (3) Common phrase: "Better than a poke in the eye with a sharp stick." (4) Last but hardly least, a "nooner" or a "quickie" is a poke.

Too many words in Italian Dialect for "shame," in my estimation.

Grand Finale Footnote: I'm amazed how many sarcastic terms we West Virginian Italians/Calabrians were keen to toss off. *Kotz.* Also how many expressions there were for shame.

About The Author

Jim Fragale has an amazing new Amazon.com novel called *Seventy-Six Trombones.*

Out of the starting gate, James A. Fragale's second novel, *F.U.! (Follow Up!) The Answer to Life Revisited*, received ten five-star reviews on Amazon. com. That work is available in paperback, Kindle, and Audio Kindle Fire.

Writer, journalist, record producer, songwriter, and blogger Jim Fragale's first novel, *The Answer to Life*, came out in April 2014 to eighteen positive reviews. Some folks referred to it as memoir-fiction. Be assured, more on that later.

While we're at it, Jim boasts five blog posts on the *Huffington Post*, listed below (and is touted regularly in New York City gossip columns).

Meat and potatoes: Triple-threat James A. Fragale got his writing start soon after college with a column in *Billboard Magazine*, "Music on Campus," later spun off as a supplement. Then four *Gentlemen's Quarterly* cover stories (Richard Gere,* Hart Bochner—they thought he was going to be a star; he did not become one—Christopher Reeve, Ryan O'Neal), a general-interest column in *GQ*, as well as a pointless article on Las Vegas.

After that, he wrote songs with Angelo (*Blue Velvet* and *Twin Peaks*) Badalamenti. Next, as "Jim," Fragale went on to produce Tony Award winner and Broadway musical actress Melba (*Purlie*) Moore's first two record albums. Moore recorded ten of his songs. At the same time, he created commercial jingles: Valerie Simpson on vocals, hit-making arranger Charlie (Four Seasons) Calello at the baton. We like touting arranger-conductor Charles Calello for creating the three notes that come after

Neil Diamond's 1969 hit *Sweet Caroline*. No one ever credits him until now. *Sweet Caroline* da-da-DA by Charlie Calello.

Then came a two-year stint as an A&R man for Columbia Records.

In *People Magazine*, Jim had stories on actress Susan Dey and a Beatles auction. Next was a *Writer's Digest* profile on writer-actor-funny duck Buck Henry, followed up by another *Digest* piece, "How to Write a Hit Song," which garnered a huge reprint from wannabe songwriters.

Not long after, he wrote profiles on West Virginia-born Jazz Age personality Ada "Bricktop" Smith for both the Los Angeles *Sunday Times* and *Chicago Tribune* that ran simultaneously with the cross-country Smithsonian touring exhibition on the Jazz Age. Then there was a controversial news-making two-parter on actor Montgomery Clift in now-defunct *Blue Boy* that got him into heated discussions. (Dueling bios by Patty Bosworth and Robert LaGuardia came out simultaneously on Clift, and some disgruntled interviewees changed their minds after speaking with Jim. He had the interviews on tape.

Soon after, as a screenwriting student, he won the John Truby Student Screenwriting Award two years in a row, which led to precisely *niente*. Not one of his fifteen screenplays was made into movies. (Jim's running joke to anyone who will listen: Don't let your daughters be screenwriters.) On the other hand, Jim's article "Who Is Syd Field and Why Does Everyone Own His Books?" in *Creative Screenwriting Magazine* garnered one of their biggest reprint requests ever. (Aspiring writers are friggin' everywhere.)

When he was just plain "Jimmy," he assisted columnist Liz Smith with her widely syndicated daily column and traveled around as well working as Smith's about-town New York leg man. (Good gams run in the family.) More recently, as James A. Fragale again, his essay on the humblest of coins, the penny, appeared in *Newsweek*. The work got hundreds of reprints (he ran off multiple photocopies himself) and thousands of online hits.

In 2012, Jim produced the pop music CD *Oil and Coal* with singer Joe Lutton. For the nine original songs, he wrote the lyrics; Joe Lutton composed the music. Check out the cuts on CDBaby.com or iTunes.

What's more, his five *Huffington Post* blogs still get daily hits; they are (a) lengthy, "Save the Music, Music, Music," (b) underground, "Books

You Hold in Your Hand," (c) sadly funny, "OLD! OLD! We Hate Old!" (d) tart, "Is It Art? Or Is It Soup?" (e) and, more recently, touching, "My Huckleberry Friends and Me."

While on the subject of fine legs, we feel compelled to add that Jim's niece Kaitlin Gates was Miss West Virginia in the 2013 Miss America competition. (He doesn't take any credit for that). His aunt Virginia Fragale was Miss Clarksburg 1934. His first cousin Rose-Emma Biafore was Gilroy, California's Garlic Queen 1955. Wait, there's more: second cousin Emelina Adams, in Las Vegas, was Miss Nevada, USA, in the Miss Universe competition 2016. The legs have it.

In closing, we'd like to chide Jim for not including in his credits above the weekly column he compiled for "The Hillbilly in Manhattan" that appeared in the late Jim Comstock's labor of love, *The West Virginia Hillbilly.* (Both opera's Eleanor Steber and comic Soupy Sales were highlighted.) Hang in here!

Note: Blowing smoke...* The controversial Richard Gere cover story in *GQ* is considered the best ever in that publication's fifty-plus-year history by *Gentlemen's Quarterly's* current editor-in-chief, James Nelson. Editor Nelson was quoted saying so in the *New York Daily News.* (Conversely, some grumps disliked the imitated Gere cover photograph; Richard Gere was holding a cigarette.)

And now there is a third Amazon novel: *Seventy-Six Trombones.* James A. Fragale was born in Clarksburg, West Virginia, studied journalism at the University of Miami in Florida, and got a BA in English at Salem College, Salem, West Virginia. Penultimately, James A. Fragale's first Amazon.com novel, *The Answer to Life,* took (off and on) more than forty years to complete (and at one point was completely lost) and then saw the light of day in early 2014. Well worth the wait? The memoir-fiction got raves on Amazon.com. And his second novel, right out of the gate, garnered ten five-star reviews: *F.U.! (Follow Up!) The Answer to Life Revisited.* We gush again: ten five-star reviews on Amazon.com.

Enough about him. Send him your "answer to life" at jamesafragale@yahoo.com. Surely you have one or two.

Made in the USA
Middletown, DE
05 October 2017